A Thoroughly

WICKED WOMAN

Murder, Perjury & Trial by Newspaper

Caitlin Press Inc.
8100 Alderwood Road,
Halfmoon Bay, BC V0N 1Y1
www.caitlin-press.com

Text and cover design by Michelle Winegar and Vici Johnstone
Printed in Canada on recycled paper.

Caitlin Press Inc. acknowledges financial support from the Government of Canada through the Canada Book Fund, the Canada Council for the Arts, and from the Province of British Columbia through the British Columbia Arts Council and the Book Publisher's Tax Credit.

Canada Council   Conseil des Arts
for the Arts   du Canada

BRITISH COLUMBIA
ARTS COUNCIL

Library and Archives Canada Cataloguing in Publication

Keller, Betty

    A thoroughly wicked woman : murder, perjury and trial by newspaper / Betty Keller.

ISBN 978-1-894759-48-9

    1. Jones, Esther—Trials, litigation, etc. 2. Jackson, Theresa—Trials, litigation, etc. 3. Trials (Perjury—British Columbia—Vancouver. 4. Murder—British Columbia—Vancouver. 5. Women—British Columbia—Vancouver—Social conditions. I. Title.

HV6335.C32V3 2010   364.1'34   C2010-904457-6

A Thoroughly

WICKED
WOMAN

Murder, Perjury & Trial by Newspaper

Betty Keller

 CAITLIN PRESS

A typical BC Penitentiary cell. NEW WESTMINSTER PUBLIC LIBRARY.
ACCESSION NUMBER 1630.

AUTHOR'S NOTE

A Thoroughly Wicked Woman is an exploration of a theft, a murder and a trial that occurred in Vancouver, BC, between September 1905 and May 1907. These events are recounted here with historical accuracy, and all the newspaper accounts quoted are exactly as they appeared in the papers of the day. I have, however, imagined the private conversations that took place within the Jones/Jackson household and events that took place in the newsroom of the *Daily Province*. Most of the remaining dialogue is reconstructed from the exceptionally detailed newspaper reports and from transcripts of the inquest, the police court preliminary hearings and the county court trial.

The only fictional characters in this account are reporters Dennis Hopkins and Michael Kelly, two men that I have created to represent the legion of nameless itinerants who made their living in the newsrooms of Vancouver's daily papers during the early years of the twentieth century.

INTRODUCTION

Although the primary focus of *A Thoroughly Wicked Woman* is a murder that occurred in Vancouver in November 1905, the story behind that murder actually began two months earlier with a case of theft. As a result of this first crime, the two female principals in the case—a mother and daughter—gained a small measure of local notoriety, so that when they turned up as principals in the main event, popular sentiment was already running against them.

This bias was compounded by the fact that the two women were more or less independent at a time when women were already causing anxiety within Canada's essentially male ruling class by pushing for equal rights. The mother in this case had left her husband some years earlier. Had divorce been an option, she would probably have chosen it, but in Canada at that time (and until 1969) the only grounds for divorce was adultery—which was difficult to prove—and even then, divorces were only granted at the discretion of the Supreme Court of Canada. As a result, only three marriages in every ten thousand ended in divorce. Most marriage dilemmas were, therefore, resolved by one spouse deserting the other and making a new life elsewhere, and until the middle of the nineteenth century it was usually the male partner who deserted. However, by that time, increasing numbers of women were also taking this time-honoured route out of their unsatisfactory marriages, simply abandoning their husbands (and sometimes their children) and travelling as far away as possible to start new lives. (The construction of railways across North America greatly facilitated this exodus.)

Unfortunately, the deserting women quickly discovered that the morals of divorced, widowed and single women of marriageable age were generally viewed askance, so most of them, upon leaving husband number one, soon looked for another, in many cases marrying again without the bother of legally ending the first marriage or waiting for the first husband to die. British Columbia was, in fact, littered with "widows" who still had living husbands back east. A second and more pressing reason to look for another husband was the fact that single women had a difficult time supporting themselves: all the respectable alternatives to marriage—teacher, milliner, dressmaker, confectioner, seamstress, nurse, stenographer, domestic worker, hairdresser, telephone operator—were very low paying. In Vancouver, however, where an extremely high percentage of the population was composed of single, young working men, there were two other occupations that allowed a decent livelihood. A woman could rent a house in the West End and offer bed and board (as did the mother and daughter in this story) or she could rent one on Dupont Street (the section of Pender Street between Abbott and Main) and offer something rather more personal. The morals of the woman offering bed and board were often suspect and the morals of her Dupont Street sister always suspect, offending the sensibilities of the churchgoing classes and causing continual debate in city council meetings, but the women in both of these occupations made a better living than the seamstresses and domestics of the city.

The two women in this tale also faced prejudice because they happened to be Americans. Anti-Americanism in Canada has had its upswings and downswings, but it has been an essential component of our national culture ever since the thirteen colonies to the south elected to break away from the Empire. Subsequently, Canadians fought Americans in the War of 1812 and again at the time of the Fenian raids, and when we emerged from those scraps to find the border between us still intact, we believed ourselves triumphant. We entertained ourselves for another century by sneering at those south of the border, comparing the Anglo-Saxon Protestant purity of our citizens—Quebec was not really counted—with their polyglot, multi-faithed rabble. At the same time, because of our inevitably intertwined economies, the level of anti-Americanism in this country rose every time there was an economic crisis. But it was America's imperialist ambitions that consistently brought out the most strident anti-American diatribes from Canadians; by the end of the nineteenth century the US had gobbled up Alaska, California, Texas, Cuba and the Philippines, and Canadians feared that their land would be next.

Nowhere was this anxiety more pronounced at the beginning of the twentieth century than in the outpost of the British Empire west of the Rockies. Here geography should have dictated a state running north and south, and thus, after the Americans took over Alaska in 1868, it seemed logical that they would attempt to absorb British Columbia in order to complete their Alaska-to-California link-up. This fear was the impetus for BC's entry into confederation in July 1871 and became the spur behind the completion of the Canadian Pacific Railway to Vancouver in May 1887. But the fear was still there in 1896 when gold was discovered in the Klondike, and pro-British cities like Vancouver and Victoria experienced a massive influx of Americans heading north, many of them lawless miners from the California goldfields. When the gold petered out, those same miners began drifting south again, many of them stopping short of the border to settle, and though they were tolerated here, every time a crime was committed, they were naturally the first suspects.

While British Columbia may have been a mere outpost of empire, its subjects expected all the trappings of British law and order. As a result, the justice model adopted here was a combination of the British county court system, which administered both civil and criminal law, and the police or magistrate's court system, which prosecuted minor offences, although it was also empowered to bind persons over for trial in the superior court. By 1900 British Columbia had three county court judges—one each for Victoria, New Westminster and Vancouver—but since they were also expected to go "on circuit" to hold sessions of court in more remote areas, none of their courts sat continuously. Consequently, a person facing trial in county court either waited in jail until a judge and jury were assembled for the regularly scheduled spring or fall court sessions, known as "assizes," in that city or opted for a "speedy trial" by judge alone, in which case he would be tried by any of the three judges who happened to be available. County court cases were prosecuted by local lawyers appointed for a single assize, while police court prosecutors were city employees. All court officials—judges, prosecutors and defence lawyers—came to court gowned and wigged in order to dispense justice with all the pomp and decorum of the British original.

As British Columbia was still frontier country, it attracted all the vagabonds, con men, thieves and ne'er-do-wells the continent had to offer, so there was never a shortage of persons willing to flout the law. There was, as a result, a steady demand for legal services, and by the end of the nineteenth century lawyers were flocking west to make names for themselves. As many as one-third of them had received their legal training in Britain. There it was possible for a sixteen-year-old legal apprentice to enter the employ of a seasoned barrister as general dogsbody, be expected to read up on legal principles after working hours and at the end of five years of servitude write state-sanctioned exams and be called to the bar. As a consequence, it was generally acknowledged that at least half of those in the British legal profession were unqualified to practise law even though they had been given full legal status in the courts. And sadly, it was often the most undereducated of these young, poorly qualified British lawyers who chose Canada as the place to seek their fortunes.

Most of the remaining lawyers were Canadian-educated, although few were the products of university law schools as there were only three of them in Canada at that time—McGill's law school was founded in Montreal in 1848, Dalhousie University Law School in Halifax in 1883 and Osgoode Hall Law School in Toronto in 1889. Instead, the average young Canadian lawyer received his legal education through "articles of clerkship," a slight improvement on the system used in Britain. As in the "Old Country," the would-be lawyer apprenticed to a practising lawyer for a period of five years, at the end of which time he wrote exams set by one of the provincial law societies in order to be "called to the bar." For the first three years of this apprenticeship, the young man—no women were accepted until the 1920s—received little payment but worked long hours copying documents, keeping records and filing; for the last two he was generally allowed to draw up documents, interview witnesses, do research and conveyancing and handle foreclosures. Unfortunately, although it was an improvement on the British system, it was still somewhat hit-and-miss, and many of the articling students received little supervision and even less positive mentoring, being expected to somehow absorb the law through osmosis.

In British Columbia, although there were acknowledged legal superstars at this time and the province's bar association was urging the establishment of a self-regulating, well-educated and ethical professional law society, the haphazard system of articling meant that the general public had considerable doubt about the competence of those who served in the courts. This attitude was nicely demonstrated by a story told by Judge W. Norman Bole who presided over the County Court at New Westminster from 1893 onward. A product of the legal training system in Northern Ireland, he was a pillar of dignity on the bench and rather conscious of the importance of his position at all times, but he was also considered a wit and enjoyed telling tales on himself.

It seems that one day while driving his buggy across the bridge from New Westminster to Surrey, the judge gave a lift to a local character whom he had sent to jail on an earlier occasion. "Ah, Paddy," said Bole, "I'm thinking it's a long time ye'd be in Oireland before ye'd be riding in a buggy with a judge."

"True for ye, y'r honour," snapped Paddy. "And it's a long time ye'd be in Oireland before ye'd be a judge, I'm thinking."

One of the results of the overall inadequate legal training was the tendency for many Canadian lawyers, especially those in the far west, to treat each court case as a training ground, a place to sharpen their debating skills, chewing on each legal point *ad nauseum* and prolonging each case via objections and adjournments while they hustled up new arguments. Much of what went on in court, therefore, had little to do with the welfare of the clients or the outcome of the case; the lawyers and judges, confident of their importance, performed mainly for each other's benefit and that of the onlookers who crowded into the courtrooms for an afternoon's entertainment. Thus, in the cases described in this book, the accused were trundled back and forth between jail and court for months, more or less forgotten, while the lawyers stood in the spotlight, enjoying the cut and thrust of debate and their own and the judge's wit.

The spotlight in which they basked was provided by newspapers, and in British Columbia there was no dearth of them either because the towns of this province were growing like Topsy. Almost entirely as a consequence of immigration—mostly from the British Isles and eastern Canada—Vancouver's population grew from an estimated 1,000 at the time of the city's incorporation in April 1886 to 13,709 in 1891 to 26,133 in 1901 and then almost doubled again to 50,379 in 1906—a period totalling just twenty years. These immigrants relied on the newspapers to provide them with their only window on the outside world from which they had come because most of the stories printed in them came "off the wire" and covered world political events and conflicts as well as sensational crimes and trials in faraway places. Only gradually did local news begin to dominate their front pages.

The three papers that served Vancouver in those early years of the twentieth century were all dailies and all were financed by money from either the Conservative or Liberal political parties. In 1887 Francis L. Carter-Cotton—a Conservative-Independent member of BC's Legislative Assembly from 1890 to 1900 and from 1903 to 1916—had merged two weekly newspapers, the *News* and the *Advertiser*, to create a Conservative morning daily called the *News-Advertiser*. Within a year John and Sara McLagan, backed at first by local Liberal Party money, established a rival paper, the left-leaning evening daily *World,* and Carter-Cotton became embroiled in a fight for his paper's survival. The influence of the *News-Advertiser* was not entirely eclipsed, however, until after Liberal Senator Hewitt Bostock raised fresh party funds to put behind his Victoria-based weekly *Province* newspaper, which he then brought to Vancouver in 1898 as a daily. For the next seventeen years the bulk of the circulation wars were carried on between the *Province* and the *World,* especially after 1905 when the latter paper was bought by American entrepreneur Louis D. Taylor.

Most stories in these papers were written by nameless reporters, although a few did become household names—Sam Robb, Norman Norcross and David Higgins of the *World,* Clara Battle who wrote for the *World's* Women's Page for many, many years and Isabel "Alexandra" McLean who did the same at the *Province,* Robert Bruce Bennett who reported first for the *World* and then for the *News-Advertiser,* and Roy Brown of the *Province* who later became city editor and then in the 1930s editor-in-chief. It is also known that in the early years of their papers John and Sara McLagan of the *World* and publisher-editor Walter Nichol of the *Province*—who, according to one former employee, was known for "his sharp, epigrammatic style" and who "loved to sting"—wrote all their editorials and lead stories. The names of other newspapermen of this period are unknown, partly because few bylines were given, but mostly because they were an itinerant group, independent-minded, poorly paid and often plagued by alcohol problems.

What kept newsmen and women of this period interested in the job was "muckraking," a type of journalism that originated with the nineteenth-century investigative writers of the American Progressive Movement who sought to expose corruption and scandals in government, the horrific conditions in industry and the poverty and lack of educational opportunities for the working classes. The muckrakers also applied this same fearless approach to reporting on events in courtrooms, feasting on sensational trials—and if they were not inherently sensational, these newsmen and women worked very hard to make them so.

And so the stage was set for the 1906 trial of *A Thoroughly Wicked Woman.*

Vancouver's first county courthouse, constructed in 1894, stood on the south side of Hastings Street between Cambie and Hamilton. CITY OF VANCOUVER ARCHIVES, BU N13

ONE

Captain William Sprague, master of the coastal steamer *Merchant Star*, clung to the gatepost of the house on Melville Street and mopped his face with a large red handkerchief. "It's this ... confounded hill," he said, his words coming on pain-filled whistles of breath. "It's ... just this confounded ... hill."

Beside him, his son, Doctor Wilfred Sprague, jiggled the baby wagon in which his own small son lay sleeping and watched his father dispassionately. There was no point in cautioning him again about his heart. The old fool never listened. "Why can't it wait?" he said. "I'll come back with you another time without the baby ..."

"No!" the old man squawked, and his moustaches quivered with the power of his indignation. "I'm here to collect ... what's coming to me and that's ... what I aim to do! If you won't come with me, I'll do it alone!" He opened the gate and started unsteadily up the path to the house, stabbing at the gravel with his ebonywood cane. "That jezebel isn't ... going to ... get the best of me!"

Doctor Sprague set his jaw in angry silence. The old man had used this ploy on him before and it wasn't going to work. Besides, he had to stay with the baby wagon to prevent it bouncing back down the hill. *He wasn't interested in taking a walk with me at all. He only wanted me to help him collect rents!* *He's as devious as a woman,* he reflected and felt a little ashamed of the pleasure it gave him that it happened to be a woman who was holding out on his father. Especially one who was—according to the captain's account—almost as devious as he was.

When Captain Sprague reached the foot of the stairs, he paused uncertainly and looked up the long flight in front of him. If Wilfred had come with him, he could have leaned on him to climb the stairs without having to admit that he needed help. *Thunderation!* The damned baby couldn't come to any harm in the few minutes it would take them to collect from the woman! But while the old man was standing there trying to decide how to force his son to come with him, his glance caught a movement beyond the oval glass panel in the door. *Damn her eyes!* She was standing there watching him. Feeling pretty smug that he couldn't get up there, was she? Well, he'd show her, he would!

He started to climb, wheezing and puffing as he hauled his bulk from stair to stair, pausing to rest only long enough to regain his breath before tackling the next one. Each time he was tempted to give up, he thought of her staring down at him. "I won't give the jade the satisfaction," he muttered.

"Hah!" he grunted when he reached the top. "Hah!" But it took him several minutes to get his breath, leaning against the porch railing where the blue trumpets of morning-glory vines, now tightly closed to the evening air, hung thickly round him. If his nose hadn't been so attuned to tar and salt spray, he might have appreciated the fragrance of the flowers, but he brushed them aside with one leathery paw and shuffled to the door. He knocked several times before he noticed the fancy handle of the doorbell, then he left off knocking and began cranking the handle until he could hear the bell pealing through the house.

He waited. But the only sounds that came to him were his own wheezing breath and the distant clanging of a streetcar.

"Hah! Think I'll go away, do you?" He cranked the handle again and yelled at the closed door, "Might's well open the door, missus, because I'm not going off without my money!"

On the sidewalk, Doctor Wilfred Sprague glanced around to see if anyone had heard the old man and discovered that a well-dressed couple had paused on the other side of the street to see what was going on. Thoroughly embarrassed, the doctor raised his hat to them and they moved on. Unfortunately, his father had never been in port long enough to understand that the kind of people who lived in Vancouver's West End didn't go bellowing about money matters right out on the porch like that—even if the woman inside the house did owe them rent money. Granted that quite a number of the houses on Melville Street took in boarders, making it not quite as "toney" as streets such as Barclay where the doctor had established his family and his offices, but it was still part of the West End and there was a certain standard of behaviour expected here.

Doctor Sprague was trying to decide whether to pretend he didn't know the old man and continue his walk with his baby son when his purpose was interrupted by a refined, extremely feminine voice.

"Why, Captain Sprague, how nice of you to come calling."

The doctor looked up at the house. In the doorway stood a tiny, fragile woman dressed entirely in black. Her costume's only ornament was a pince-nez dangling on a chain attached to a brooch on her bosom. *This* was the terrible battleaxe who had defied his father on two previous occasions, even defied the bill collectors he had sent around? Doctor Sprague shook his head in exasperation.

His father, however, was looking straight into the eyes of Esther Jones, and he was convinced now more than ever that he should not have confronted her alone again. There was something about the cursed woman that terrified him. She was too small to physically molest him, though he had known wiry little women like this to have quite remarkable strength. And it wasn't that her features were ferocious—they were quite regular, even patrician. No, it was something about the way her small, dark-brown eyes were set closely above a slightly hooked nose and the ghost of a smile that never left her face that told him she was as cunning as any of the heathen he had met in his younger days in the wicked Orient. And he had always taken care never to do business with any of *them* without a half-dozen burly crewmen along to back him up.

"What do you want?" Esther Jones asked. Her voice was pleasant—even rather musical.

The old man was momentarily confused. What did she mean by asking him what he wanted? She knew exactly why he was here! He shifted his feet, then suddenly inspired, he tried a new strategy. "Is Mrs. Jackson at home?" he demanded.

"Why have you come to see her?"

"You know deuced well why I come," he said truculently. "It's about these here promissory notes she signed for the rent owing to me for my house on Westminster Road."

"She's not here, and anyway your business is with me, as you are well aware. I endorsed those notes. I will pay them." Smiling graciously, she stood aside to let him enter the house. "Come in."

But the captain, immediately anxious, turned and called down to his son, "Doctor Sprague, you'll be needed to witness this! Park the wagon by the stairs here and come up." There! She wouldn't try anything smart in front of a doctor!

But before the doctor could open his mouth to answer, the

lady in black stepped out onto the porch, grabbed his father's arm and, giving him a shove that almost toppled him, propelled him into the house. She closed the door and turned the key in the lock. The old man let out a yelp of anxiety.

"What are you afraid of?" she mocked him. "I am a lone woman. If you're not man enough to face me by yourself, I won't pay you."

"There should be a witness to this ..."

"How many notes do you have?"

Belatedly he remembered to remove his hat. "Two of them," he told her. "One for ten dollars and one for five. The rest of them's at home."

"How much is it altogether?"

"All the notes? You know right well how many there is! There's seven of them altogether. That's sixty-five dollars you and Mrs. Jackson still owes me."

"I will pay them in full. You can write me out a receipt."

"I'll come back with the notes tomorrow then." The captain started for the door. "I'll come back with the notes and make you a proper receipt."

"That's not necessary," she said, barring his way. "You can write out a receipt on a piece of paper." She took his hat from his hands and placed it on the hall table. "Come along. There's pen and paper on the desk in here." Just inside the front parlour she pulled out a chair that faced a writing desk and motioned for him to sit down.

"I want my son to witness this," the captain complained, but when she said nothing, only continued to point imperiously to the chair, he sat and began writing.

"Make sure you date it," she ordered. "September 11, 1905. And for the full amount—sixty-five dollars."

On the sidewalk in front of the house, Doctor Sprague jiggled the wagon back and forth, watching his son's sleeping face. He was determined that the boy would never feel about him as he felt about his own father. Of course, he would be stern with the boy, but he would be fair ...

"Wilfred! Wilfred!"

Purple in the face, Captain Sprague had burst onto the porch where he now stood clutching the railing and bellowing for his son. It was obviously an apoplectic fit, and Doctor Sprague reacted instantly, shoving the wagon into the yard. As he bent to set its brakes, Esther Jones popped out of the house behind the old man, stuffed his hat into his hands and disappeared into the house again.

"Stay calm!" the doctor yelled, bounding up the stairs. "Just stay calm," and he tried to force his father to sit down on the top step.

Behind them the door slammed and the lock turned.

"Stop!" the old man shouted, wrenching away from his son to return to the door. "You can't do that! You have to give me my money!"

"For Heaven's sakes, what's happened?" his son demanded.

"She took my receipt! The jade took my receipt and she won't give me my money!" the captain cried. "Open up in there!" he shouted, pounding on the door so hard that the glass vibrated. "I want my money!"

Across the street a small crowd had gathered.

"Come away, father," Doctor Sprague said, fastening both hands onto his father's arm. "People are staring at us."

"She took my receipt!" the old man yelped.

"Go away!" Esther Jones shouted back through the door.

"You hear the jade? You hear her?" The old man struck out at his son to free himself. "Leave hold of me!"

"You're making a fool of yourself! People are staring at us, father!"

"Damn them all to hell!" the old man shouted and pounded on the door again. "You won't get away with this, missus!"

With his outraged face close to the captain's ear, his son whispered angrily, "It may not be important to you if you make a fool of yourself, but I have my medical practice to think of!"

"Go away then! Go away! If you can't be any help to me, don't be a hindrance!" But in spite of himself he turned to peer down at the people on the sidewalk below.

Finally, muttering bitter complaints, the captain allowed himself to be led down the stairs and away from the house. Once on the sidewalk he grew more belligerent again. "That's not the end of it, no sir," he announced loud enough for the onlookers to hear. "Not by a fathom or two. I'll sue the slut, I will. I'll take her to court and ruin her." But in his heart he still quailed at the memory of those cunning little brown eyes.

His son retrieved the baby wagon from the yard and began pushing it determinedly down the sidewalk.

The old man stayed to shake his walking stick at the house. "I'll ruin you, missus, see if I don't!" Then reluctantly he began trudging after his son, though stopping now and again to look back at the house and mutter imprecations.

On the street outside the offices of the *Vancouver Daily Province*, Dennis Hopkins mounted his wheel and began pedalling toward the Police Courthouse at the corner of Cordova and Westminster (Main) streets. There really was ample time to do the four blocks on foot, but this was only the fourth or fifth time that he had been assigned to the police court beat—the regular reporter having fallen off the wagon a few days earlier—and he was savouring his importance. Besides, the bicycle was new and Hopkins was young enough—barely twenty-one—to enjoy showing it off. At the corner of Hastings and Carrall on a sudden impulse he turned right onto Carrall and steered among the wholesalers' drays and produce carts until he came to the middle of the block. There he dismounted and walked so that he could look up at the second-storey windows of a red brick building that had been the scene of the city's biggest gambling raid only two years earlier. To his disappointment there were no signs of returning life, and thus no story to report. He mounted again and turned the corner onto Dupont Street, pedalling slowly so that he could peer into the brothels. There was no one else on the street, no one entering or leaving the houses, and lace curtains effectively blocked his view of the interiors.

Thwarted again, he turned north on Westminster Street and steered toward the Vancouver Police Courthouse. He was beginning to believe that all the city's gamblers had packed it in and all the ladies of the demi-monde—as city editor Roy Brown euphemistically referred to them when he wasn't calling them soiled doves or doxies—had become respectable. How was an apprentice police reporter supposed to write exciting copy if all the exciting things in Vancouver had already happened? It was already September 16 and he hadn't filed a story this month that had drawn anything more than a grunt from his editor. If only a few drunken loggers would hit town to disturb the peace, they would provide him with a story, but there was little hope of that happening until after the snows came to the hinterlands.

At the courthouse, renovated just a year earlier when the police department was moved out of the building's ground floor to new quarters down the street, he went around to the back and pushed open the door leading to the cells. He paused to take in a deep breath of fresh air before wheeling his bicycle inside.

"Full house today, Mr. Grady?" he said, closing the door and parking his bicycle beside jailer John Grady's desk. He had already learned that the intensity of the odour of excrement and unwashed bodies was directly related to the number of inmates in the cells. But today's odours were made worse by the stifling warmth within the building. The heating system had obviously turned itself on again when it wasn't wanted.

Grady ignored his question and frowned pointedly at Hopkins's bicycle.

"You don't mind, do you, Mr. Grady?" the reporter said. "I can't leave my wheel out there while I'm in court."

Grady mopped the perspiration from his face with a tattered handkerchief. "Huhn! So you think it's safer in here with this lot?" He waved a hand toward the cells where a half-dozen men clung to the bars of the windows in their cell doors.

"How many are going up today?" Hopkins asked, hoping to turn the conversation away from his bicycle.

Grady consulted his book, his gray head bowed over the handwriting, his finger following the letters while he sounded out the names. Hopkins waited patiently. Michael Kelly, the *Province*'s regular court reporter, had warned him never to offer to help the jailer decipher the names on the court roster. Grady was intensely sensitive about the lack of schooling that had prevented him rising above the rank of jailer, and he had a ferocious temper when he thought that anyone was being condescending to him. It was said that he had once killed a prisoner by kicking him down the stairs from the courtroom, though he was never charged because no one had been willing to come forward as a witness.

"That's seven," Grady said after a lengthy study of the book, "and I got two of them doxies in the back." Grady was referring to the women's cells at the back of the jail. They were supervised by a matron who came on duty only when women had been

Magistrate Adolphus Williams had learned the law through "articles of clerkship" in Toronto and practised in Welland, Ontario, before setting off for Vancouver in 1889. As police court magistrate, he was far more familiar with drunk and disorderly charges than cases of stolen receipts and stylish American ladies. CITY OF VANCOUVER ARCHIVES LP 365

apprehended by the law, but she was directly responsible to Grady.

"Well, we should get through the lot of them inside an hour, what d'you think?"

Grady shook his head. "McIntosh's got a couple of complaints on the docket as well, so that'll stretch it out a bit."

"Right," Hopkins said and began to climb the steps to the courtroom.

When he was almost at the top, Grady called after him, "I ain't being responsible for that there bye-cycle."

"Yes sir," said Hopkins again and escaped into the slightly cooler atmosphere of the courtroom. Finding a seat next to a window, he spent a few minutes wrestling the sash up, then before he sat down, he rescued a well-thumbed copy of the *World*, Vancouver's other evening newspaper, from the floor under his bench. He searched his pockets for a pencil then began marking the items in the paper that related to his own beat. Across the aisle Norman Norcross, the *World*'s man, grinned before he went back to checking his copy of the *Province*. At precisely ten o'clock the portly police magistrate, Adolphus Williams, entered immaculately wigged and gowned as usual, and everyone in the courtroom rose, seating themselves again only after he had taken his seat.

For a full minute the magistrate stroked the ends of his voluminous white moustaches as he examined the crowd in front of him, then he demanded, "Am I to assume, Mr. McIntosh, that this city's criminals are all on holiday?" He waved a hand at the vacant dock.

The court clerk, Peter McIntosh, preparing to announce the first case, raised his head to stare at the dock in consternation. Grady had forgotten to bring the prisoners up. He must be napping again. But before McIntosh could reach the door leading to the stairs, the door opened and the prisoners began straggling in, with Grady bringing up the rear. One of the men, a wiry little fellow in seaman's clothes, was holding a bit of rag to his face. The cloth was soaked with blood.

"What is the matter with that man?" the magistrate asked as the prisoners filed into the dock.

"Fighting in the cells, your honour," Grady said flatly, looking Williams in the eye.

At the end of the line were two women, the most bedraggled and wretched-looking creatures that Hopkins had ever seen, and although they were proof that not all of the demi-monde had become respectable, he couldn't see his editor getting excited about this pair. When the dock gate had been slammed behind them, the court clerk took up his ledger again and called the first case.

There's no story here, Hopkins thought in disgust, and he let his eyes rove over the room while the court began dealing with Grady's criminals: a couple of drunk-and-disorderlies, two breaking-and-enterings, a ship jumper and two gaming house found-ins. It was while Hopkins was looking over the spectators that he spotted

Doctor Sprague. *Now what is a West End doctor doing in Police Court?* he asked himself.

"Lester Lawler, also known as Lester Lawrence," intoned the court clerk, "charged with breaking and entering. Daniel MacKay, also known as Peanuts MacKenzie and Danny MacRitchie, also charged with breaking and entering."

Maybe Sprague's the injured party in the B&E, Hopkins thought and listened carefully to the details of the charges against the two men. But no, there was no mention of Doctor Sprague in the evidence, and anyway he seemed to be totally uninterested in it. The gaze of the doctor was, in fact, fixed on two women who had entered late and taken seats near the far wall. Both were dressed very stylishly in brown walking suits and wore large hats with veils, but even from where he sat, Hopkins could see that the younger one was pretty in a doll-like way. *No wonder the doctor was staring,* Hopkins thought, but when he checked on him again, he saw that Doctor Sprague had turned to speak to the person next to him. Hopkins couldn't see who it was because he or she was short and hidden by the doctor's shoulder.

Finally it was the turn of the two bedraggled prostitutes to face the magistrate and they stood sullenly in the dock while the clerk read the charges and the magistrate handed down their sentences. There were no surprises either for them or for the court. Ninety days or a fine of fifty dollars—which they could not pay. They would serve their sentences in the women's section of the penitentiary in New Westminster, a move that would at least get them out of Grady's clutches.

These two being the last of the day's malefactors, Grady opened the gate of the dock and ushered them back down the stairs. As soon as the commotion died away, the clerk intoned, "Number Eight: Information and complaint of William W. Sprague of the

City of Vancouver, aforesaid master mariner, who saith that Mrs. Esther Jones of 1284 Melville Street, Vancouver, on the 11th day of September, A.D. 1905, unlawfully did steal one piece of paper, the property of the complainant, on which was written a receipt for the sum of $65 as payment of seven certain promissory notes payable to the said complainant by one Theresa Elizabeth Jackson and endorsed by the accused under the initial and style of E. Jones, said receipt being signed by the complainant and dated September 11, 1905."

"Are the complainant and defendant both in court?"

"Yes, your honour. Mr. David Grant is appearing for the complainant and Mr. Stuart Livingston for the defendant."

Both lawyers rose to their feet, their clients beside them, but since both of the stylish women in brown stood up, Hopkins was unable to decide which one was the defendant. He turned his attention to the complainant and saw a portly man of sixty-odd years clutching the rail attached to the top of the bench in front of him. The resemblance was unmistakable: the old man had to be Doctor Sprague's father.

"How does your client plead, Mr. Livingston?"

"Not guilty, your honour. She has consented to be tried by this court."

The women and their lawyer took their seats, and the old captain was ushered into the witness box. Mr. Grant, a tall man given to pointing one long finger repeatedly at accused and witnesses alike, began the examination of his client. "Calling your attention to the 11th of September, did you see the accused, Mrs. Jones, on that day?" The long finger stabbed in the direction of the two women.

"Yes sir. At 1284 Melville Street where she lives now."

"How came you there?"

"Another of these notes of Mrs. Jackson's was due that day. I went to collect on it."

"Is this Mrs. Jackson in court?"

"Yes sir."

So one of the women is Mrs. Jones and the other is Mrs. Jackson. And that means that pretty little thing is married, Hopkins thought with just a twinge of disappointment.

"Will you point Mrs. Jackson out for the court, please."

"She's sitting over there nigh the wall," said Sprague.

The doll-faced woman bowed her head in embarrassment.

Ah-ha, so the young one is Jackson, thought Hopkins. He checked his notes—the clerk had given her name as Theresa Elizabeth Jackson. *She's not using her husband's first name so there's a good chance she's a widow ...*

"And what was this note in payment of?" Grant asked his client.

"For the rent that was owing to me for my house on Westminster Road. She was short of cash when I went to collect but she tells me that Mr. Jackson has made a strike in the Cassiar and would be bringing money as soon as he sold his claim. So I lets her give me the promissory notes."

"Mr. Jackson is a prospector?"

"So she says, but I ain't seen hide nor hair of him nor his money all these long months!"

"What took place when you went to collect on your note, Mr. Sprague?"

While Sprague told his story, his voice quavering with indignation, Hopkins watched the women. *Well, I'll be darned!* he thought. *The old girl is smiling! How's that for arrogance, eh?*

"When I finished writing out the receipt," continued the captain, "she puts on her glasses and picks it up and carries it to the front door."

"She carried the receipt to the door?" asked Grant.

"Yes sir. To see it better, you see. 'This seems to be all in order,' she says to me after she looks it over, and she tucks my receipt right into the front of her dress. Then she smiles and she says to me, 'Now get out of my house and don't come back!'" The captain's voice rose to an outraged squeak. "'Where's my money?' I says to her. 'I want my money!' And right then I starts for the door to call my son. 'You can't get away with this!' I tells her." By now the old man's face was mottled with rage.

"Calm yourself, Captain Sprague," Magistrate Williams interjected.

The captain paused for a few moments to get his breath then launched into his story again. "I tries to open the door, but it won't open, so she just reaches past me and unlocks it and then pushes me outside. 'Get out!' she says, 'I'm not giving you anything!' Then she shoves my hat at me and locks me out of the house!"

"And Mrs. Jones had the receipt at this time?" asked Grant.

"Yes. She picked up the receipt and tucked it in her bosom."

"Did you see any money?"

"She paid me no money and I seen no money."

The defence lawyer's cross-examination began with the old man's departure from the Melville Street house. "When you took up your hat, Mrs. Jones understood that you wanted to leave, isn't that correct? And that is why she opened the door for you."

"She *told* me to leave!" the captain said indignantly.

"So you took your hat and left."

"She shoved it at me and I took ahold of it!"

"Who opened the door?"

"She did. I tried to open it but it wouldn't open so she came and unlocked it."

"You tried to open the door before you got your hat?"

"Yes, I did. I was going to call my son."

"So she believed you had forgotten your hat."

"She said get out of the house and take your hat with you. That's what she said!"

"Why did you draw up the receipt when there was no money in sight?"

"She said she was going to pay me and she wanted a receipt."

"And then she took hold of you and shoved you out of the house. And you did not resist?"

The captain was affronted. "I'd never resist a lady, sir."

"Do you think a lady would steal, Captain Sprague?"

Too late the old man realized he had been tricked. "She's a woman, sir," he huffed, "and every woman's entitled to be called a lady."

Livingston's face remained bland while he played his trump card. "Do you recall visiting Mrs. Jones last November to collect the rent? This was at the house you rented to her on Westminster Road."

"I do, sir."

"Did you not on that occasion think that the money she paid you had been mislaid? Did you not search all your pockets for it?"

Captain Sprague looked extremely uncomfortable. "Yes, that's true, but I—"

"And did you not accuse Mrs. Jones of taking your money at that time?"

"No, no. I found it in my pocket. I never accused her. I had put it in my outside pocket and I was hunting all the time in my inside pocket."

"You are careless with money at times, are you not, Captain Sprague?"

"No!" Sprague thundered. "I'm not a careless man, by the Lord Harry! I put it in my outside pocket is all ..."

As Hopkins listened to the old man's answers, it occurred to him that he just might have the makings of a story after all, and he began taking shorthand notes as quickly as he could. Of course, old Sprague could simply be forgetful, but if he was to be believed, this Esther Jones was not what her appearance suggested. *But what would make her think she could get away with a confidence trick like this one? On the other hand, the old man might be just taking advantage of a couple of defenceless women. In a way it was too bad that the victim wasn't the Jackson woman. She'd make a far better story ...*

Dennis Hopkins glanced up from his typewriter toward the windowed corner office. Although most of his stories went to city editor Roy Brown for editing, any reports of court happenings went directly to publisher/editor Walter Cameron Nichol, and Hopkins could see him now, glowering as he hunched over the day's copy. Nichol had learned the newspaper business at the *Spectator* in Hamilton, Ontario, but after coming west in 1897, he had been recruited by lawyer-rancher-journalist Hewitt Bostock (who was also the Liberal MP for Yale-Cariboo) to edit his weekly *Province* newspaper in Victoria. The next year Bostock had moved the *Province* to Vancouver as a daily and Nichol came with it. At first he had done much of the writing himself, but after Bostock was appointed to the Senate in 1904, Nichol bought control of the paper and thereafter delegated more of the writing to his reporters. Unfortunately for them, he was an excellent newspaperman himself, and because he was never satisfied with his own work, he never satisfied with theirs. In fact, his employees were convinced that he always thought more highly of the men on the rival paper, the *World*, than he did his own people, though one of his former employees would later point out that, whenever Nichol managed to poach one of the *World*'s reporters, that man would "lose caste" as soon as he began to draw a *Province* pay cheque.

Now as Hopkins watched surreptitiously, from time to time

Nichol would wave a sheet of paper in the air and bellow the name of some unfortunate reporter who would scuttle into his office to receive a scathing reprimand, generally climaxed with a demand for a rewrite. Very occasionally he approved a story, yelling for a copy boy to take it to the typesetters, and the reporter would return to his desk noticeably happier. But it was more than an hour since Hopkins had given his story on Sprague vs. Jones to a copy boy to deliver to Nichol, and still his name had not been called. He didn't know whether to feel hopeful or expect the worst.

"Hopkins!"

"Yes sir." He dashed into Nichol's office and stood just inside the door. "Right here, sir."

"What the hell d'you mean by turning in a story like this?"

"Like what, sir?"

"Like this! What the hell's the outcome? Is she going to trial or not?"

"The outcome? Oh, yes sir. She's remanded to the Fall Assizes on $200 bail."

"Well, why didn't you say so?" As the editor scribbled the information on the bottom of the story, he commented, "That's a hell of a lot of money for such small potatoes."

"But she's an *American,* sir. The judge figured she might skip town."

"I don't see that anywhere in your story."

Hopkins advanced toward the desk. "It's right there, sir. First line."

The editor grunted. "You think she did it?"

Startled to be asked his opinion, Hopkins said, "Mrs. Jones, sir? I don't know, sir. She's pretty small to have pushed the captain around like he says. And there was something funny happened when they got his son, the doctor, on the stand—I'd swear he didn't believe his father's story even though he was there when it happened."

"How come he didn't believe it then?"

"Well, he was on the sidewalk, you see. Myself, I think the old man pocketed the money." In response to his editor's raised eyebrows he added hurriedly, "On the other hand, if the way the old man tells it is what really happened, it'll make a better story, won't it?"

His editor ignored the collegiality implied by Hopkins' question. "Is she out on bail?"

Hopkins nodded. "I checked back with McIntosh an hour ago. Some fellow named Exall came in at lunch time and signed the bonds for her. Englishman, about my age, maybe twenty-one or twenty-two. Apparently he boards at the Jones house. McIntosh thinks he's got something going with Mrs. Jackson because he was jumping through hoops for her. She's a peach, all right."

"Well, keep an eye on the case. Get some background. We don't want the *World* getting ahead of us on this one. And next time don't forget the punch line." He yelled for a copy boy, dismissing Hopkins without a word of commendation.

On the other hand, Dennis Hopkins decided, *he didn't hand me any brickbats either.*

When the last car of the *Imperial Limited* slid out of the Canadian Pacific rail yards, Ernest Exall closed and locked his ticket window and prepared to cash in his receipts for the day. As he counted the money and added up the columns of figures, his stomach growled. He'd gone without lunch in order to go to the Bank of Montreal on Granville Street and take out his savings then catch the street-car across town to pay his landlady's bail at the Police Courthouse.

His hunger pains were made worse by his anxiety: it had taken almost every cent he owned to provide Esther Jones with bail. But what else could he have done? He took off his glasses and began polishing them vigorously as he thought about his encounter with his landlady's daughter earlier that day. Theresa—dear sweet Tessie—had stood clinging to the bars of his ticket window, her eyes welling with tears.

"But you must help, Ernest, you must help! Mother and I have no one else to turn to, and if we don't get the money, she'll have to stay in that awful jail until the Fall Assizes!" One trembling hand, its nails bitten to the quick, pressed a lace hanky to her mouth. "Oh, this is all so terribly unfair!"

Ernest looked around anxiously to see if his supervisor was listening. "There, there ... Mrs. Jackson," he said loud enough for the supervisor to hear, "the *Continental* is always on time and I'm sure your son will be on it." Then he lowered his voice to a whisper and leaned close to the bars. "What about Harry? Why can't he pay her bail? He's your cousin, isn't he?"

"Harry doesn't have any money." And she began to sob.

"Neither do I," he told her.

She leaned toward the bars, her wet brown eyes imploring him. "But you told me you had money in your savings account, Ernest!"

Ernest Exall slid a hand under the bars of his wicket and touched Theresa Jackson's fingertips. He saw the dusting of powder on her cheeks, the tiny scar above the bridge of her nose. He closed his eyes and inhaled her cologne.

Only a complete cad would have refused, he thought. Besides, he reassured himself, there was no question of Esther's innocence and he'd get his money back as soon as she was exonerated. But he couldn't understand what on earth had possessed the old man to accuse her of taking the receipt. Of course, Esther Jones was no shrinking violet, but Exall was positive she would never have taken it if she hadn't given the man his money. Obviously the captain was pretending he never got it so he could collect the rent all over again. Tessie was right. It was all terribly unfair.

Exall signed his daily tally and carried his box to the end of the line of ticket agents waiting to turn in their money to the head cashier.

"Hey, Exall, you know your landlady made the front page of the *Province* this afternoon?" Plummy Wilson, grinning from ear to ear, stepped into line behind Exall.

"The front page?"

"Bold as brass, right there on the front page. *American Lady Charged With Stealing Receipt.* One of my customers showed it to me." He laughed at Exall's obvious embarrassment. "Better be careful, Exall. The CPR's gonna start worrying about the company you're keeping!" And he laughed again.

Plummy was right, of course. It was exactly the kind of thing the railway's management would take an interest in.

The head cashier counted the money in Exall's box twice and carefully checked the numbers on his ticket stubs before he made out his receipt. He too had seen the afternoon *Province*. In the agents' cloakroom Exall hurriedly traded his eyeshade for a black derby, shrugged into his street jacket and rescued his umbrella from the back of the employees' coat cupboard before Plummy could catch up to him. He was almost running by the time he got to the newspaper kiosk at the corner of Granville and Hastings. And yes, there it was on the front page of the newspaper:

> Mrs. Esther Jones, a stylish American resident of Vancouver, was charged today with stealing a receipt for $65 last Monday. The complainant, Mr. W.W. Sprague, a master mariner, told a hard luck story at the police station. If his version of the affair is true, Mrs. Jones is a woman of finesse and strategy.

According to Mr. Sprague, his financial relations with the accused involved seven promissory notes aggregating $65, payable by Mrs. Theresa Jackson and endorsed by the accused. When the last of the notes came due, Mr. Sprague called upon Mrs. Jones. Adopting a suggestion from Mrs. Jones, the master mariner wrote out a receipt before receiving the cash. Mrs. Jones, he avers, then grabbed the receipt and taking him unawares, hustled him into the hallway and snapped her door with a spring lock. Mr. Sprague pleaded for readmission but in vain.

Now the master mariner will seek to prove that Mrs. Jones was guilty of theft by keeping the receipt without giving the equivalent. Mrs. Jones will be tried in the Fall Assizes.

Exall folded the story to the inside of the paper, tucked it under his arm and walked quickly toward Melville Street. He would certainly be needed.

"Dinner's almost ready, Ernest. We're just waiting for Harry," Esther Jones announced, "so you've still got time to wash up." She turned back to the stove and began stirring the soup. Through the doorway he could see Theresa in the dining room setting the table and humming tunelessly as she worked. She looked quickly away when she caught sight of him.

Where were the tears, the wailing and tearing of hair that he had expected? How could Esther Jones stand there calmly with a soup ladle in her hand when she had spent the morning being humiliated in police court, when her name was splashed all over the front page? And where were the outpourings of gratitude that were surely his due?

For a moment he hesitated, cleared his throat, then unable to think of anything to say, he walked dumbly down the hall and up the stairs to the bathroom. When he returned to the kitchen, the women were already waiting in the dining room. Harry Fisher was standing at the sink washing some black goo from his freckled hands.

"Molasses!" he snarled at Ernest. "Your goddam railroad sent us another stove-in barrel of molasses! Look at me! Covered in the bloody stuff!" He pulled at the buttons of his shirt and stripped it off, then as he let it drop to the floor, he swore. The molasses had seeped right through the shirt and stained the front of his singlet.

Harry Fisher simmered with perpetual outrage at the injustices the world bestowed on him, but especially those that occurred on the job at Webster Brothers' Groceries. A small man, he had the kind of rounded baby face that—when he was wearing a hat—suggested he was no more than a freckle-faced boy. Hatless, the receding line of his faded red hair made it apparent that he was approaching thirty. His eyes were brown like his cousin Theresa's, but while hers were soft and frequently wet with tears, his were small—and frequently venomous.

Ernest Exall would have preferred to live far away from Harry Fisher, but moving to a new boarding house would mean parting with Theresa Jackson. And now there was the additional factor of the money that Esther Jones owed him. He would just have to make the best of it. Tonight he certainly didn't feel like defending the CPR but to avoid a conflict with Harry he said mildly, "I'll check with the freight people in the morning." There was nothing, of course, that a mere ticket clerk could do about the condition of arriving freight and Ernest knew it. So did Harry.

"I'll check with the freight people," Harry mimicked Exall's West Country English accent. "You just been promoted to president of the railroad?" And he swaggered into the dining room in his undershirt and took his seat.

Ernest followed. Standing in front of her own place at the table, Esther ladled soup from the china tureen then carried the first bowl to Harry, placing one hand on his shoulder as she put it in front of him. Viciously he pushed her hand away.

"Think I'll help you if you toady up to me, don't you?" he snarled. "Don't kid yourself! I don't owe you nothing!"

Esther's glance flickered toward Exall, and for an instant he thought he could detect a flash of fear on her face, but it was gone so quickly that he couldn't be sure. *But what reason would she have to fear me?* he wondered. The next moment her usual half smile played around her lips. Then suddenly Exall had another thought: *Maybe it's Harry that she's afraid of … and what did he mean about owing her?*

At the other end of the table Theresa Jackson raised her napkin to cover her mouth. Her eyes had filled with tears.

Harry stopped eating and waved his spoon at Exall. "You ever kill a rat, Exall?"

The young man shook his head, hoping that would be the end of the topic. But it wasn't.

"Strychnine, that's the ticket for them. Got fifteen of them in the traps at Webster's warehouse this morning. Big as cows they were! Ever seen what happens when a rat gets into strychnine? Twitches all over like it's got St. Vitus's dance." He stood up and, carefully watching Exall's face, began demonstrating the actions of a rat in its death throes.

Suddenly Esther's voice sliced across his laughter. "Stop it!" Her voice dropped to a whisper. "Eat your dinner and behave yourself!"

With his mouth still open Harry darted a look at her then let his eyes slide briefly to Exall before he sat down and hunched over his plate again.

TWO

Wednesday, November 8, 1905, was rainy and chill, and by early evening great banks of fog had crept up from the harbour and draped themselves over the city, muffling the sounds of auto engines, streetcars, horses' hooves and wagon wheels as they moved through the streets. In the West End the heaps of leaves piled ready for the street cleaners' drays had been scattered by the winds of the previous week and now lay wet and rotting under the passing traffic.

On West Pender Street a bell clanged continuously as a streetcar began to move cautiously west toward Stanley Park. At the rear of the car the conductor chatted to a mackinaw-coated man. "So you came in on the *Camosun*, did you?" he asked.

"Yes. She was delayed in the fog, but after seven months up north a few more hours don't seem like much."

"That was Burrard Street we just passed, sir," the conductor told him. "Your stop is next." He pulled the overhead signal cord.

"I don't know how you can tell one street from another in this stuff," the man said, but he shouldered his duffle bag. The black dog that lay curled at his feet rose in anticipation.

"Oh, you get used to it," the conductor said.

"I'll never live long enough for that!" And the man laughed.

A moment later the car stopped and man and dog stepped down into the fog and darkness. On the sidewalk the man paused to pull his hat lower and get his bearings, but the dog was already pulling on the leash, heading up Thurlow Street. Not quite trusting the animal to remember the way home, the man walked with one hand outstretched to locate trees and utility poles before he collided with them. He had only lived in the house for a few weeks the previous spring, but he remembered that it was just one short block south from the streetcar line, then west for a half block. Number 1284 Melville Street. He remembered it as a tall gray house with a picket fence and peculiarly shaped gateposts. Not that this would do him much good in the fog. He would have to rely on the dog to turn in at the right gate.

At 1284 Melville, dinner was over. To everyone's relief, Harry Fisher had slipped out into the fog to make his way to Murphy's Billiard Hall. As usual, he would return long after they were all in bed. In the front parlour Ernest Exall read and re-read the same paragraph of *The Virginian.* He had positioned his chair so that he could listen to the women's talk in the kitchen where they were washing and drying the dishes, but neither of them had said a word since they rose from the table.

Exall, anxious about Theresa's health, decided that she was the bravest little woman he had ever known, sticking gallantly by her mother in spite of the awful cloud over the old woman's head. In the two months since her mother's arraignment, Theresa had lost weight and dark shadows had formed beneath her eyes. Esther Jones seemed physically unchanged, but the half smile seldom played around her mouth anymore. Exall was convinced that waiting for the trial to begin had proved harder than either of the women would acknowledge, but it was still two weeks away, and there seemed to be nothing he could do to help.

Ever since their court appearance the women had been repudiated by the community. In shops the clerks ignored Esther, responding only to Theresa as she stood watery-eyed, her little hanky held to her mouth with her bitten-nailed fingers. No one came to call anymore, and not even their nearest neighbours invited them to tea. Their social life, meagre though it had been, had come to a standstill. With the onset of the November fogs, their isolation was complete.

So no one in the house was prepared for the doorbell to ring. Exall's reaction was to slam his book shut, half rise, then sit again. As a mere boarder it was not his place to answer the door. In the kitchen Theresa dropped the cup she was drying and it shattered into a dozen shards. Esther froze with her hands in the dishpan.

The doorbell rang again.

Whimpering, Theresa dropped to her knees and began picking up the bits of china.

"Answer it, Tess," Esther hissed.

"I've got to clean this up," and she began sobbing as if it had been the last cup in the house.

"Answer the door!" Esther pulled her daughter to her feet and shoved her toward the front hallway. "Whoever it is, I'm not here, you understand?"

In the parlour doorway Ernest Exall stood undecided what to do. His darling Tessie was obviously in no condition to answer the door, and he was about to intercede when he caught Esther's fierce eyes fastened on him. Without a word he retreated into the parlour.

Theresa approached the door cautiously, glancing back at her mother in the kitchen doorway, hoping for a reprieve.

The bell rang again and she stopped in her tracks.

"Get on with it," Esther hissed and disappeared into the kitchen.

Slowly Theresa slid back the deadbolt, turned the handle and inched the door open.

"Who is it?" she asked. In the fog and darkness of the porch stood the bulky figure of a man, hat in hand, a huge duffle bag mounted on his shoulder. The porch light glistened on his bald head and on the damp fur of the dog that strained on its leash toward her.

"Tessie?" he said. "Tessie, it's me!"

"Thomas?" she said in a terrified voice.

"Yes, love, it's me! I'm home!" He swung the duffle bag off his shoulder in order to push the door open and take her in his arms, but by this time Theresa Jackson was lying in the front hall, fainted dead away. Thomas Jackson and Ernest Exall reached her at the same moment.

"What have you done to her?" Exall demanded, bending to pick her up.

Jackson, already on his knees, glanced up angrily into the other man's face. "Who the hell are you?" The dog, wedging himself under Jackson's arm, tried to lick Theresa's face.

"His name is Ernest Exall," Esther announced calmly from the kitchen doorway. "He's the boarder I wrote you about, Thomas. Ernest, this is Mr. Jackson—Theresa's husband." Turning back to the newcomer, she said flatly, "Welcome home, Thomas." Pushing the dog out of the way, she stooped over her daughter as she lay cradled in her husband's arms and snapped open the little vial of smelling salts that Theresa wore on a chain around her neck. Waving it under the young woman's nose, she ordered, "Wake up, Tess." Then raising her voice very slightly but not bothering to turn and look at him, she said, "Ernest, this is family matters." And she dismissed him to the parlour with a wave of her hand.

Her husband! Since no one had ever mentioned the man, Exall had just assumed that he was dead. Immobilized by despair as he watched Jackson bending over the woman he had hoped to claim as his own, he stood in the parlour doorway until she began to revive, then at last he retreated, pulling the door shut behind him.

But he's too old to be Tess's husband! Exall's mind reeled with the shock of this new development. *And if he is her husband,* he asked himself, *why is she so terrified of him? She actually fainted when she saw him at the door! Oh my god, I'll bet he beats the poor little thing! That's why she's so scared. And just where's he been all this time?* he wondered. *Oh my god, I bet he's just out of jail! That's why they've never mentioned him. They were too ashamed.* And now the man had come back to claim his wife again. "I won't let him," Exall said aloud. "I won't let him have her!"

Outside the parlour door Jackson struggled to his feet with his wife in his arms. Exall shuddered as he listened to the man's footsteps mounting the stairs. Oh god, his beautiful Tessie would be going to bed with this old man, this jailbird, and he was powerless to save her. *But I will, Tess, I will,* he promised.

When Exall came down to breakfast the next morning, Esther Jones and her nephew were deep in conversation. He caught the words "strike" and "Skeena" before they noticed him and stopped talking. But they had given Exall the clues he needed to decide where Jackson had been—probably not in jail after all, but prospecting along the Skeena River where the latest gold strikes had been made.

Exall slid into his chair at the kitchen table as Harry Fisher bent his head over his dish of oatmeal and resumed spooning it up in silence. Behind him Esther Jones moved from the stove to the table with Exall's breakfast. Matching Harry's silence, he began to eat. It was beginning to dawn on him that there was much about this family that he didn't understand. *Maybe I should ask for a transfer to Saskatoon or Winnipeg and clear right out of here,* he thought, but there was the matter of the bail money to be considered. If he left town, he might never recover his savings. And he would never see Tessie again, either. *She needs me,* he told himself.

"Coffee, Ernest?" Esther asked.

He shook his head and rose from the table. "No," he said. "I'm late for work." He grabbed his coat from the peg near the door. He was, in fact, early for work but he was totally unnerved by Harry Fisher hunched wordlessly over his plate, and he couldn't stay in the house any longer straining his ears for sounds from upstairs.

"Are you working this Sunday, Ernest?" Esther asked, handing him his lunch bucket.

Why did she ask him that every week? "Yes. I have to work every Sunday until the end of February." He fled out the door. He would have to make excuses to avoid being around the house so often in the evenings. Maybe he'd take Plummy up on one of his invitations to play billiards or go dancing.

It was after six o'clock on Saturday, November 11, before Exall again dined with the family at 1284 Melville Street. Esther Jones was preparing to serve roast beef and Yorkshire pudding. Theresa stood counting out cutlery at the sideboard. Beside her Thomas Jackson was pouring what was very obviously not his first beer of the evening.

"Exall," he shouted jovially, "sit down and have a beer with me."

Exall's eyes slid from Jackson to his wife, but Theresa began fussing with the napkins and the place settings, careful not to look at him. He studied her face for signs that her husband had abused her, but except for her heightened level of tension and an almost deathly pallor, she seemed much as she had been when he last saw her on the night of Jackson's arrival.

"No, thanks," he told Jackson. "I'm not much of a beer drinker."

"No, no," Jackson insisted, "you're having a drink with me." He put the glass into Exall's hand. "There. Now, young fellow, sit down and tell me all about yourself. I want to get to know you." He pulled out the nearest dining chair and pushed Exall into it then sat down across from him.

But Exall was saved from launching into his life's story by the arrival of Fisher who went straight to the sideboard to pour himself a drink.

Jackson, seeing him, said, "I finished the last of the stout, Harry, but I bought a half-dozen Red Cross this afternoon. Where'd I put 'em, Tessie?"

But it was Esther Jones, just entering the dining room with the roast on a platter, who answered. "You left them in the pantry right beside those packets of salts you brought home."

"Oh," her daughter cried out anxiously, "I'll get it for you, Harry!" She hurried toward the kitchen, but Harry was already on his way, and she stopped in the doorway between the dining room and the kitchen to watch him. In the pantry Harry picked up one of the paste-board packages of Epsom salts and, knowing that the others could not see what he was up to, he balanced it on his palm and smiled tauntingly at her.

"Harry," Jackson called after him, "I'm trying to get this Exall fellow here to tell me about himself." As Theresa fled back to the sideboard, Jackson, laughing, put out an arm to snag her around the waist and pull her to him, but she quickly extricated herself and returned to her duties. Swinging his attention back to Exall, Jackson asked, "Did that young scallawag ever tell you how I found him?"

Exall shook his head. Could Jackson really be referring to *Harry* as a scallawag?

Jackson laughed and slapped Exall's knee. "I was down in Seattle on business … This was five years ago just after Tess and I got married, you see … and I was in this tavern having a drink at the bar, and this young fellow come up and stood right next to me. 'Where you from?' he says to me, and I tell him Alberni. I had the old Arlington in Alberni in those days, you see, and he said, 'Now that's a coincidence. I've got an aunt that works in Alberni. Name's Esther Jones!'" Jackson laughed happily and knocked back the remaining beer in the glass he was holding. "Isn't that the damnedest? Here was Esther working for me and she never even mentioned she had a nephew in Seattle, and there we were in that great big town and the two of us end up side by side at the bar!"

Fisher had returned to the dining room with a bottle of Red Cross beer, and throughout Jackson's story he and the two women had been watchfully quiet, but as Jackson finished, Esther slammed shut the drawer of the sideboard. With a startled cry, Theresa Jackson dropped the cutlery to the floor and began to sob.

Jackson's laugh died immediately and he started to get up to go to his wife, but Esther had moved more swiftly. "Stop that this minute," she ordered. Theresa's tears ceased on one long indrawn breath.

Jackson laughed and settled into his chair again. "There, there, nothing to get upset about, Tessie. I'm going to give you a dose of those salts when I take mine. That'll fix your nerves up!"

Suddenly Exall had the awful feeling that something momentous had just happened—not merely the slamming of the drawer and the dropped cutlery—but some turning point in the family's life, the exhumation of some secret that the others were privy to and he and Jackson were not. It was a few moments before he found his voice. "You mentioned the Arlington? What's that?"

"My hotel," Jackson explained. "Me and couple of partners. Esther come along a couple of years later to housekeep, and my little Tessie come with her to wait table till I married her." As his wife passed on her way to the kitchen, Jackson reached out again and pulled her onto his knee. "So I brought Harry home with me and put him to work in the Jolly Jack. You should have seen their faces when we stepped off the boat together! Isn't that right, Harry?" He roared with laughter then gave his wife an affectionate squeeze. "That was some surprise, wasn't it, Tessie? Get me another beer, there's a good girl."

"What's the Jolly Jack?" asked Exall.

"A bloody hole in the ground," snarled Harry Fisher, "that nothing good ever came out of."

Jackson laughed good-naturedly. "Ah, poor Harry come along when we'd about done with the old Jolly Jack. She was a pretty good producer up till then, but she petered out a couple of months after he came. Now the Black Diadem, that was a real mine. You should have been there for her, Harry. She was a producer!" He turned to Exall. "I sold her to buy the Arlington back in 1900."

"Dinner's on the table, Thomas." Esther obviously wanted her son-in-law off this topic, but Exall was not quite sure why. "We'd better sit down and eat before it gets cold."

"Coming, Mother," Jackson said, apparently oblivious to the fact that he had annoyed her, and he gave her a playful hug before he took his seat. "All right, let's have this beautiful dinner you've been so busy preparing."

Her face never changed expression. "I've promised Mr.

Soames we'll visit him this evening," she said as she began serving. "He goes into hospital in the morning and he phoned to say he could do with some company."

"Soames?" asked Jackson. "Willie Soames? What's he going into hospital for?"

Esther coughed primly. "It's not dinnertime conversation, Thomas."

"Oh," he said. "Well, you and Tessie go. I'm taking Harry and Exall here to the Stag and Pheasant. I'll drop in and see old Willie tomorrow."

Exall opened his mouth to protest that he had other plans but Harry was faster.

"I have to work until nine tonight, Tom," he said. "We'll have to make it another night."

"All right, but I'm taking Exall tonight. I want to get to know this boy."

Across the table Harry Fisher looked pleased with himself, and once again Exall had the feeling that something important had just clicked into place within the family's little circle, but what it was he had no idea. By this time he had changed his mind about turning Jackson's invitation down; he would take the opportunity to study his enemy at close range.

"Harry?" Theresa Jackson called out as she and her mother removed their coats in the front hall. "Harry, are you home?"

"Don't be silly, girl!" her mother snapped. She kicked the black dog that lay on the hall carpet and the animal retreated.

"But he said he would be finished work at nine, and it's half after ten …"

"And when did he ever come straight home from work?" Esther Jones hung her coat on the hall stand and started up the stairs.

"I just thought … Are you going to bed, Mother? Shall I bring you a cup of tea?"

Esther shook her head and continued plodding upward.

"Good night, Mother," Theresa offered. Her mother made no response, but Theresa stood watching her climb to the top of the stairs before she scurried down the hall, into the kitchen and then into the pantry, turning on lights as she went. The dog followed her expectantly. On the pantry counter sat the two packages of Epsom salts that her husband had brought home that afternoon. Snatching them up, she scuttled back into the kitchen, stopping in panic in the middle of the room. Just then she heard the front door opening and the dog raced out of the room to meet his master. Turning, she darted back into the pantry with the packages, climbed on top of the trunk sitting in the corner, and wedged the packages between the biscuit boxes on the top shelf.

"Tessie!" Jackson yelled. "You home?" And he lumbered down the hall with Exall and the dog in his wake. "Tessie?"

She popped anxiously from the kitchen. "Mother has gone to bed, Thomas." She put her hand up to shush him. "You must be quieter."

Decidedly the worse for drink, he grabbed her hand playfully and raised it to his lips. "Sh-h-h," he told her. "We're being quiet as mice. Aren't we, Exall?"

"Come," and she urged him toward the kitchen. "I'm making tea."

"Tea?" He laughed uproariously but allowed her to lead him. "What do we want with tea?"

"I'll have some, Tess," Exall said, pulling out a chair at the table.

Without acknowledging him, she went to the sink to fill the kettle.

"I can't make this fellow out, Tessie," Jackson said, coming up behind his wife, wrapping his arms around her waist and nuzzling her neck. "I don't know no more about him now than I did before! Would you believe it—I did all the talking."

"And all the drinking, I think, Thomas," she offered timidly.

He laughed. "You wouldn't grudge me that, would you, pet? Not after all those months in the bush?" He kissed the back of her neck and moved unsteadily toward the pantry, returning moments later with two bottles of beer. Exall, using his foot, pushed a chair out for him, and Jackson sat heavily. "Did I tell you about the time we run out of tea on the Babine, Ernie? Well, it was August, you see, and me and my partner, old Boyd McKenzie, we'd been prospecting up there for nigh on three weeks and we were ready to give up on her and trek out when we had this snowfall. This was in August, mind you ..." The dog leaned against Jackson's leg, and the man's hand reached out automatically to caress the dog's head. "So there we were way to hell and gone up that river, and it started snowing ..."

Jackson was still telling stories a few minutes before midnight when Harry Fisher finally arrived home, entering silently through the back door. "Harry," Jackson cried, "I was just telling young Exall here —"

"Would you like tea, Harry?" Theresa asked, getting guiltily to her feet and rushing to tend to the fire.

"Where's the beer?" Fisher demanded, eyeing the empties on the table.

"There's more in the ..." she said, but he had already gone into the pantry. She fluttered after him, but by the time she arrived, he had snatched up a bottle of Red Cross and was wrenching the metal cap off. She hesitated in the doorway then retreated, and he returned to the kitchen to stand wide-legged before the stove, tipping his head back and draining half the bottle in one long swallow.

"I was just telling young Exall here," Jackson began again, "about this new property of mine on the Skeena. She's a winner this time, Harry!" He stood. "What say you come back up there with me in the spring? We'd have a great old time, you and me —"

"But, Thomas," Theresa protested, "you said you had a buyer for that claim —"

But Fisher was shaking his head. "And slog around in the mud again?" He drained the rest of the bottle, put the empty on the table and headed for the front hall.

"Not this time, Harry, old boy!" Jackson said, catching up to him. "It's halfway up a mountain."

Theresa followed, anxiously calling after him, "Don't wake Mother ..."

"This time I've got me a real honey of a claim," Jackson said, trudging after Harry up the stairs. "Wait'll you see it —"

"I don't need to see it —"

The dog, after a final mournful glance at Theresa, went up the stairs behind Jackson. Theresa watched them anxiously. "Don't wake Mother," she repeated.

Behind her, Exall rose from his chair. "Tessie?"

"Not now, Ernest," she said and, without looking at him, scurried past him into the pantry. "I must clear away and put out the breakfast things."

He hesitated. He was desperate to talk to her alone, but she was quite right. This was not the time. "Good night," he whispered and left the room.

Minutes later, as she was washing the teacups, she heard a woman's voice upstairs and hastened back to the hallway. *Mother will be so cross in the morning,* she worried as she started up the stairs, but at that moment she heard her mother's laugh and breathed again. It would be all right, after all. Back in the pantry, no sooner had she raised her skirts in order to climb onto the trunk to retrieve the packages of salts when Jackson came clumping back down the stairs.

"Tess," he called, "what did you do with my salts?"

By the time he reappeared in the kitchen, she had turned out the pantry light and was standing by the sink.

"I'm going to need that dose of salts in the morning," he said as he wandered into the pantry and turned on the light again. "What did you do with them?"

"What salts are you talking about, Thomas?"

"The Epsom salts I bought at the chemist's this afternoon."

"I didn't see them."

"They were right here," he said and he patted the counter in the pantry. "I put them right here."

"Well, they're not there now," she offered tremulously. "We'll find them in the morning."

"I put 'em right here so they must be around here someplace. Maybe Mother put 'em away." He moved toward the hallway again but Theresa was there before him.

"Mother," she called up the stairs, "did you see the salts Thomas brought home this afternoon?"

"They were on the counter in the pantry," her mother called down.

"Well, they're not there now," he called up to her.

Theresa attempted to steer her husband toward the stairs again. "We'll find them in the morning, Thomas."

Instead Jackson returned to the pantry, and when she followed, she saw he was pointing up at the packages she had stowed away earlier. "What's that up there?" he asked. "On the top shelf. That looks like 'em." He started to climb onto the trunk then thought better of it. "Here, Tess, you do it." He put his hands on her waist and began hoisting her onto the trunk. "That's my girl! Don't worry, I've got you!" He caressed her bottom as she straightened up.

"I don't think I can reach them, Thomas. I'll get one of the boys to get them in the morning."

She would have climbed down but he held her there. "No, no, they're right there beside your hand. That's it. That's my girl." He took the package she handed him, helped her down from the trunk, grabbed a bottle of beer from the pantry counter and headed for the hallway. "Bring a couple of glasses when you come, will you, pet?" Then as he started up the stairs, he called back, "And a spoon."

On Sunday, November 12, the city of Vancouver was still enveloped in a thick grey fog, nurtured by a thousand coal and wood-burning furnaces and kitchen stoves. At eight that morning Ernest Exall sat down to eat his breakfast alone at 1284 Melville Street with Esther Jones hovering nearby, determined to heap his plate with bacon and eggs.

"No, thank you. I just want toast." Then after a minute or two of chewing he added, "I'm going to St. Alden's for the service tonight so I won't be home for dinner."

"Yes, you told me. Well, you'd best hurry or you'll be late for work. Your lunch pail's in the pantry."

"There's plenty of time," he said.

Esther vanished in the direction of the front parlour, leaving Exall to his thoughts.

Around three in the morning while he had been on his second cold, barefoot journey to the bathroom, he had heard Tess cry out as he passed the Jacksons' bedroom door. In spite of being the recipient of Jackson's hospitality all evening, he'd had a momentary wild impulse to break down the door and kill the man on the spot. Instead he'd returned meekly to his room and imagined himself holding his darling Tessie in his arms and comforting her. Since Jackson had returned, he hadn't once been alone with her. If he could just talk to her, he knew he could convince her to run away with him as soon as the old lady's trial was over and he got his money back.

At four in the morning Exall had gone downstairs to the pantry where he prepared himself a bicarbonate of soda. In bed again he had fallen into a fitful sleep. So on this Sunday morning as he dawdled over his coffee and the kitchen clock ticked off the minutes, he was experiencing the giddy euphoria of one with much on his mind and too little sleep. Still he lingered, convinced that any moment now Tess would suddenly appear for an early breakfast, he would pour out his plans for their future, and she would rush into his arms. But there was no sound from upstairs, and at last he was forced to grab his coat and lunch bucket and race out the door.

As she heard him leave, Esther gave a snort of amusement, then returned to the kitchen where she cleared the table and sat down to peel apples for a pie. It was now 8:35 a.m. Upstairs in the darkness of the early morning Theresa Jackson lay awake beside her sleeping husband, her body rigid, her eyes wide and staring as she waited for him to wake. In the room at the far end of the hall Harry Fisher slept the deep sleep of the innocent.

It was well after nine when Thomas Jackson woke. The night's drinking had left him with a thick tongue and a full bladder, and he stumbled out of bed without a glance at his wife and wrenched open the bedroom door, which always stuck in wet weather. In the bathroom after emptying his bladder, he stripped to the waist and gave himself a cold wash at the sink. When he returned to the bedroom, shoving his arms into the sleeves of his long johns, Theresa was already dressed and with trembling fingers was trying to pin her hair up.

"I must get downstairs and help Mother with the breakfast," she said, scraping the door open again.

"Make me up a dose of salts before you go," he said, combing his hair in front of the mirror over the bureau.

She stopped in the doorway.

"I'll just take my usual." He walked over to the washstand, opened the package of salts and held it out, then put it down again while he reached for the bottle of beer. "And some for yourself. It'll do you good."

"Thomas, I ... I don't ..." She came slowly toward him.

"Did you bring a spoon?"

She retrieved the spoon from the washstand and showed it to him.

"Just put some salts in the glass for me, there's a girl." He pierced the metal cap on the beer bottle and peeled it back.

With shaking hands, Theresa Jackson spooned salts into a glass, put it down on the washstand and turned to leave.

"That's not a dose, pet. I usually take half a packet!" He picked up the package and poured more of the salts into his glass then poured a small quantity into a second glass. "It'll do your nerves a world of good!" And he proceeded to fill his glass with beer. When he raised the bottle to pour beer into the second glass, she put her hand over it.

"No, Thomas." Her face had gone ashen, but she picked up the water jug and poured some into her glass.

He smiled encouragingly while he stirred the concoction in his own. "Nothing to be afraid of, pet, and you'll feel ever so much better." And he drank his medicine down, refilled his glass with beer and drank that down, too. "Now you," he said and watched while she sat on the edge of the bed and with an unsteady hand raised the glass to her lips and drank the contents. "There now. That wasn't so bad, was it?" He picked his shirt off a chair and began putting it on. "Where's my trousers, pet? Oh, here they are on the floor where I dropped 'em." He laughed. "I've been in the bush too long, I can see that." He sat beside her to put on his slippers. "Come on, let's see what Mother is cooking for breakfast. I smell bacon!"

"Good morning, Mother," Jackson said as he entered the kitchen. He planted a kiss on Esther's cheek.

"Good morning, Tom." Esther Jones ran the spatula under the eggs sputtering in the frying pan and flipped them expertly. "Make the toast, Tess," she ordered as her daughter trailed in after Jackson. Theresa, pale and shaking, went to the sideboard and began cutting bread.

As Jackson took his seat at the kitchen table, the dog came out from behind the stove and settled at his feet. "Harry still in bed, Mother?" Jackson asked.

She nodded. "He always sleeps late on a Sunday." And she began piling Jackson's plate with eggs, bacon and fried potatoes.

He held up a hand. "Not so much, Mother. I took a dose of salts and I'm feeling a bit strange."

"Have you finished the toast, Tess?" Esther Jones demanded. Turning, she discovered her daughter clinging with both hands to the sideboard. "What's the matter with you, girl?"

"I insisted she take some salts," Jackson said, "and I don't think they agreed with her." He rose from his chair just as Theresa bolted for the pantry, retching ineffectually. He followed. "What's the matter, pet?"

Theresa, her face now flushed, clutched at her stomach but seemed unable to speak.

"Come and have a cup of coffee," he coaxed her. "I'm feeling a bit queer myself but a cup of coffee will make it all right. Come along." He put an arm around her and led her to the table where Esther was pouring coffee. Seating her, he put the cup into her hands. "You drink that and you'll feel better." Then without warning, he slumped into his own chair and clasped his arms to his belly. "Could I have some coffee, Mother?" he groaned.

The dog skittered away from Jackson's chair and stood at a distance, watching warily.

"What's the matter, Thomas?" Esther asked. His face had gone deathly white. "Are you sick?"

Before he had a chance to reply, Theresa, reaching out a trembling hand to put down her coffee cup, missed the table and the cup crashed to the floor. Moments later she slipped off her chair and crumpled into a heap in the middle of the spilled coffee and broken china. Jackson stumbled to his feet again. "Tessie!" he cried as he knelt beside her. "Tessie, what's wrong?" And he tried to take her in his arms.

"I'm dying," she whimpered, but with his help she slowly pulled herself to a sitting position.

Abruptly Jackson clutched at his stomach again. "Oh, god!" Clumsily, he started to rise then fell to his knees, moaning in pain. "Get the doctor, Mother!"

"Harry!" Esther screamed, running into the front hall and up the stairs. "Harry! Come quickly! Tom and Tessie are dying! Come quick!" She pounded on Harry's door. "Harry! Harry!"

After a few moments Harry opened the door a crack. "What's the matter?"

"Phone for the doctor! I think they're dying!" She started for the stairs again.

"Who's dying?"

"Tessie and Tom! I think they're dying!" She ran down the

stairs to find Jackson on the hall floor, twitching uncontrollably.

"Air," he whispered. "I need air."

She hurried to the front door and flung it open to the raw November morning. "Harry!" she screamed again as her daughter staggered into the hall from the kitchen. "I think they've been poisoned! Call Dr. Riggs!" And she ran toward Theresa just as the young woman sank to her knees. Esther dragged her through the archway to the dining room and pushed her into the steamer chair next to the sideboard.

"Tess!" Jackson groaned and began crawling to where his wife lay slumped in the chair. "Tessie darling, don't die!" Then catching sight of Harry on the stairs, he cried out, "She's dying, Harry! For god's sake, get the doctor!"

Harry, his eyes widening as he saw Theresa lying as lifeless as a rag doll in the chair, ran to the hall phone. "What's his number?"

"It's there by the phone!" Esther shouted. "Hurry!" And she ran through the kitchen to the pantry, snatched up a container of mustard, ran back to the sink and, after dumping some of the mustard into a glass, filled it with water. Back in the dining room, she pried her daughter's mouth open and began pouring the mixture down her throat. Next she knelt beside Jackson where he sat on the floor and tried to make him drink some of it, but he could not swallow and it splashed down his chest and onto the floor. She bolted for the kitchen again, this time returning with a basket of eggs, and proceeded to crack one of them open and force its raw contents down Theresa's throat. But as soon as she turned to administer the same to her son-in-law, her daughter roused, struggled to sit up and vomited mustard, water and egg all over herself and her mother.

Harry, coming into the dining room from the hallway at that moment, asked fearfully, "What do you want me to do?" He went toward Theresa then backed off at the smell of vomit.

"Is the doctor coming?" Jackson begged.

"Yeah, he's on his way," Harry said.

"Help me get Tom onto the couch," Esther ordered, nodding toward the settee at the end of the room.

But Jackson waved them weakly away. "Look after Tessie," he begged, but as Esther Jones persisted in her attempts to move him, he was seized with a convulsion and landed heavily on the floor again where he was racked with violent spasms. Standing over him, Harry watched in fascination. "Just like the rats," he muttered.

Esther, on her knees trying to wedge a spoon between Jackson's teeth, looked up in alarm. "Strychnine?" she whispered. "Harry ..."

Harry's gaze was cool. "You want me to put him on the couch?"

Still staring at him, she shook her head. Then as Jackson's spasms ceased, Harry turned away and walked to the front window. "Doctor's here," he said.

Esther rushed to the front door. "Hurry, doctor!" she called down to him.

"What's the trouble here?" he asked as he mounted the stairs.

"They've been poisoned!" she said, ushering him into the house. "Hurry!"

Jackson had managed to seat himself on the settee by the time Riggs entered the room. "See to my wife, doctor," he whispered. "Don't worry about me." And the doctor turned away and put his bag down beside Theresa who was retching again.

"Some kind of irritant poison, I think," he said. "I'm going to wash her stomach out." And he sent Esther to the kitchen to get a basin and fill a jar with warm salted water. Harry watched these proceedings anxiously from his post by the window, but when Jackson began to groan again, he headed for the hallway. "I'll need more help," Riggs called after him. "Phone for Dr. Underhill to come. His number's 51L."

"Harry? Did you hear?" Esther demanded. "Phone Dr. Underhill at 51L."

"I heard," Harry said from the hall.

"Tell him to bring a stomach pump," Riggs called after him without turning his attention from Theresa. "There, that should do it. Now hold the basin, Mrs. Jones, while I see to this fellow." But as Riggs stood up, Jackson was seized with another convulsion and slid from the settee. Down on his knees beside him, Riggs began preparing a hypodermic.

"Underhill's at church," Harry reported from the archway.

"Call Dr. Young," Esther ordered. "His number's by the phone." Harry vanished into the hall again. "He's Tess's doctor," she told Riggs.

Theresa, having vomited up the salt water, now began whimpering at the sight of her husband jerking and twitching on the floor. "Thomas!" she cried weakly. "Oh, Thomas ..."

"Take your daughter to the kitchen, Mrs. Jones. It's not doing her any good to see her husband like this."

Esther pulled Theresa to her feet and half-carried her out of the room.

"Young's on his way," Harry announced from the doorway. Once again he was mesmerized by Jackson's convulsion.

"Here, help me hold him still," the doctor ordered.

But as soon as the two of them held Jackson down, the violence of the convulsion increased and they were forced to let him go. Now he was gasping desperately for air.

"He's going to asphyxiate," Riggs muttered, and reaching out, he held Jackson's arm tightly for a moment before jabbing the hypodermic needle into it.

"What's that?" Harry asked.

"Morphia. It should calm him." But it had no immediate effect and minutes passed before the spasms began to subside. By this time he had stopped breathing. "Help me turn him over," Riggs ordered, and together they got Jackson onto his stomach. Riggs immediately straddled him and began artificial respiration. Five minutes passed with the doctor pumping rhythmically before Jackson breathed freely again, but Riggs had barely climbed off him when Jackson was overtaken by yet another convulsion. Riggs reloaded his morphia syringe, but this time there was no opportunity to inject it as the patient flailed and jerked with such violence that he could not be restrained for even a moment. When at last the flailing began to subside, Riggs plunged the needle into his arm. Moments later the convulsions began again. Then asphyxia and resuscitation. And then again.

Half an hour later it was all over. In the midst of a final paroxysm, he ceased moving altogether, and the terrifying sounds of his struggle for breath ended. In the silence that followed, the doorbell rang. Harry rose, left the room and returned with Dr. Young.

"He's gone," said Riggs. "Asphyxiated."

The dog slunk into the kitchen and hid behind the stove.

THREE

"Hopkins!" Walter Nichol shouted as he put down the telephone.

All heads in the *Province* newsroom turned toward the young reporter, some merely curious, others affording themselves a smile at his discomfort in being singled out by their hard-driving publisher. Dennis Hopkins rose warily and went to stand in the doorway of Nichol's office.

"Your lady friend's making news again."

"My lady friend, sir?"

"Jackson. Theresa Jackson. She and her husband have been poisoned." Nichol tossed him the sheet of yellow paper on which he had taken down the phone message.

The young man felt his heart contract. "She's dead?"

"No," Nichol said, picking up another sheaf of copy to read. "*He* is, though. Chief North says it was strychnine."

"I bet that old lady did it. Did he arrest her?"

"That's for you to find out. Get on your bike and get yourself over to the police station."

"Me, sir? You want me to interview the police chief?"

Nichol didn't even look up. "You don't see anyone else with the name Hopkins standing around, do you?"

Hopkins hurried back to his desk, thanking god that Michael Kelly had apparently fallen off the wagon yet again and had failed to show up for work. "Doctor Herbert Riggs reports," he read from the yellow paper as he stowed a notebook and pencil in his pocket, "that Thomas W. Jackson, 48, died Sunday morning around ten. Strychnine. Mrs. J. also poisoned but survives."

"Get a date for the inquest!" Nichol bellowed as Hopkins slipped into his overcoat and scurried out the door.

"It's murder, my boy!" Chief Samuel North exulted. "Murder! And you can tell the *World*'s readers that they can expect an arrest before the day is out!" North tilted his chair back and hooked his thumbs into his waistcoat pockets.

"I'm with the *Province*, Chief," Dennis Hopkins ventured.

"Well, no matter. You can tell 'em that Chief North won't let the dastardly villain that done this get away with it!"

In May 1901 when Samuel North had won the post of chief of police—thereby becoming the sixth police chief in the fifteen years since the city's incorporation—there had been no other bidders for the job. His predecessors had, after all, spent more time fighting off the criticisms of local politicians and the carping of newspaper editors than getting on with the job of law enforcement. But North had been with the force since 1890, rising through the ranks from patrolman to sergeant in charge of the chain gang, and he thought he knew the pitfalls to avoid in carrying out the job. He was wrong, of course, and in November 1905, when Thomas Jackson died of strychnine poisoning, most of Chief North's energies were employed in an ongoing war with the mayor and council. Quite a number

When Walter Cameron Nichol moved the *Province* newspaper from Victoria to Vancouver in 1898, the city already had two daily newspapers, so the Jones/Jackson case became a primary battleground in the circulation wars. Nichol and his *Province* were ultimately victorious, and the other two newspapers faded away. CITY OF VANCOUVER ARCHIVES, PORT P1504.

of their skirmishes were over brothels. The aldermen wanted them removed from Dupont Street (that portion of present-day Pender Street between the Sun Tower and Main Street) where they had become prominently established, but the politicians were unwilling to decide whether to ban them altogether from the city or allow their inmates to find suitable premises in less conspicuous districts. North, on the other hand, believed that the brothels were easier to control in a concentrated "red light district" and was quoted as being "unalterably opposed to cleaning out Dupont Street and allowing the ladies to scatter over the city." Most of North's remaining battles with council concerned the Sunday closing laws: the aldermen contended that North was deliberately allowing bars to open for business on the Sabbath, while North cited his lack of personnel—he had only five men on daytime duty and sixteen at night for the whole city—as his reason for failing to keep the bars closed. Thus, the Jackson case came as a godsend to him, a chance to divert some attention from brothels and bars—for a while at least.

"Was it the old lady who did it, Chief?" Hopkins, writing furiously in his notebook, demanded.

"What old lady?" asked the chief.

Hopkins paused in his writing. "Mrs. Jones." And when the

chief still looked blank, he explained, "Jackson's mother-in-law."

"Don't be daft, boy! Jackson took the poison in a glass of beer and Epsom salts—no woman could've masterminded a job like that! No, my boy, I got my eye on the killer and when the time is ripe, I'll swoop down and nab 'im."

"Who is it, Chief? Is it the boarder ... what's his name ... Exall?"

"Wait and see, my boy. Wait and see."

The *World*'s Norman Norcross, having arrived during this final exchange, interrupted with, "What about fingerprints, Chief?"

"Fingerprints!" North scoffed. "You don't want to go believing all that fancy hogwash that them Frenchies is putting out. It's good old-fashioned detective work as what brings 'em in every

The Vancouver City Police force posed in front of the Police Courthouse in 1903. The notoriously brutal jailer, John Grady, is seated at the far left in the front row. Police Chief Samuel North is seated in the centre of the front row. Both Grady and North were dismissed from the force in June 1906. CITY OF VANCOUVER ARCHIVES POL. P4

time, Norcross, and don't you forget it. I've got the finest detectives in the country to do it."

"So it's true you've put Jim Preston on the case?" Norcross said.

"That's right. Preston's the man for the job."

James Arthur Preston was not the only detective on Vancouver's police force and not even the head of that department. That role was filled by Detective Sergeant Michael Mulhern (although Preston would replace Mulhern as head of detectives in 1907). But Preston had recently solved a series of robberies in the city and had therefore become the darling of the media.

"When's the inquest, Chief?" Dennis Hopkins asked.

"You'll have to ask the coroner that, my boy." He stood up. "Well, that's it, gentlemen."

Dennis Hopkins stuffed his notebook back into his pocket and prepared to leave. "Oh, just one more thing, Chief. The wife ... Mrs. Jackson ... is she going to live?"

"Nothing wrong with that little woman that a good thrashing wouldn't cure!" And he laughed heartily as he ushered them from his office.

The police constable who sat behind the front desk of the coroner's office was not very forthcoming. Dr. William J. McGuigan was not in. No, he didn't know when he'd be back. Yes, there would be an autopsy. No, he couldn't tell him when, and no, he didn't know when the inquest would be resumed either.

"What do you mean resumed?" Hopkins asked.

"Dr. McGuigan empanelled a jury this morning and two of the witnesses gave evidence, but it had to be adjourned, didn't it?"

"Why?"

"Because they need an autopsy, don't they?"

"And you don't know when the autopsy will be held?"

"That's for Dr. Poole to decide, isn't it? He does the autopsies."

Hopkins's next stop was the surgery of Dr. Herbert Riggs, and he found the doctor more helpful.

"Strychnine? It's very bitter. Exceptionally bitter," Riggs said.

"So you'd know right away if that's what you'd been fed?" Hopkins asked.

"Well, not necessarily, young fellow. Not necessarily. You see ..." And he proceeded to give the reporter a half-hour lecture on the properties of strychnine and its effects on humans. Much of this Hopkins did not really understand and what he did understand gave him a strong urge to throw up, but he never stopped taking notes. However, as he pedalled back to the *Province*'s offices, it was not the unpleasant effects of strychnine that he was thinking about. It was fingerprints. He was thinking that if Preston had taken the fingerprints on the glass that held the beer, they'd have the dastardly villain who did this terrible deed just like that! And Hopkins was absolutely sure of this because he had read all about fingerprinting in the latest edition of *Argosy* magazine.

Back at the *Province*, Hopkins began typing up the results of his interviews, and then, after watching Walter Nichol put on his overcoat and sally out of the office, he dug the pulp magazine out of the bottom drawer of his desk and reread the article, stopping to ponder the sentences that read:

> In Canada the fingerprint system has been adopted by the police chiefs of all the big cities and it is soon to be placed in active operation. Already many of the larger detective agencies are employing it.

Except in Vancouver, Hopkins thought wryly before reading on. According to the *Argosy* story, the Chinese had known for centuries that handprints could be used to identify people, and the government there had used them on land transfer documents. But it was in

Prague in 1823 that a Czech physiologist named Johannes Purkinje first demonstrated quite conclusively that the pattern of ridges and whorls on fingertips was unique to the individual. Unfortunately, European police forces, which were just being organized at this time (Scotland Yard was founded in 1829), did not get around to making use of this information for another sixty years. Instead, in 1882 the French police adopted the system of criminal identification known as "Bertillonage," developed by the French anthropometrist Alphonse Bertillon. He had taken thousands of body measurements—the size of skulls, the length of finger bones—and discovered that no two human individuals are exactly alike. It was not until 1892 that Scotland Yard—having been assured by the eugenicist Sir Francis Galton (Charles Darwin's cousin) that fingerprints really were unique and that the chance of two individuals having identical fingerprints was one in 64 million—began collecting fingerprints to identify the country's professional criminals. The French, having at last found the Bertillon system too time-consuming and not especially efficient in identifying criminals, followed the British example in 1898. By 1905 Scotland Yard had a gallery of 800,000 impressions, and the London police were making an estimated 5,000 identifications each year by fingerprinting alone.

But that bloody stupid North doesn't believe in fingerprinting because he thinks the "Frenchies" invented it, Hopkins mused. *And Jackson's killer is going to get away scot-free …*

"Hopkins!" Nichol bellowed as he strode past the young reporter's desk. "Where's the story on the Jackson murder?"

"I'm typing it up right now, sir," Hopkins said, stuffing the magazine back into the drawer. *Now where was I …* And he began typing again.

> Strychnine comes in colourless crystals which are prac-
> tically insoluble in water but may dissolve in alcohol.

It has an exceptionally bitter taste. Symptoms usually appear within twenty minutes, starting with stiffness at the back of the neck, twitching of the muscles, and a feeling of impending suffocation. The patient is then seized with violent convulsions; the body arches and the head bends backwards. Then after a minute or two, the muscles relax and the patient sinks back exhausted. During this stage a touch, a noise, or some other stimulus will cause convulsions to recur or they can recur spontaneously every few minutes. Death comes from suffocation or exhaustion. Dr. Herbert Riggs says that a person suffering from strychnine poisoning should be promptly administered charcoal or egg white but not emetics as they will bring on more convulsions. The patient should be kept very quiet. Artificial respiration may be necessary ...

"Where the hell have you been?" Nichol bellowed from his office doorway. Startled, Hopkins looked up, but Nichol's question was directed at the man who had just entered the newsroom from the street—Michael Kelly, stubble-chinned and bleary-eyed but upright.

"Jackson inquest," Kelly said cheerfully. "But McGuigan adjourned it for a week to wait for Poole's autopsy report."

Nichol had long ago realized that chastising Kelly only provoked further disappearances, and since he was by far the best reporter on the paper and had a phenomenal nose for news, he merely growled, "Give your notes to Hopkins to type up and get in here. I want you to get over to the mayor's office ..."

On his way to Nichol's office Kelly flipped his notebook to Hopkins. "Here, kid," and then he added apologetically, "Lemme know if there's anything you can't read."

All of it! Dennis Hopkins thought as he stared at the court reporter's sketchy shorthand notes. Then as he became used to the scrawl, he realized that Kelly had taken down the testimony almost verbatim—a feat he was far from accomplishing himself. He read rapidly to the end before he began typing, his imagination soaring as his fingers flew.

> Mr. Thomas Jackson, a mining man who returned from the North on the steamer *Camosun* last Wednesday night, died under tragic circumstances yesterday forenoon at the residence of his mother-in-law, Mrs. Esther Jones, 1284 Melville Street. He passed away in terrible agony an hour and a half or two hours after taking a dose of Epsom salts in a glass of beer. His wife, a daughter of Mrs. Jones, shared the beer with him and was also taken violently ill and may not recover. It has not yet been established whether she, too, drank any of the salts. Everything points to poisoning by strychnine.

> Pathos and devoted conjugal love are woven into the weft and woof of this sad affair. While writhing on the floor in inexpressible agony as the deadly poison began to contract his limbs, the thoughts of the dying man were concentrated on the welfare of his wife who, being the first to feel the deadly effects of the poison, lay in a comatose state, the only symptom of life being the involuntarily frothing at the mouth and the twitching of her arms and jaw. "Oh my god, my god, my wife! Do what you can to save her life!" shouted the dying man to Harry Fisher, who lives in the Jackson/Jones household and had been awakened from sleep by Mrs. Jones. There was an unfortunate delay of fifteen minutes before Dr. H.W. Riggs, who was the first physician found, reached the house.

Detective Preston attended the residence a few minutes after death had ended Mr. Jackson's sufferings. He had the body removed to the undertaking establishment of Messrs. Center and Hanna where Dr. McGuigan, the coroner, empanelled the jury. The first witness, Mr. Harry Fisher, deposed that he has lived in the Jones household for the past six months and that he is a grocery clerk in the employ of Webster Bros. He told the court, "The other occupants of the house Saturday night were Mrs. Jones, who is a relative of mine, her daughter, Mrs. Jackson, and her husband, Mr. Thomas Jackson, and Mr. Ernest Exall. I usually work late Saturday nights and am in the habit of sleeping until noon on Sunday. Yesterday morning between nine and nine-thirty I was awakened by Mrs. Jones, who rushed into my room screaming out that Tom and Tess were dying and imploring me to get medical assistance. I called up Dr. Riggs three times before I could get him and this occupied about ten minutes. In all fifteen minutes elapsed before the doctor arrived. When Detective Preston arrived, I handed over to him the empty beer bottle and the two packages of Epsom salts."

In answer to the coroner's question Mr. Fisher explained, "After Mr. Jackson pleaded with me to help his wife, he told me that he had had a bottle of beer, though I am not positive on that point, but afterwards I found a bottle and two glasses in their bedroom. Mrs. Jones told me that they had drunk the beer upstairs in their bedroom before coming down for breakfast."

When questioned further by the jurors, Mr. Fisher said, "The relations of every member of the household were of the most harmonious character. Mr. Jackson had been away from the city since last April. He was a very temperate man and not given to drinking, but we always had beer in the house. Everybody was well the night before when I returned from work about 11:30. Nobody had retired. They were all in a good humour, laughing and chatting." Then in reply to another juror he repeated, "There was not a happier home in Vancouver."

Mr. Ernest Exall, who rooms and boards with Mrs. Jones, also gave evidence. He was not present in the house when the poisoning occurred.

Dr. McGuigan, who placed the jurymen under a $100 bond to appear next Monday to resume the inquest, dwelt on the gravity of the case. He said that he hoped in the interests of justice that every juror would be present at that time. He will take steps to have an analysis made of the contents of the bottle and glasses by Dr. Frederick T. Underhill, City Medical Health Officer, and will have an autopsy performed.

The deceased was a vigorous-looking man of forty-eight in the very prime of manhood. His life was insured for several thousand dollars and he owned considerable property. He was his wife's senior by many years as Mrs. Jackson, according to one of the witnesses, is only twenty-three or twenty-four years old.

Mrs. Jones recently figured as the defendant in an Assize case in which Captain W.W. Sprague was plaintiff.

Dennis Hopkins picked up the sheaf of typed paper, sat back and reread his story before calling for a copy boy. He was confident that Kelly could not have done better.

On Tuesday morning Kelly, well-shaved and obviously freshly bathed, got the plum assignment of attending Police Court for the remanded case against four boys who had burned down the cricket grandstand in Stanley Park. Dennis Hopkins spent his morning at a meeting of the Fire and Police Committee during which they argued endlessly over the awarding of a contract to provide the city with a new eight-hundred-gallon fire engine. When they finally agreed on the contract, he pedalled back to the office in sleety rain. He had just finished typing up his report when he heard Nichol bellow his name.

"Yes sir?"

"The Jackson funeral is at two o'clock. I want you to cover it and see if you can get an interview with this chap Fisher. Says he's related to the Jones woman."

Hopkins looked at the office clock. Not quite twelve-thirty. He could bicycle over to Melville Street first and see if Fisher would talk to him there. Much easier than accosting him at the funeral. He pulled on his rain cape and galoshes then snapped bicycle clips onto his trouser legs before heading out again into the wet November day.

The man who opened the door at 1284 Melville Street had thinning red hair and a baby face. His jaws worked rhythmically as he finished chewing a mouthful of lunch. A blob of brown grease rested on his chin.

Hopkins, standing on the porch, found himself looking down on the top of the man's head from his own five foot eleven inches of height. "Mr. Fisher? Harry Fisher?" he inquired. "I'm Dennis Hopkins of the *Province*."

Fisher finished chewing then asked, "What do you want?"

"The *Province*'s readers would like to know how Mrs. Jackson is doing."

"Yeah, sure," Harry sneered. He wedged a fingernail between his front teeth to loosen some food lodged there. "Bet you're the guy we've got to thank for bringing up that old charge against Aunt Esther again, don't we? Just had to revive that scandal, didn't you?" Hopkins, unprepared for the attack, said nothing and Fisher went on, "There's two sides to the charge that old bugger Sprague made, you know. Anybody will tell you he boasted he would do for her, but I know she paid him because I gave her the money to pay him, and I want to testify at the trial, but she won't let me —"

"I'm sure Mrs. Jones's lawyer will —"

"And now people are saying she had something to do with Tom's death. Isn't that the way of the bloody world?"

"I'm sure no one has suggested such a terrible thing —"

"And it's a lie. She was devoted to Tom and Tessie. *Everybody* in this house got along just fine, even if she did turn Tom down when he offered to share that bottle of beer with him and Tess."

"Is that so?" Hopkins paused in his note-taking.

"She don't drink, you see. Won't even take a glass at Christmas time."

Hopkins looked up from his book. "You mean Mrs. Jones doesn't drink? Then why did Mr. Jackson offer to share the bottle of beer with her?"

"He was making a joke."

"I see. And Mrs. Jackson? Does she take a drink from time to time?"

"Tess? Nah. Only when Tom insisted. And she didn't take any Epsom salts."

"She didn't?"

"No, she didn't," he said belligerently. "And that's very, very important to the police investigation, see? They're not going to find any poison in the salts. If there was any poison at all, it was in the beer. Tessie wasn't in the habit of taking salts and she never took any on Sunday. I told them that at the inquest yesterday and they paid no attention. The poison was in the beer ... Not that we suspect anyone would deliberately plot to poison them ..."

"Where did Mr. Jackson get the beer?"

"He bought it Saturday afternoon. Brought a half-dozen home with him."

At that moment, Esther Jones, her face blotched with weeping, appeared behind Fisher in the hallway before heading upstairs. Fisher moved to close the door.

"And Mrs. Jackson's condition?" Hopkins asked again.

"The doc says it's fifty-fifty whether she's going to die."

Halfway back to the office, Hopkins turned into an alleyway, dismounted and parked his bicycle in the woodshed behind a tall brown-shingled house. No point in going all the way back to the office before he went to the funeral home on Hastings Street. He retrieved a sandwich from an inside pocket of his jacket, sat on the woodpile and began mentally composing his story while he ate.

> It was a sorrowful household at 1284 Melville Street which a *Province* representative visited at one o'clock today. The members of the family and a few intimate friends were eating a hurried lunch prior to going to the funeral of Thomas Jackson, who died on Sunday. In reply to the inquiry of the interviewer, Mr. Harry Fisher said, "Mrs. Jackson is still unconscious and her recovery is in grave doubt."

Should he report what Fisher had said about Mrs. Jones being responsible for Jackson's death? No, probably not. Anyhow, the beer bottle and the glasses the Jacksons used that morning were found upstairs so how could Jackson have offered Mrs. Jones some of the beer if she was already downstairs making breakfast? Fisher had obviously got the story mixed up. But his remarks about old Sprague's charges had been interesting. Maybe he should take another look at his notes from the hearing back in September. He was sure there had been no mention at that time of Fisher providing the money for her to pay the promissory notes and it was the boarder, Exall, who had put up the bail money. Maybe he should interview Exall before the case came up in the Fall Assizes ...

After sitting through the funeral at the undertaking parlour of Messrs. Center and Hanna on Hastings Street, Hopkins decided to return to the office to write his story instead of pedalling out to the city cemetery. He was already cold and wet enough.

"This is all you got from Fisher?" Nichol asked when he called Hopkins in to account for the brevity of his story.

"Yes, sir. Well ... not entirely, sir. He went on at me about the *Province* bringing up Captain Sprague's charge against Mrs. Jones again and ..."

"And?"

"Well ... he said something about people accusing Mrs. Jones of having something to do with Jackson's death ... and he insisted the poison was in the beer not the salts—"

"I don't see any of that in your story!"

"Well, I wasn't sure ..."

Nichol thrust the paper back at him. "Write the story."

Chastised, Hopkins went back to his typewriter. This time he typed:

"It is a brutal shame," Harry Fisher told the *Province*'s reporter today, "that uncharitable people in our hour of trouble darkly hint that Mrs. Jones has had some connection with the death of her son-in-law and the condition of her own daughter. But that's the way of the world," he added vehemently. "It was enough that Mrs. Jones should have been charged with a crime in order to revive the breath of scandal. This is a cowardly piece of work in the hour of her affliction. There are two sides to the charge preferred against her by Mr. Sprague. It is well known that he boasted he would undo her. Why, I gave Mrs. Jones the money to pay Mr. Sprague and I know she paid him. I wanted to testify at the trial but Mrs. Jones would not allow me."

Harry Fisher continued with intense animation, "Mrs. Jones was devoted to her daughter and her son-in-law. The relations of the members of the household were of the most harmonious character, and Mr. and Mrs. Jackson were devoted to each other. No one is more anxious to clear up this mystery than every member of this family. That Mr. and Mrs. Jackson were both poisoned is undoubtedly true, and the medical analysis should place the blame where it belongs. One thing is certain and that is that Mrs. Jackson did not take the salts with her husband. She did share the beer with him, and this, in my opinion, narrows the question down to ascertaining whether the beer contained poison or not. Not that we suspect that anyone would have any designs on them or would deliberately plot to poison the beer. Yet there is a grave mystery which we are only too anxious to fathom. When Mr. Jackson came downstairs he said he was going to take his usual medicine, meaning the salts he was in the habit of taking with beer, and he asked Mrs. Jones if she would like to share the bottle of beer with Mrs. Jackson and himself. Mrs. Jones, however, declined. She's a very abstemious woman and even at Christmastime has refused to take a glass of wine."

When asked why Mr. Jackson would offer to share the bottle of beer with Mrs. Jones when he was aware of her habits, Mr. Fisher suggested that he "uttered the invitation in the spirit of jest." He continued, "The medical analysis will, in my opinion, show that if any poison existed, it must have been in the beer. There were several other bottles of beer in the same package that Mr. Jackson brought home, and all bore the same label and all are sealed with metallic stoppers."

During the conversation, Mrs. Jones, her eyes and cheeks reddened by weeping, came into the hallway. She seemed overwhelmed by grief.

This time when Nichol reviewed Dennis Hopkins's story, he made no comment, simply passed it to a copy boy to take to the type-setter. The lesson Hopkins took from this was that embellishing the story was definitely better than condensing it.

On Wednesday morning Michael Kelly was assigned to inter-view the medical health officer for the Jackson story, and at the last minute Nichol ordered Hopkins to accompany him.

"It needs two of us to interview one doctor?" Hopkins asked Kelly as they walked toward Dr. Alfred Poole's surgery.

Kelly grinned. "You ever cover an autopsy before, kid?"

Hopkins shook his head. "No, but didn't Poole do the autopsy on Jackson two days ago?"

"That's right. And today we're going to find out what he and Underhill discovered inside him."

Poole's surgery was a small windowless room centred by a large marble-topped table. Against one wall was a bank of cup-boards and counters and against another were rows of cages con-taining frogs, mice and rats. The whole place stank of blood and excrement. But Poole himself, a paunchy, red-nosed, bespectacled man in his forties, beamed a welcome toward the court reporter. "Well, who have you brought me today, Michael? The *Province*'s latest novice?"

"Alf, this is Dennis Hopkins. He's covering the Jackson case with me."

The doctor put out his hand and grasped that of the young reporter. "I'm very pleased to meet you, young man."

"How do you ..." Too late, Dennis Hopkins realized that the hand enclosing his own was covered in gore.

The doctor laughed uproariously. "Oh my dear, will you look at that?"

He tossed Hopkins the towel that had been lying on the end of the marble-topped table. The young man was assiduously wiping the gore from his hand when he realized that he was replacing it with something even more noxious. The towel had obviously been used to mop up after an operation of some sort. While the doctor and Kelly laughed, he flung the towel back onto the table, fished out his handkerchief and carefully cleaned his hand. His problem now was that the handkerchief was not fit to be returned to his pocket and he flung it, too, onto the table. Once more the doctor and reporter dissolved in fits of glee.

When at last he could control his laughter, Kelly asked, "Where's Underhill?"

"In bed with gout, poor chap. So I'm doing all the preliminary work in connection with the analysis to determine the cause of death." Poole was suddenly all business. "I've made considerable progress, too. Removed the viscera of the deceased including the stomach, the liver and one kidney. The stomach, by the bye"—he reached into an enamelled basin and held up Jackson's stomach, both orifices tied off with catgut—"showed no indications of an irritant poison, which pretty well confirms Riggs's theory that death must have been due to an alkaloid."

Hopkins recoiled involuntarily from the dreadful object, but Kelly merely asked, "How long will it be before you know the cause of death?"

Poole frowned. "Oh, the process of discovering the character of the fatal drug—that is, if any was actually contained in the beer Mr. Jackson drank—is a long and slow one. I've taken two samples of the contents of the stomach by making a small incision into the organ right here"—he thrust Jackson's stomach toward Hopkins and poked a pudgy finger at an incision that had been stitched shut with catgut. "By adopting this little precaution, we can make further tests if the authorities should deem such a step necessary. The samples I took are comprised of digestive ferments and animal tissue, and I've got them macerating in separate solutions of sulphuric acid and hydrochloric acid right now." He threw the stomach back into the basin and trotted over to a cupboard to retrieve two beakers in which some disgusting mix was percolating. "After a period of twenty-four hours, I will slowly boil my samples to eliminate the fat and animal tissue, leaving a residuum in which the poison—if any exists—will be contained. I've reserved check samples in order that Dr. Underhill can make further tests if he deems them necessary."

Hopkins, determined to match Kelly's *savoir faire*, asked, "So how will you know if it's poison?"

"A very good question, young man. The final and most important test of the whole process is the physiological one. I will take a sample of the residuum and inject it into one of my little friends." He waved a hand at the caged animals. "If it contains poison, the fact will soon be known as the animal will die."

"And that's it?" Hopkins asked. "What about the remains of

the beer in the bottle and the packages of Epsom salts? Will you be analyzing them?"

"Ah, yes, my boy, but not yet. I still have to run tests on the mucous membrane of the stomach, likewise the liver and kidneys. After that, I will get to the Epsom salts and the beer bottle."

On the way back to the office, Kelly stopped at Brogan's Delicatessen to buy a sandwich for his lunch. Hopkins waited for him down the street, unable to bear the sight and smell of the bloodied meats hanging in the window.

When Hopkins set off after five that afternoon for his boarding house in the West End, it was already dark and fog had settled thickly over the city. As he walked his bike, his thoughts returned to the Jacksons—or more specifically to Theresa Jackson—and he found himself detouring to Melville Street. He leaned his bike against the gatepost and climbed the stairs. It was Esther Jones who opened the door to him.

"What do you want?" she said as the light from the hall fell on the lanky young reporter standing on the porch.

"I'm Dennis Hopkins from the *Province* ..."

She slammed the door shut.

"I just want to know how Mrs. Jackson is doing," he yelled at the closed door.

After a minute she opened it a crack. "She's a little better. The doctor says she might recover." She began to close the door again.

"Did she take any of the Epsom salts her husband took?"

"Yes."

Before the door closed completely, he asked, "And the beer?"

"Yes."

The door closed and he heard the bolt slide into place. As he walked back down the stairs, he was thinking, *But that's not what Fisher told me ...*

Coroner William J. McGuigan, presided over the inquest into the death of Thomas Jackson in November 1905. He had been Vancouver's mayor for one term, alderman for seven years and served on every education and medical board in the city. He died of "consumption" in 1908. CITY OF VANCOUVER ARCHIVES PORT P.222

The coroner's inquest did not resume on Monday, November 20, because the city's medical health officer, Dr. Underhill—the pain of his gout somewhat lessened but his good humour unrestored—had decided to run all of Dr. Poole's tests again. Coroner William Joseph McGuigan took this news stoically then informed the jurors that their services would not be required for another fortnight.

A fifty-two-year-old, bull-necked, heavily moustached Irish bachelor with both medical and law degrees, McGuigan was considered the "most educated man in the city." He had come to the West Coast for his health in 1885, a year before the city of Vancouver was incorporated. Since then, as well as carrying on a medical practice and acting as coroner, he had spent seven years on city council as an alderman and one year as mayor, chaired the free library board and BC Council of Physicians and Surgeons and served on the school board. As a result, he commanded considerable respect. But McGuigan was not a well man (he entered hospital a year later and remained there until his death in 1908), and his constant pain translated into a very short temper. Thus, when he formally extended the jurors' hundred dollar bonds to appear before him again in two weeks' time, most of them knew enough to accept their lot in silence. One of the jurors was, however, a man new to the city and unaware of McGuigan's reputation, and he made the mistake of smilingly announcing that he was willing to forfeit his bond in order to take a little holiday trip to the sunny climes of California. Fixing him with a cold eye, the coroner told him that the city of Vancouver had "a fine jail and provided the best of sustenance." The juror ceased smiling.

"What day will it be two weeks hence?" McGuigan then asked Detective James Preston who sat—large, handsome and moustachioed—in the front row.

"Monday," replied Preston with a smile as he nudged the detective who occupied the seat next to him.

McGuigan was not amused. "What *date* will it be?" he snapped.

It was the court clerk, Peter McIntosh, who responded. "December fourth."

"And what are we to do in the meantime?" inquired juror J.A. Pelkey. "We are getting the evidence piecemeal through the newspapers!"

"They're not getting any information from us!" Preston snarled.

"Nor from me," McGuigan rebuked Pelkey.

But the editorial departments of Vancouver's newspapers had their own sources of information and they were not about to let two weeks go by without action on the Jackson murder. The *World's* reporter visited the owner of the Gold Seal Liquor Company, which bottled Red Cross Lager, and was told that Jackson's bottle could not have left his bottling works with anything in it that hundreds of other bottles didn't contain. This was because all Red Cross Lager bottles were filled on an extremely modern conveyor belt system and automatically capped at the end of the line. The owner of Gold Seal then issued a challenge: his company would pay one thousand dollars to the Vancouver General Hospital if "injurious substances" could be found in any bottle of his beer, ale or stout. To show he meant business, he sent a cheque in that amount to be held by the *World*'s new owner, Louis D. Taylor, and the *World* promptly trumpeted this challenge to the city's drinkers.

A little ferreting within the medical community produced the information that Jackson had bought his Epsom salts at Pill-Box Drugs at Hastings and Seymour on Saturday afternoon. The druggist, a man named Morrow, showed reporters the drawer where the salts were stored as well as the locked room in which his poisons were kept. "I weigh the salts out myself into these little paste-board packages," he protested, and he insisted that it would be impossible for them to become contaminated while in his store.

Meanwhile, Dr. Poole had communicated privately to his friend Kelly at the *Province* that there had, in fact, been no poison in the dregs of beer left in the bottle from which Jackson had supposedly drunk, and this news made Walter Nichol itchy to prod the authorities to get on with the investigation. While not wanting to offend Detective James Preston, who had a habit of pursuing those who crossed him with as much vigour as he sought out criminals, Nichol ordered Kelly to write a story that would give the police a nudge. On November 21 Kelly's lead story in the *Province* was headlined: *How was Poison Given to Jackson? Did he Commit Suicide or Was He the Victim of Cold-Blooded Murder?*

> The case of the poisoning of Thomas Jackson is altogether one of the most remarkable in the police annals of the city of Vancouver. It presents features of intricate and unusual character, and today the investigation is practically at a standstill, not because the authorities are not working to solve the problems presented but because the mystery is so exceedingly complicated that progress is very difficult.

Yesterday the inquest was adjourned for the purpose of allowing the completion of the analysis of the stomach contents of the dead man and an examination of the Epsom salts and beer which he and his wife drank on that fatal Sunday. Everyone is looking on with interest, waiting to see if there is any poison, where it will be found if it does exist, and what kind of poison it is. But to what extent will the mystery be solved even if all these questions are answered?

As a matter of fact, the results of the examinations now being made cannot possibly have much effect on the outcome of the case. While the medical evidence has so far not been formally submitted, it is a practical certainty that when Mr. Jackson died a week ago last Sunday morning, the cause of his death was poison. More than that, he exhibited all the symptoms of poisoning by strychnine. Now, even if strychnine should be found in the dregs of beer still contained in the bottle, does that go at all to prove that the beer contained the poison when it was bought? If the unfinished package of Epsom salts should be found to contain the fatal powder, is

James Arthur Preston, who had the distinction of being the Vancouver Police Department's first Canadian-born policeman, led the investigation into the murder of Thomas Jackson. He joined the department as a patrolman in 1899, was promoted to detective in May 1903 and became detective-sergeant and head of the detective squad in 1907. He left the force in November 1908. CITY OF VANCOUVER ARCHIVES LP 269.

that any proof at all that a hideous mistake was made in the drugstore and that death was the result of a frightful accident?

The facts as already contained in the *Province* all point in the other direction. It has already been established on authority practically indisputable that the beer contained no poison when it was taken from the store to the Jackson home the night before the tragedy. Besides the stated fact, there is the inferential argument—and it is the strongest kind of evidence—that if the beer had contained anything out of the way of natural ingredients, widespread death would have resulted in the city for hundreds of bottles would have contained the same poison as this single one. It can be taken as a settled fact that there was nothing wrong with the beer. Now practically the same thing can be said of the salts. There is no conceivable way in which poison could be introduced into packages of salts by mistake in the drugstore, considering the fact that poisons are kept under lock and key, that they are in a separate room and that they are seldom sold.

Now the case resolves itself into an inquiry whether Jackson took the dose with the intention of ending his own life or whether the strychnine was mixed with either the beer or the salts with the deliberate intention of killing somebody. It has been suggested that possibly the combination of beer and salts might in some way supply a draught that would act as a poison. This, however, is not possible for the ingredients of neither contain anything that would act upon a man like strychnine. In beer there is berberine, which may or may not be obtained from hops and which gives the bitter taste to the beverage, then there is some sugar, water and alcohol, and that is about all. There is nothing in that which, if mixed with salts, could make a poison.

The beer was contained in a bottle with a metallic cap of the kind that cannot be corked up after having once been opened. If the poison was in the beer in that bottle, it looks very much as if the case ends right there as one of suicide, for Jackson was the only person who could have introduced poison into that bottle of beer. On the other hand, the package of salts was easily reached by anyone who might wish to introduce a poison because it could be opened and closed without showing that it had ever been tampered with. Enough strychnine to kill a dozen persons could have been placed in the top of the package at any time while the members of the family were asleep on Saturday night.

If indeed Jackson killed himself, it seems to be reasonable to suppose that he intended to carry his wife to the Beyond with him. But he acted, when the doctors came, in the manner of a man who wished to save the life of his wife and who was not trying to kill himself either. Apparently he was in the throes of an agony which caused him just as much surprise as it seemed to cause other members of the family. Jackson's friends also declare that the possibility of his having committed suicide is remote. He was a man of cheerful disposition, and the very fact that he had come home after a long summer's absence naturally made his heart lighter. Then, too, there is nothing in the statements made by Harry Fisher or young Mr. Exall, the boarders, at the inquest or by Mrs. Jones that would indicate that Jackson had any intention of ending his own life.

There is no strychnine lying around the Jackson house at the present time, but one would hardly expect to find any. If Jackson killed himself, it seems reasonable to suppose that he would have taken good care, unless indeed he had openly vowed suicide beforehand, to leave nothing lying around to show what had been the method. It is also true that if anyone deliberately intended to end Mr. Jackson's life, no trace of the poison would remain either because of the possibility of the police tracing the purchaser of the poison.

"That should put a flea in Preston's ear," Kelly commented as he whipped the last page of his story from his typewriter.

At the desk behind him Hopkins was labouring over the latest developments in the downtown real estate boom. His morning interview with Abe Goldstein, a Cordova Street merchant, had uncovered the information that he had cleaned up a good profit on two deals that fall. Four months earlier he had paid $10,500 for the land and buildings on the southwest corner of Cordova Street East and Westminster Avenue (which would later become known as Main Street) and had sold them for $15,500, a "clear profit of a thousand dollars a month." Goldstein's second sale involved two lots on the western side of Beatty Street that he had bought two years earlier for $2,300; the sale price was $7,950.

"I am in the wrong business," Hopkins told himself as he handed his story to the copy boy.

FOUR

When the coroner's court resumed on December 4, 1905, Walter Nichol sent both Kelly and Hopkins to cover the event. As they took their seats in the courtroom at Cordova and Westminster Road, Kelly exchanged nods with the *World*'s Norman Norcross and the *News-Advertiser*'s Bruce Bennett who were already seated at the other side of the room, their notebooks out and pencils ready. They could all feel the tension in the air. There would be no more delays in the inquest because Theresa Jackson was sufficiently recovered to testify, and Dr. Underhill was at last satisfied with the results of all the tests on Jackson's stomach contents, the beer bottle, the glasses and the Epsom salts.

The first to be sworn in was the widow. Veiled and dressed all in black, she walked unsteadily from her seat and seemed close to tears as she put her hand on the bible and swore to tell the truth. Then in response to prompting by court clerk Peter McIntosh, she said in a faint voice, "My name is Theresa Jackson and I live at 615 Davie Street, but at the time of Mr. Jackson's death I lived at 1284 Melville Street."

"Please take a seat, Mrs. Jackson," the coroner instructed, "and tell us what happened, beginning with Saturday, November 11."

Theresa Jackson sat, paused, wrung her hands and looked imploringly toward her mother. When Mrs. Jones only turned her head away, the new widow slowly began reciting, detail by exquisitely tiny detail, the sequence of events leading up to her husband's death, her voice so low that everyone in the courtroom leaned forward, straining to hear. After close to a half hour of testimony, she concluded with "I remember nothing further than that the doctors did come and that Mr. Jackson got up and walked about while I was lying on the chair. I don't remember what he said but I know he was speaking."

When the frail voice ceased, there was a moment of silence before the provincial prosecutor, William E. Burns, stood up to ask, "When were the beer and salts brought into the house?"

"Mr. Jackson brought them home about half past four in the afternoon. He had with him three packages—a package of stout, one of beer and one that contained two packets of salts. He said to my mother, 'I have the salts and beer to take my usual medicine,' and he put the packages down in the pantry and opened a bottle of stout and asked me to have a glass with him, which I did. Late at night he asked me for a packet of the salts, and I found them and gave him one. He took it and a full bottle of beer upstairs and when I went upstairs the preparations for taking the salts were all on the washstand."

"Did Mr. Jackson leave the bedroom at any time between bringing the salts and beer to the room and consuming them?"

"I have already told you that he went to the bathroom in the morning to wash."

"And you remained in the bedroom where the beer and salts were on the washstand while he was in the bathroom?"

"I have already said that," she said, her voice becoming firmer. "Mr. Jackson was only in the bathroom long enough to have a wash, and I was still dressing when he came back and said that he would take his usual medicine. He was standing at the bureau combing his hair when he said that, and then he walked over to the washstand and asked for a spoon. I went to the washstand to get the spoon, which was in plain view. He had picked up the bottle and was opening it and told me to pour a good dose of salts into a glass for him. The flaps of the package were already open and I put three or four spoonfuls into the glass—not that one over there with the handle but a big water glass without a handle that would hold half as much again as that one. He said I had not given him enough so I pinched the package like this and poured more into the glass. He said I should take some, too, but I told him I did not care to, but when he pressed me, I took a spoonful and put it in a glass."

"You are not in the habit of taking salts?"

"I have not taken salts more than once or twice in my life."

"But you took a spoonful of salts on the morning of November 12?"

"Yes, but only because he pressed me to do so. He started to put beer in my glass and I said, 'I won't take beer with mine. I would rather have water.' And I filled my glass half full of water and drank it. Then I took a small wineglass about half full of beer. Mr. Jackson finished what was left in the bottle by drinking it from the glass he had taken the salts in."

"It is my understanding that you have been under a doctor's care for a nervous disposition during the past year. Is this true?"

"I have been under the doctor's care at different times during the year," she said defensively and then added defiantly, "Before that I was constantly under his care, and for three or four months I took electrical treatments for general nervousness and weakness."

The foreman of the jury now got to his feet. "Was your husband in the habit of having poisons in the house?"

Her voice sank to a whisper. "Not to my knowledge. The only poisons used in our home would be laudanum and iodine and such things as that."

The coroner interrupted with "Please speak up, Mrs. Jackson."

She raised her voice a little. "I said the only poisons in our home would be laudanum or iodine."

"Thank you. You stated in your testimony that the package of salts was already open."

"Yes. When I first saw the salts, the packet was closed, but in the morning when he called to me to get the spoon, the packet was open. I did not actually see him open it."

But the foreman was not finished. "I understand your husband had been away prospecting, Mrs. Jackson, and that he owned a hotel in Port Alberni."

"He was a partner in the Arlington Hotel until two years ago when he returned to prospecting. Mr. Jackson's financial affairs are very poor now. He leaves little money to speak of and has outstanding bills. He had an insurance policy of $1,000 with Imperial Life. That is all."

"So what are you and your mother living on?"

"I have some money of my own and we had money coming into the house from the boarders, and —"

"And the boarders are Mr. Exall and Mr. Fisher."

"Yes. Mr. Fisher is my first cousin. Mr. Jackson also sent me some money by post office order, but he did not send it regularly because he was not working for wages most of this summer. He had bad luck with his prospecting the past year or so, but he brought a small nugget with him when he came back in November. He told me he had located a new property for himself and he was expecting some papers concerning it to be delivered on the *Tees*. I don't know where the property was, but I know he had been working around Port Essington and in the Skeena River country."

"Did your husband have enemies, Mrs. Jackson?"

"None that I know of ... but he had many friends."

The questioning continued, going back and forth again and again over the same details, but finally, two hours after she took the stand, Theresa Jackson was excused. The prosecutor and coroner then had a hurried, whispered conference, and before she could seat herself next to her mother, the coroner called her back to answer more questions.

"You have said that the glass that is exhibit 'D' is not the glass that your husband drank from. Is this correct?"

"The glass Mr. Jackson used didn't have a handle. It was a water glass much bigger than that one."

"What happened to the glass that he drank from?"

"It was in our bedroom when we went downstairs. I don't know what happened to it."

After another half hour of questions, she was once again excused. At this point McGuigan declared a recess for lunch. Kelly led Hopkins to the Boulder Saloon at Number 3 West Cordova Street where they drank their lunch, a first for the young reporter. Norman Norcross from the *World* also enjoyed his lunch at the same bar, but knowing that Esther Jones would be next on the stand, none of them was late for the afternoon session. Unfortunately, during the lunch break the courthouse's erratic heating system had turned the place into a boiler room again, and the court clerk had first to fling all the windows open before the hearing could resume.

After being sworn, Esther Jones told the story of Thomas Jackson's death from the beginning again, but unlike her daughter, her voice was firm and confident.

After she came to the gruesome finale of the story, Mr. Burns asked, "You say you took a glass of beer with Mr. Jackson on the afternoon of Saturday, November 11?"

"Yes. In the late afternoon Mr. Jackson brought home six bottles of beer or porter and asked me to take some. I seldom take any, but that afternoon—it was between four and five o'clock—I took a glass of beer or porter—they are much the same to me. But afterwards it made me sick and I vomited."

"Mr. Jackson told you he was going to take his usual medicine?"

"Yes. He said nothing to me about taking salts or buying salts until he brought them home, and then he said he was going to take his usual medicine. He made a habit of taking salts so I paid no attention at the time. He did not say whether he was going to take them at night or in the morning. It has been suggested by someone else that I told him that he should take them in the morning, but I do not remember saying that. I have gone through too much to remember everything."

"You told Detective Preston that—"

"I don't remember what I said to Detective Preston that Sunday," Esther Jones snapped. "I was working over Mrs. Jackson in the kitchen and I didn't know if she was going to recover. I was crazy at the thought that all I had in the world were dying!"

There was a pause before the jury foreman ventured, "When you called for the doctor, how did you know that Mr. Jackson had been poisoned?"

"I am somewhat familiar with sickness. I have been employed as a nurse in the past. When they both complained of sudden sickness of the stomach and had the twitching, I thought of poisoning. That was why I gave them emetics."

"Have you ever bought poison?"

"I have never bought poison in my life!" Esther Jones's voice was sharp-edged. "I know of no poisons being in the house and I keep no medicine chest. I have some laudanum for medicine. I concluded that the poison, if that was what was affecting my daughter and son-in-law, had been in the beer or salts because they had not eaten anything."

"Mr. Jackson placed the beer and salts in the pantry when he brought them home in the afternoon. Then you all went out for the evening. Was the house locked when you were out?"

"Yes."

"Is there a window in the pantry?"

"The pantry has a window and it is not locked, but it opens down from the top. It would be difficult for anyone to enter that way. And there is also a door leading from Mr. and Mrs. Jackson's room to the upper veranda that was never locked because it had no key."

"And everyone stopped by your room that night to say goodnight before going to their rooms?"

"Mr. Fisher did not always come to say goodnight, but he did that night. He is my nephew."

"To your knowledge did anyone enter or leave Mr. and Mrs. Jackson's room during the night?"

"I don't think that's possible. Their door is very hard both to open and shut. It has to be closed with a bang and pushed with the shoulder to open."

When Esther Jones was at last excused, Dr. Alfred Poole took the oath. He outlined the test procedures and their outcomes in a very professional manner but produced very little that was new as far as the newspaper reporters were concerned. He and Underhill had found no poison in the beer or salts, but they had determined that Jackson had ingested about ten grains of strychnia, a half to two grains being enough to kill a man. Poole then added that a half grain would not necessarily kill, depending on the man's size and stamina, but it would act more quickly and effectively on an empty stomach. He and Underhill had verified the type of poison by feeding parts of Jackson's organs to two dogs, which both died "in a fashion typical of strychnine poisoning." When questioned by one of the jurors, Poole said that the poison could have lain on top of the salts and not penetrated down into the package, and if four spoonfuls were removed from the top, that might have taken most of them. However, they had not found the slightest trace of poison in the salts remaining in the opened package.

Poole was followed to the stand by Dr. Herbert W. Riggs who had attended the victim on the morning of November 12. He described Jackson as "sitting on the couch very quietly" when he arrived, but that Mrs. Jackson was "very much excited, trying to vomit and throwing herself around. Judging from her actions that some irritant poison had probably been taken, I inserted the stomach tube, and after several ineffectual attempts succeeded in washing her stomach out. Just as I finished the stomach washing, Mr. Jackson was seized with a convulsion and slipped onto the floor."

As soon as Riggs finished outlining the course of Jackson's demise, the coroner interrupted with a question. "Am I to understand, Dr. Riggs, that Mrs. Jackson's symptoms were not the same as her husband's?"

"That is correct."

All eyes were suddenly focussed fully on the doctor, and in spite of the torpor that all the reporters were experiencing in the overheated room, their pencils began moving rapidly across the pages of their notebooks.

"I concluded that Mr. Jackson's death was due to strychnine poisoning, which has since been verified. Mrs. Jackson had nothing approaching a tetanic convulsion. None of her muscles were rigid.

She is not a robust woman and is inclined to be extremely nervous. In fact, I have attended her once or twice during the last two years and have seen her in a hysterical condition. I cannot say for sure that her actions on the Sunday that her husband died were due to hysteria, but many of her actions did *conform* to hysteria, and I do not know of any poison which would cause the symptoms she displayed."

As Riggs left the stand, Kelly leaned toward Hopkins. "Riggs is saying that she gave him the poison then got so scared it made her sick ..."

Dennis Hopkins turned to look at Theresa Jackson where she sat beside her mother. That pretty little thing could not have poisoned anyone, of *that* he was quite sure.

After Dr. George P. Young was sworn in and had recited his part in the Sunday morning tragedy, the jury foreman asked if he had seen any symptoms in Mrs. Jackson that would be compatible with strychnine poisoning. "Well, yes," he said slowly, "there was some spasmodic flexure of the arms. She had them every one or two minutes for nearly half an hour, and there was also some contraction of the abdominal muscles concurrent with the arm movement, but I saw nothing else to simulate strychnine poisoning. The movement of the arms might have been part of a hysterical action." Then after further questioning, he concluded, "I did not find any symptoms that would lead me to believe that she had taken anything that would cause her death."

Kelly was now whistling silently between his teeth. He already had tomorrow's headline in mind.

The next up was Detective James A. Preston, the Ontario man who had become the city's first-ever Canadian-born policeman when he joined the force as a patrolman six years earlier. In 1903, having made a reputation as a crime-solver, he had been promoted to detective. Now at age forty he was very conscious of his profile in the community and he took the stand with a degree of arrogance that Hopkins found almost comical. He verified that Harry Fisher had handed him a glass, a spoon, two full bottles of beer, a bottle containing a small quantity of beer, which was said to be the bottle from which Jackson had drunk, and two packets labelled Epsom salts, one of them opened.

Dr. Frederick Theodore Underhill was next but he had nothing to say that had not already been said. Finally, at the end of the day the evidence that Harry Fisher had given on the first day of the inquest was read into the record. The jury members were thus reminded that it had been Harry who, having been told by Mrs. Jones that the Jacksons had consumed the beer and salts in their room, went upstairs to collect the bottle, glasses, spoon and packet of salts. "I kept charge of them," he said, "till I handed them over to Detective Preston. There was nothing peculiar about the salts that I noticed." Fisher had also stated that he had made his home at 1284 Melville Street since coming to Vancouver six months earlier when he took the job at Webster Brothers, and that even earlier, when he had worked in New Westminster, he had come to Mrs. Jones's home every Saturday night.

Ernest Exall's testimony was also read into the record. He said he had roomed and boarded with Mrs. Jones for nine months and had always seen peace and harmony in the family. He had been at work when he got a telephone message that there had been an "accident" at 1284 Melville Street. "I went up as quickly as I could. I was met by Mr. Fisher who told me that Mr. Jackson was dead and Dr. Young and Dr. Riggs were working over Mrs. Jackson. I helped carry her upstairs and stayed all night with her. She was still unconscious in the morning but more natural."

It was late afternoon when the inquest was adjourned. For

the newspaper reporters who had covered it the working day had just begun. As Norman Norcross hurried off into the pea-soup fog toward the *World's* offices at the corner of Homer and Pender streets, Hopkins and Kelly turned up their collars and marched rapidly down Hastings to the *Province* building. Once back at their desks, Kelly instructed Hopkins to type up his notes on the afternoon's events. He would handle the widow's testimony himself. But first, sliding a hand into the inside pocket of his jacket, he retrieved a flask, took a surreptitious swig and then settled down to work. For the next hour their cries of "Copy!" rang out across the room.

FIVE

When three days had passed with no new developments in the Jackson murder case, the newspapers returned their attention to Police Chief Sam North's running battle with city council over the problem of the "ladies of the night." Council had decided to extend Pender Street to Dupont by filling in the gulley that separated the two, thereby adding an extra link between Granville and Westminster Road. As it was out of the question that the ladies should ply their trade on such an important thoroughfare, council had sent eviction notices to all those living on Dupont, after which North was ordered to find them somewhere to settle that would be less objectionable to the respectable members of the public. North fought back via the newspapers, making it known that he saw nothing wrong with them living on Dupont Street and that he was "unalterably opposed" to them setting up shop in the East End, West End, Fairview or Mount Pleasant. The residents of those areas agreed wholeheartedly with his stand and were fully in favour when he suggested the ladies move to Park Lane, a dandy little street sandwiched unobtrusively between Westminster Avenue and

False Creek just south of Prior Street—and only a stone's throw from the ladies' old haunts on Dupont Street. Naturally council was "unalterably opposed" to the ladies settling there. And the battle continued.

The only newsman in town not caught up in this battle was young Dennis Hopkins, who lay awake for hours each night, thinking about Thomas Jackson's pretty widow and from there allowing his mind to wander over all the anomalies in the inquest. However, it was not until Friday afternoon when he was in the middle of typing up an obituary that he finally decided to share his thoughts on the subject. "Why do you suppose Harry Fisher insisted that they'd find the poison in the beer?" he asked Michael Kelly's back.

"Don't know." Kelly continued typing.

"At the inquest Mrs. Jones said it was Saturday afternoon when Jackson offered her that glass of beer," Hopkins continued.

"Yes, and she drank it," Kelly said, finally swivelling in his chair to face Hopkins, "and then she got sick and vomited. But if it had strychnine in it, she would have done more than vomit. And so would Jackson if he shared it with her."

"But that's not my point," Hopkins said before Kelly could turn away again. "When Fisher told me that people were accusing Mrs. Jones of having something to do with Jackson's death, he said it was *Sunday morning* when Jackson offered her the beer and that she *didn't* drink any of it. It was as if Fisher was telling me that Mrs. Jones knew it was poisoned and that's why she refused it."

Kelly scratched his bald spot thoughtfully. "But Poole and Underhill have proved there wasn't any poison in that bottle of beer …"

They were interrupted by Walter Nichol who had emerged from his office and come to stand in front of Kelly's desk. He was carrying a copy of Monday's newspaper, folded to the story of the inquest. "Why hasn't North announced an arrest in the Jackson case?" he asked.

Kelly swivelled his chair around to face his boss. He shook his head. "Too busy with the ladies, I expect. He just keeps putting me off with 'Wait and see, Mr. Kelly. Wait and see!' But I don't think he's got a clue who did it ..."

"What about Preston?"

"He won't even talk to me ... But it's got to be the wife that did it and then got rid of the evidence. Poole says there was no poison in the bottle and none in the remaining salts in the packet ..."

"So where did Jackson get it?" Nichol tapped the newspaper. "Poole says he had as much as ten grains of strychnine in his body."

Kelly offered, "Maybe it was already in the glass ..."

"You think he wouldn't notice that there were strychnine crystals in his glass before he poured the salts into it?" Nichol demanded.

"But," Kelly said, "he didn't put the salts in the glass. It was the *wife* who did it. And that would explain why she didn't get any strychnine. She shared the same salts and drank beer from the same bottle that he did, but she used her own glass."

Nichol rubbed his jaw line thoughtfully. "But Poole says there was no poison in either of the glasses they used —"

Kelly interrupted, "In any case, Riggs and Young figure she was just hysterical. They're convinced she wasn't poisoned."

"But she had symptoms before he did, didn't she?" Nichol asked, searching the story in the paper for the information he wanted.

Kelly agreed. "She was trying to vomit then collapsed into a chair. Jackson had just handed her a cup of coffee when he suddenly clutched his belly in pain."

"So she didn't become hysterical because her husband had been taken sick. She ..."

Kelly finished his sentence, "... got hysterical because she knew damned well he'd been poisoned even though he didn't show any symptoms yet!"

Hopkins, who had been silent all this time, suddenly ventured, "We only have Fisher's word for it that the bottle and glasses he gave to Preston were the ones he took from the Jacksons' bedroom."

Both Nichol and Kelly turned to look at him appraisingly.

Hopkins continued, "And Mrs. Jackson complained that the glass entered as evidence wasn't the one her husband drank from."

"That's right," Kelly said slowly. "She said the one he used didn't have a handle and it was much bigger ..."

"But North won't use fingerprinting so we'll never know for sure!" Nichol growled. "Bloody incompetent nincompoop!" Scowling, he headed back to his office.

But Dennis Hopkins was still thinking about Theresa Jackson's statement about the glass used by her husband. "But if she was the one that put the poison in the glass, why would she say it wasn't the right glass? She would have been much smarter to just go along with everybody thinking that there hadn't been any poison in the glass he drank from, wouldn't she?"

Kelly shook his head. "Maybe she's not very smart ..."

Nichol had paused in the doorway to his office. "Jackson had a hotel in Alberni, didn't he, Kelly?"

"The Arlington," Kelly said.

"Get over there and see what you can find out about him and the Joneses."

"Today, sir?"

"Of course today!"

Unfortunately for Kelly, the *World*'s new hands-on proprietor, Louis D. Taylor, had already sent reporter Norman Norcross off to Alberni to ferret out information about the Jones family. Norcross had quickly discovered that Jackson had sold his share in the

Arlington more than three years earlier and that his two partners in the venture had long since left town. A diligent search turned up a neighbour who said that one of the partners, Auguste La Belle, had gone placer mining at Pine Creek near Skagway. This was not a lead that Norcross was eager to follow up in the cold of December; however, the neighbour also reported that Jackson's other partner, Hector Fitzgerald, was rumoured to be running a dry goods establishment in Victoria, and Norcross immediately set off for that city by steamship.

When Kelly arrived in Nanaimo a few days later, he followed his usual modus operandi of investigating all the bars in town, and in one of them he met a mining man who had known Jackson well. Not being at this point in his bar rambles totally inebriated, Kelly took notes, and a couple of days later when he sobered up briefly, he was able to decipher them—more or less—and telegraph word to the *Province* that:

> Thomas Jackson was one of those whole-souled fellows that take well in any mining camp, and while in Alberni made a number of friends who regretted to see him turn his back on the camp and were glad when news came that he was on the road to "something good" in the upper country.

> Jackson arrived in Alberni some time in the winter of the year 1896. His free miner's certificate, taken out shortly after his arrival, bears the date January 7, 1897. He prospected, mined and occasionally trapped in the area, but a lucky strike, followed by a sale to a mining company, allowed him in the early autumn of 1900 to go into partnership with Hector Fitzgerald and Auguste La Belle and lease the Arlington Hotel in Alberni.

Mrs. Esther Jones had been the housekeeper in another hotel in which La Belle had an interest, and La Belle moved her to the Arlington after the trio took it over. An informant says that Mr. Fitzgerald quit the partnership after an argument in which he claimed that Mrs. Jones had stolen from him and from their customers.

Having telegraphed his story, Kelly returned to the saloons of Nanaimo, all thought of Walter Nichol and his newspaper dismissed from his mind. It would be many days before he resurfaced.

Walter Nichol had not forgotten Kelly, however, and on Friday, December 15, he made some very pointed remarks about the court reporter's ancestry after the *World* trumped the *Province* with a banner headline that read: *New Development in Jackson Poisoning Case.* And beneath it a secondary headline asked: *Is Mr. Fisher a Son of Mrs. Jones?*

A light of an extraordinary nature is thrown on the Jackson poisoning case by a letter received by *The World*, although as a light, it serves chiefly to deepen the darkness of that tragic mystery. The letter, written by one whom *The World* has ascertained to be a man of reliability and good repute, states that Fisher, who figured so largely in the evidence given at the inquest, is a brother of Mrs. Jackson and a son of Mrs. Jones, the mother-in-law of the deceased. We quote from that letter:

To the Editor of the World,
Sir: In reading the Jackson poison case I think they are trying to defeat the justice of the law. Knowing all the parties well, the man that calls himself Fisher is not his name, only an assumed name. His name is Jones. He is brother to Mrs. Jackson. Mrs. Jones is his mother. As I have known them

ever since they came to British Columbia, I think I can throw some light on the mystery.

This is a most remarkable state of affairs. Never once at the inquest of the deceased Jackson did any one of the three, Mrs. Jones, Mrs. Jackson or Fisher, let slip any expression showing any other relationship than that of cousin. In fact, Mrs. Jones, in speaking of Fisher made the direct statement, "He is my nephew." Mrs. Jackson in her evidence stated that Fisher was a cousin and only when quoting what she heard her mother call out at the time of the poisoning did she refer to Fisher by the Christian name of Harry. In Fisher's case the contrast of his evidence with the fact of his alleged relationship is also remarkable. He never once lapsed into such expressions, which would have been natural to a son and brother, as "my mother" or "my sister" but stated in an impersonal way that he had made his home with them ever since he came to Vancouver.

Taking the statement that Fisher and Mrs. Jackson are the children of Mrs. Jones, brought up together and brother and sister, it shows extraordinary schooling of themselves to the use of terms natural to the assumed relationship. What their reasons may have been for the adoption of such a course, if the facts are as alleged, might very properly be made a subject of investigation under the circumstances, these being about as peculiar and distressing as they could be made.

Walter Nichol arrived at his office the next morning in a state of near apoplexy at being scooped by the *World*, a paper that had more or less ceased to provide real competition for the *Province* after its first owner, John McLagan, had died in April 1901. Nichol had certainly not rejoiced in the man's death, but he didn't mourn the fact that the *World* went downhill in the years that followed as McLagan's wife, Sara, and her brother, Fred Maclure, took over its management. Meanwhile, the *Province,* with Hewitt Bostock's western Liberal Party connections still bankrolling it, had surged ahead in circulation. Unfortunately, the purchase of the *World* by Louis D. Taylor in June 1905 had changed the entire picture because Taylor, an American who had managed to get solid eastern Liberal Party cash behind him, wanted to make a name for himself as the friend of the working man and champion of rights for women. He hired more staff, and as he began aggressively courting advertisers, the paper's circulation boomed. But what really galled Nichol wasn't the *World*'s new prosperity; it was the

Louis Denison Taylor and his *World* newspaper used sensational reporting of the Jones/Jackson case to increase circulation, but a few years later he sank all his money into building a new home for the paper, the World Building, and went broke. CITY OF VANCOUVER ARCHIVES, PORT P1765.2.

fact that Taylor had been employed as circulation manager by the *Province* for the previous seven years, and in all that time Nichol had been entirely unaware of the dapper little man's aspirations to compete with him. It was bad enough being scooped but absolutely unbearable to be scooped by a former employee.

The *Province*'s veteran reporters had quickly learned to make themselves scarce whenever the *World* scooped their paper, but Dennis Hopkins had not been around long enough to know this so he was busy at his typewriter when Nichol entered. He took the full brunt of his boss's wrath.

"Where the hell is Kelly?"

"I don't know, sir. Working on a story, I guess ..."

"A hangover, you mean! Find out who wrote that letter!" he demanded.

"The letter, sir?"

"The letter in the *World*. Find out who wrote it!"

"How, sir?"

"How the hell should I know? Just get out there and don't come back till you track him down!" And he stormed into his office, slamming the door so that the windows rattled.

Once out on the street, Hopkins asked himself what Kelly would do with this assignment. The answer, of course, was to prowl

The *World* newspaper editorial staff, 1901. Left to right: Harold Sands, Sam Robb, Alexander Baxter, R. Bruce Bennett and Sam Gothard. The picture was taken by Roy Brown who became city editor of the *Province* in 1903. By 1905, Bennett was reporting for the *News-Advertiser*; only Gothard still worked for the *World*.
CITY OF VANCOUVER ARCHIVES STR. P.84

the city's hotel bars and saloons, but he had none of the older man's almost uncanny ability to ferret out information over a tankard of ale, and at the end of the day he was no wiser about the identity of the *World*'s letter writer. Fortunately, when he returned—a little less than cold sober—just before quitting time, Nichol had left for the day. But Hopkins dreaded Monday morning.

On Saturday, December 16, the *World* did it again. According to that paper's headlines, Fisher, Mrs. Jackson and Mrs. Jones, provoked by the newspaper's accusations, had actually visited the *World*'s editor that morning to accuse him and his so-called reliable source of lying. The editor, although not quite sure at this point who was telling the truth, managed to persuade the trio to sign statements to the effect that Fisher was not the son of Mrs. Jones, and Fisher even provided the editor with the names of his parents—Henry and Mary Fisher of Cleveland, Ohio. The newspaper published their affidavits in that evening's paper, informing its readers at the same time that their reliable informant was "an old-timer in British Columbia" named Betts, "at present residing in the provincial home in Kamloops." He was a "man of good repute and considerable ability" who had known the Jones family since their arrival in the province many years earlier. The *World* left its readers with a choice: was Betts telling the truth or was Fisher really Mrs. Jones's nephew as the family said he was?

The paper did not leave them to make this decision on their own for long. Monday's edition of the *World* provided even more sensational information:

> Hardly were the affidavits of the Jackson-Jones family
> declaring that Fisher was not Mrs. Jones' son deposited
> in the *World*'s safe, and hardly had the story of those
> affidavits—as it appeared in the *World* on Saturday

night—become the talk of the city, than despatches arrived from Victoria and Alberni, giving the antecedents of the family and stating that Fisher had changed his name from Jones after serving three years in the penitentiary for forgery.

According to the *World*'s sources, Mrs. Jones's husband, John H. Jones, had come from Ohio in 1886 and purchased five acres on Glenfield Avenue in the Lake District, about three miles outside Victoria. In 1890 he sent for his family—his wife, Esther, a twelve-year-old son named Fred and a nine-year-old daughter named Theresa. After their arrival, Jones also rented an adjoining farm owned by a man named Foote, a bedridden but well-to-do rancher, and when Mrs. Jones left her husband just a few years later, she was engaged by Foote as his live-in housekeeper. All went well until the fall of 1896 when Foote died, and the executors of his estate had her arrested and began criminal action for theft, claiming she had made "extravagant purchases on the estate account." She was subsequently acquitted, and in October 1897 she brought an action for damages for wrongful imprisonment against the executors; she lost this lawsuit and was charged with all the costs of the case—which she never paid. She then moved to Alberni where she became the housekeeper in a hotel owned by Auguste La Belle.

In the meantime, Fred—now eighteen years old—had been getting into trouble with the law, and on May 24, 1897, he had "feloniously entered the business premises of Major Wilson, commercial agent, and stole cheques." One of these he forged and attempted to cash, but the forgery was detected and he was arrested, tried, convicted and sentenced to three years in the penitentiary at New Westminster. The record shows that he was admitted there on July 20, 1897. At that time this prison on the north bank of the Fraser consisted of a single concrete and stone structure containing ninety cells that were intended to accommodate one hundred and thirty prisoners. However, as these were boom years for British Columbia, there was a steady stream of felons, fraud artists, thieves and murderers arriving on every train and ship, and all who were caught, convicted and sentenced to more than a month in prison had to be accommodated there. As a result, most cells held three or more prisoners, making it possible for all of them to learn brand new skills from their cellmates before they returned to the law-abiding world.

While Fred was in jail, his mother spread the word that he had died there. In fact, the prison records show that Fred Jones was released from the penitentiary on January 12, 1900. Shortly after this, a young man named Harry Fisher was hired by Rae's Grocery Store in New Westminster, and he apparently worked there for more than a year before leaving for Seattle where he found work with that city's streetcar company. It was in a Seattle bar in early July 1901 that Harry Fisher met Thomas Jackson who offered him a job in his Jolly Jack Mine on Vancouver Island.

Fred Jones's sister had in the meantime found trouble of her own: on August 2, 1899, eighteen-year-old Theresa Jones was arrested for stealing a screen door valued at $1.50 from a merchant named Wallenstein who did business on Yates Street in Victoria. In court her lawyer, Frank Higgins, pleaded that she had found it in the alley behind the store and thought it was "of no value and not wanted by the owner." She wept and was acquitted. She then followed her mother to Alberni and shortly thereafter married Thomas Jackson. It was in Alberni in July 1901 that Jesse Betts met up with the Jones family again. He had come to stay at the Arlington Hotel and discovered Theresa Jones—now Jackson—waiting on tables.

When Ernest Exall picked up a copy of the *World* on his way home from work that Monday, December 18, and read this history of the Jones/Jackson family, his first impulse was to bolt. He would quit his job with the CPR, pack his bags and head east. Unfortunately, there was the small matter of the $200 that he had paid out for Esther Jones's bail, and if he left now, he would definitely never see it again. And, of course, there was darling Tessie.

Toward noon on Wednesday, December 20, Theresa Jackson telephoned Walter Nichol at the *Province*, and after he hung up the receiver, he came to stand in his office doorway. "Hopkins," he said in a conversational tone, "get in here." And he returned to his desk.

Dennis Hopkins, accustomed to being bellowed at, sat with his fingers poised on the keys of his typewriter, his eyes fixed on Kelly's empty chair at the desk in front of him. For two whole days Nichol had said nothing about Hopkins's failure to find out who wrote the letter to the *World*, but this was it. He was about to be fired. At last he stood, straightened his tie and marched toward Nichol's office. The job had been too good to be true, anyhow, he told himself.

"The widow wants to talk to you," Nichol said, his tone curiously jubilant.

To Hopkins the words made no sense. "Widow?" he repeated blankly.

"The Jackson woman. She wants to talk to you."

He wasn't being fired!

"Well, get going!"

"Yes sir!" Hopkins started to leave then turned back. "What about, sir? I mean, what does she want to talk to me about?"

"How the hell should I know?" Nichol snapped. "Maybe she wants to marry you!" When Hopkins only stared at him in confusion, he continued, "It's what *we* want to know that counts,

Hopkins! Is Fisher her brother? Who killed her husband? Is she going to move back to the States? That kind of stuff …"

"Yes sir." Then he risked one more question. "Sir, Mr. Kelly usually covers the court …"

"Mrs. Jackson specifically asked for *you!*" Nichol roared. "Now get on your bike!"

As Hopkins headed for the door, Nichol leaned back in his chair. The kid would do the job just fine. In fact, he showed considerable promise—not aggressive enough yet and hesitant when it came to taking the initiative but smart, inquisitive and a good writer. He didn't have the nose for news that Kelly had but he could be trained. And he didn't have a drinking problem. Nichol summoned his bookkeeper. "If that drunken Irishman shows up again, give him his pay packet and tell him not to come back."

The house at 615 Davie Street to which the mother and daughter had moved two weeks after Thomas Jackson's death was a modest affair but had been comfortably and tastefully furnished. Theresa Jackson, dressed all in black, was sitting primly upright on a horse-hair-upholstered settee in the front parlour into which Esther Jones ushered Dennis Hopkins. As heavy drapes allowed little daylight into the room, he could barely make out the widow's pale features. After the older woman sat down, Hopkins extracted his notebook and pencil, groped for a chair and sat gingerly on the edge of it, facing her daughter.

"You wanted to speak to me?" he asked.

She nodded but didn't respond.

His eyes becoming accustomed to the gloom, he realized that two framed photographs of the Jacksons in their honeymoon days had been placed strategically on the table beside her. He began making rapid shorthand notes. Whatever else happened, he knew he had to come back with a story of some kind.

> The severe ordeal that Mrs. Jones and her daughter
> have survived has left sad traces. Mrs. Jones has aged
> very much since that eventful day, while Mrs. Jackson
> is scarcely recognized by her former friends, so harrow-
> ing have been her experiences. After all, women are
> mostly human, and the worry and cross-examination
> they have been subjected to by detectives, lawyers and
> journalists would be calculated to upset the nerves of
> any other persons placed in the same trying circum-
> stances.

As the silence stretched on, Hopkins looked up to discover that the women were watching him and he gradually stopped writing. But when he smiled encouragingly at the widow, she only looked away. Turning to her mother, he asked, "Was it something about Mr. Jackson's tragic death that you wanted to tell me?"

"No," Esther Jones said phlegmatically. "We want to talk to you about Mr. Fisher." She exchanged a glance with her daughter before continuing, her voice unemotional, "Surely a mother ought to know the number of children she has given birth to, don't you think? Mr. Fisher is not my son. He was born in Ohio, the same state I hail from. His father was my brother and he died suddenly of a haemorrhage many years ago."

"And his mother?"

"Poor woman, her death occurred in childbirth." And she sighed.

Suddenly Theresa Jackson joined the conversation. "That's true," she said. "I've known him since childhood, but my recent statements have been misconstrued. I never meant to convey that I had only known him for five years. You see, we left Ohio about fifteen years ago when I was still a child, but about five years ago Mr. Jackson met Mr. Fisher in Seattle—he was working for the streetcar service there—and Mr. Jackson persuaded him to come to work with him at the Jolly Jack Mine in Alberni. They became warm friends and ..." she retrieved a lace-edged hankie from her sleeve and wiped her eyes, "and they expected to be mining and prospecting together for a long time."

Hopkins had the distinct impression that this speech had been carefully rehearsed, but he couldn't bring himself to challenge her. Instead, he turned to Mrs. Jones and asked inanely, "And you are positive you never had a son?"

"Never," she snapped. "I only wish I had one to help and defend me now in my old age. The world is cruel and cowardly, and we have been terribly misrepresented and slandered. But just wait. This affair is not over. We have been attacked and slandered beyond all endurance but—" She bit off the last word of her angry outburst then continued in a calm voice, "Mr. Fisher is not my son and he never served a term in prison."

"Of course, we can at the proper time make all the necessary explanations," Theresa Jackson interrupted. "It is true that Mr. Fisher was in the employ of Mr. Rae's grocery in New Westminster and he spent two seasons at the Fraser River canneries. But I know who started these lies. It was a certain Alberni hotelman who is now unlawfully living with an Alberni woman who is not his wife. My mother had no rows with anyone there. I was married to Mr. Jackson in Seattle, and when I returned to Alberni, I lived in a private house, not in a hotel as stated in the press." Then suddenly bursting into tears, she cried out, "Oh, poor Tom! Poor Tom! Those people in Alberni won't let him rest in his grave."

Hopkins took notes furiously but he was having great difficulty following the abrupt detours in the widow's outburst. In an effort to control the interview, he asked, "But why doesn't Mr. Fisher establish the record of his parentage? He would only need to show his birth certificate ..."

"But they don't keep a register of births back there," Theresa Jackson replied. "I never even heard of that system until I came to British Columbia."

"It will be impossible to prove his birth," Mrs. Jones agreed, "as there are no records available. Why, I would be in the same position myself if I were asked to do the same. But Harry was raised in Cleveland and his poor mother paid for his existence with her life."

"What was his mother's maiden name?" Hopkins asked.

"We can't tell you that," Mrs. Jones said as her daughter nodded agreement. "It is not your business."

"Scores of people in this city could not prove their own births," resumed Theresa Jackson. "Why, I was never baptized, although Mother and I have been regular attendants at the Congregational Church."

"The *World* said that you were in some trouble in Victoria, Mrs. Jackson," Hopkins said. "Is that true?"

But it was Mrs. Jones who snapped back angrily with "Well, that matter need not have been revived! She was not convicted and I have the papers upstairs to prove it."

At this point Theresa Jackson indulged in a hysterical bout of weeping, then pulling herself together, she said, "This will be a sad and mournful Christmas. One has got to have troubles in this life, I suppose, but I sometimes wish I were dead and lying beside poor Tom, so cruel has been the world to me now. This experience has revealed to us our real friends. Those who should have remained steadfast proved worthless in the hour of trial, and those on whom we had no claim—utter strangers—consoled us. Never shall I forget the thoughtfulness of the Reverend Mr. Owen in calling on us in our hour of affliction. But that is the way of the world. I have gained much wisdom during the past five weeks." She paused and mopped her eyes before taking up her monologue again. "I can truthfully say that I have not tried to seek sympathy, knowing that the stain on our reputations will be cleared. But it seems cruel to have to lose a devoted husband and then be gossiped about from one end of the country to the other." Suddenly she raised a hand as if to stop Hopkins from interrupting. "Oh, before I forget, I want to repeat that Mr. Jackson was not, as far as my knowledge goes, in the habit of carrying poison." The hand remained raised.

Hopkins waited.

"And he was always on the best of terms with my cousin, Mr. Fisher." The hand returned to her lap.

Hopkins tried a new tack. "It is reported that you are going to move back to the United States."

Her aggressive response took him by surprise. "Whose business is it if I do? But it doesn't look like it, does it, after I went to the expense of moving here from that house of sorrow on Melville Street?" She pressed her hands to her reddened eyes, and Hopkins realized for the first time that her fingernails were bitten to the quick. "But what chance do I have to secure employment here with the public's gaze directed at me suspiciously? None whatever. I will tell you, however, that if I leave Vancouver, it will be of my own accord. After all, I am free to go if I want to. To detain me, it would first be necessary to lay a charge. But you have to satisfy the morbid taste of the public, don't you? So I will state that I have no intention of leaving Vancouver at present. My heart is heavy with care and troubles over my loss but public opinion counts for little with me." She sighed deeply then stood up and, trailing the scent of lilies of the valley, left the room.

Hopkins jumped to his feet. "Thank you for the interview, Mrs. Jack—" he said, but she had already gone.

Mrs. Jones had also risen, and with a nod to indicate that the interview was over she led the way to the front door. Without a word she handed him his cap, showed him out and closed the door behind him.

It was raining again, a sullen, heavy downpour, and from the carrier on his bike Hopkins hurriedly retrieved his rain cape and pulled it on. As he fastened the clasps, his mind went back over the interview. The whole thing had been rehearsed, of course. But what had been the purpose of it? To get their side of the story across, perhaps. Or maybe to cultivate a friendly newspaper. And why had they asked especially for him? He pulled the gate open, wheeled his bike into the street and mounted it. As he pedalled back to the office, the rain slanting into his face, he thought about the widow and realized he was no longer infatuated. Where was the frightened little thing who had so touched his heart when she gave evidence after Sprague charged her mother with theft? The woman he had just interviewed seemed almost as tough as her mother. Maybe Kelly was right. Maybe she had poisoned her husband. *No,* he thought, *she didn't kill him ... but I think she knows who did!*

At six that evening, as Harry Fisher was hanging up his coverall and preparing to go home, John Webster, the elder of the two brothers who owned and operated Webster Bros. Groceries on Granville Street, called him into the tiny office beside the door that led to the rear loading dock. All day long he and his brother had been quietly taking inventory, and now they were fairly certain that there had been a steady theft of supplies—tea, cigars, tobacco—and cash from the till. There was nothing to prove that the theft had been carried out by Fisher, but all indications pointed to him as the culprit.

As Fisher entered the office, John Webster held out a small brown envelope. "Mr. Fisher ... or should I call you Mr. Jones? Here's your pay packet. We won't be needing your services after today."

Fisher's face did not change expression. He snatched the

packet, grabbed his coat from the hook by the door, collected his bicycle from the yard and left.

"I've been fired!" he announced as he entered the kitchen at 615 Davie Street.

Neither woman spoke. Esther Jones removed a pot from the stove and carried it to the sink. Theresa Jackson began to cry.

"Shut up!" he screamed at the widow. "Shut up!"

Jackson's dog, which had been waiting for its dinner, fled behind the stove. Theresa Jackson stifled her sobs.

"What the hell am I going to do now?" he demanded.

"Dinner is almost ready," Esther said imperturbably. "Go and wash up. Ernest telephoned that he will be late so we will eat without him."

"Didn't you hear me? I've been fired! What am I going to do?"

She turned and asked with icy calm, "What did you expect?" When there was no response, she said again, "Go and wash up."

They ate in silence. At the end of the meal Esther asked, "Will you go back to Seattle?"

"I don't have any money."

"You could sell your wheel."

Fisher had already thought of that, but it wouldn't bring much. He'd bought the bicycle second-hand, and he hadn't taken care of it. But he would ride it over to the docks in the morning to see if one of the navvies there would buy it.

"Be careful. The police are watching the house," Esther said.

Startled, Fisher stared at her. "How do you know?"

"I've seen them."

Theresa began crying soundlessly into her napkin.

Later that night some thoughtful individual at Webster Bros. Groceries telephoned the *World*'s editor to provide him with the information that Harry Fisher had been sacked, hint that there might also be a theft charge laid and suggest that Fisher would probably try to leave town. The following morning at precisely 8:10 the *World*'s editor telephoned to Police Chief North to warn him that Fisher planned to decamp.

As the murder of Thomas Jackson was the most sensational crime to have occurred in Vancouver in years, North really needed to solve it in order to boost his sagging reputation in the city. He had three prime suspects—the mother-in-law, the wife and the brother-in-law (he had eliminated Exall as he had been at work at the time of the murder)—but as yet he had no proof against any of them that would stand up in court. At present, the most he could charge them with was perjury at the coroner's inquest because it looked like they had all lied about Fisher's identity. Now with the news that Fisher was about to bolt, North decided that he had no choice but to arrest the man for this lesser crime. At least this move would give the police a few more days to investigate before the man was freed on bail. The chief sent two plainclothes men to watch the house on Davie Street and a patrolman to check on the people departing on the CPR's morning train. Then, since Fisher was an American and would probably try to make his way back across the line, he took the precaution of ordering a man to the Great Northern train station and another to the interurban depot. After they set off to take up their posts, he phoned the New Westminster police department and gave them a description of the suspect. No point in counting on his own men to catch the fellow.

Long before North received his phone call from the *World* that morning Harry Fisher had pushed his bicycle through the fog to the docks. He had taken Jackson's dog with him, tied it to a railing on one of the quays and left it there. When, toward noon, he realized that he was not going to make a sale, he started pushing the bike homeward. The dog strained after him, whimpering, but he ignored it. Back at the Davie Street house, he parked the bicycle in the shed off the alleyway, but when he entered the kitchen, Esther Jones was not preparing lunch. He found her standing at the window in the darkened front parlour, staring out at the fog-shrouded street.

"You'll need to leave quickly," she told him.

He came to stand beside her, peering through the lace curtains at the two men on the opposite side of the street. Hunched into their mackinaws, they were walking up and down to keep warm in the grey dampness, but they never strayed very far from where they could see number 615. "You're sure they're coppers?" He took her silence for assent, hurried out of the room and up the stairs.

She followed a few minutes later and found him stuffing clothing into a battered suitcase. "No," she said. "They'll arrest you the moment you step out of the door with that case."

"What am I going to do?" He was shaking now, his unshaven baby face pale and sweaty.

From her apron pocket she retrieved a small handful of bills of various denominations and a few coins and handed them to him.

He started for the door. "I can make the two o'clock to Blaine."

"No," she said. "Go out the back way and catch the street-car as far as the tram car depot on Hastings. It will be safer. The tram will get you to New Westminster and you can take the Great Northern from there."

At the back door she cautioned him to wait while she recon-noitred the alley then beckoned to him. He turned up the collar of his pea jacket, pulled his cap low and slipped past her without a word. Within seconds he had disappeared into the fog, walking west toward Granville Street. Once there, he hovered inside the mouth of the alley until he heard the clickety-clack of an electric streetcar coming across the wooden-spanned Granville Bridge, waited nervously while it travelled the three blocks to Davie, then dashed out and hopped aboard at the rear door. There were no more than a dozen people on the car, and after dropping his coins into the fare box, he moved quickly up the aisle to the sideways-facing benches at the front where he could keep a surreptitious eye on each new rider coming aboard. Fortunately by the time the car had travelled north as far as Georgia Street, most of the seats had been taken by Christmas shoppers, and he began to relax in the anonymity they provided, although he remained watchful.

The streetcar made the downhill run toward Burrard Inlet and, its bell clanging to warn pedestrians, swung east onto Hastings Street behind a similarly laden car. When more shoppers invaded it at the stop just beyond Seymour Street, Fisher reluctantly gave up his seat to a large and intimidating woman who came to stand over him. Now he was forced to cling to an overhead strap, counting off the streets as the car continued eastward—Richards, Homer, Hamilton, Abbott ... When the interurban tram terminal was just a block ahead, he began easing between the other shoppers standing in the aisle, making his way toward the exit at the back of the car. His only problem now would be whether he was on time for one of the tram's regular hourly runs to New Westminster. If he had to wait around in the station, he risked being spotted.

His progress toward the rear door was soon halted by the mob of shoppers planning to get off there, and as the car swayed to a stop just short of Carrall Street, he found himself sandwiched between two large ladies clutching umbrellas and loaded down with parcels. The car just ahead of them on the track had already stopped to disgorge its passengers, so the conductor delayed opening the doors, and Fisher, anxious about missing the tram, peered out the window and was reassured as he caught a glimpse of its jade green sides and gold trim as it sat on the tracks inside the station. This was working out very well! Then just as the streetcar's doors opened and the line of people in the aisle started to move toward the rear exit platform, he glanced out of the window again. There, emerging from the fog in front of the depot and eyeing each person who alighted from the first car, was a man he recognized from the inquest—Detective James Preston.

Desperately Fisher extricated himself from the parcel-laden ladies fore and aft—"Here! Watch what you're doing, young man!"—and pushed his way back down the line to sink into a seat on the opposite side of the car. He hunched down, pulled up his collar and stared at the oiled wooden floor, holding his breath until with a clang, clang, clang, the car finally started up again, passed the junction with Columbia Street and then a block later swung south onto the Westminster Road. There was nothing for it now but to stay on until the streetcar reached its terminal in Mount Pleasant, the last stop where he could transfer to the interurban.

The tram reached New Westminster's interurban terminal on the south side of Columbia Street between Eighth and Begbie just after two o'clock, but Fisher delayed rising from his seat. Through the window he could see that a lone policeman stood at the far end of the platform watching the passengers as they alighted. Could he be looking for him? It didn't seem likely but, in any case, if he waited too long to leave the tram, he would be conspicuous. Besides, how would a copper in New Westminster know how to recognize him? He joined the queue in the aisle, stepped down from the car without looking in the direction of the policeman and headed for the docks to find a café. He hadn't eaten since breakfast and as he spooned up the only food he could afford—a bowl of fish soup—he began to feel confident again. He had easily eluded the stupid police.

Meanwhile, Constable Mackenzie of the City of New West-minster Police Department hurried back to the station with the news: Fisher had just arrived on the tram and was dining at a café on the dock. The officer on the desk immediately telephoned Vancouver's police department to ask for instructions. Should they arrest the man? But Chief North was in a meeting with the mayor and could not be disturbed, and knowing their chief's volatility, no one else at the station was willing to hazard what his instructions would be. Instead, they promised that North would call back when he emerged from his meeting. But North didn't call and conse-quently the New Westminster police only stood watching when, two hours later, Fisher climbed aboard a Great Northern train bound for the border.

Three years earlier Jim Hill had pushed his Great Northern Railway (GNR) north from a point just east of Blaine, Washing-ton, right up to the south bank of the Fraser at New Westminster, but he'd had to wait until July 23, 1904, for the completion of a double-decked, road/rail bridge across the river in order to finish his line to Vancouver. Fortunately for Fisher, within the city of New Westminster the GNR shared the CPR's tracks to a depot not far from the interurban station and it was just a matter of Fisher waiting nearby until departure time.

Belatedly realizing that he had missed his chance to catch Fisher, Chief North consulted with a lawyer who advised him to wire the US marshal at Blaine, a man named Kingsley, and tell him to arrest Fisher. Marshal Kingsley was happy to oblige, and at 5:30 when the train pulled up at the border, he arrested Fisher and conveyed him to the local jailhouse. For the next hour, while the two men shared dinner—Fisher behind the bars and Kingsley seated outside them—Fisher told the marshal a hard-luck version of his life story. At 6:45, having finished dinner, Kingsley phoned the Vancouver police station to say that he had Fisher in charge and what should he do with him?

Detective Sergeant Mulhern took the phone. "Keep him under lock and key," he ordered then asked to speak to Fisher himself.

Kingsley passed the phone through the bars.

"Fisher?" Mulhern said. "You there?"

"Yes."

"I'm going to send one of my men down there to bring you back."

There was no reply.

"You hear me, Fisher?"

"Yes."

"You'll come peaceably?"

"Yes."

Mulhern was satisfied.

As Kingsley hung up the telephone receiver, he asked Fisher, "You going to let 'em take you back just like that?"

"What choice do I have?"

"Make 'em extradite you," said Kingsley.

"What's that mean?"

"That's the law, son. They gotta give you a proper court hearing before they can take you back across the border—unless you agree to go peaceable-like."

Fisher was silent for a moment. "You mean I could do that? I could insist on a hearing?"

Kingsley grinned. "You're in the United States of America, son, where every man is entitled to a fair trial."

The next morning, Friday, December 22, Mulhern saw Detective George Jackson off on the Great Northern with a warrant for Fisher's arrest for perjury. But at Blaine, the detective was in for a surprise. Fisher would not come peaceably. He would wait out extradition proceedings in the Blaine jail under Kingsley's fatherly care.

Back in Vancouver, Chief North received the bad news by telephone. In his entire career he had never extradited anyone, so once again he consulted a lawyer from whom he learned it would cost three hundred dollars to initiate extradition proceedings. This was a sizable fee, but since catching Fisher was part of a high profile murder investigation, he was sure the provincial government would be happy to provide the money. He was wrong. The Attorney General advised him that, since the man was only wanted for perjury, it was a city policing matter and North would have to pay for it out of his policing budget. There was, however, no money in the Vancouver City Police budget for such processes, and North turned to Mayor Frederick Buscombe for aid.

Buscombe hated North for opposing his plan to get rid of the brothels of Dupont Street, and he now blamed him for having allowed Fisher to cross the border in the first place. But the city's honour being at stake, the mayor announced, "This dastardly criminal will not escape again! The city's treasury and credit will stand behind our police department!"

As a result, the United States extradition commissioner in Blaine, a man named Montfort, having been assured by Detective Jackson that North was proceeding with a legal request for Fisher's extradition, issued a warrant for his arrest—though he was already in custody. The case would come before his court the next day, Saturday, December 23.

SIX

At noon on Friday, December 22, Esther Jones, standing at the front parlour window, saw the paddy wagon stop in front of the house, watched as two policemen emerged, tugged their jacket uniforms down and straightened their helmets. She walked into the hall, picked up her hat from the hall table, placed it on her head and began pinning it to her hair. "Tess," she called up the stairs, "get your hat and coat on!"

Just as the first knock sounded on the front door, Theresa Jackson arrived at the bottom of the stairs, her coat on and her hat in her hands. Her face was white and her hands were trembling, and she paused to await her mother's further instructions.

"Just a moment!" Mrs. Jones called toward the door, then turning to her daughter, she said, "Put your hat on."

Tess obeyed, but before the hat was securely pinned in place, the knocking came again.

"One moment!" Mrs. Jones called, this time with a little more temper, then with a nod of her head indicated that her daughter should answer the door. She struggled into her coat and began buttoning it.

Theresa Jackson put the last pin into her hat, walked slowly toward the door, paused to look back pleadingly at her mother, then moved forward, drew back the bolt and opened the door. "Yes?" she said.

There was a shuffling of feet on the front porch. Both of the policemen standing there had arrested women before but they had been the ladies of Dupont Street, most of them as tough as any man. These were *real* ladies that they had come to collect and they didn't quite know how to go about it. Finally the sergeant cleared his throat and took a step closer to the widow.

"I have a warrant here for the arrest of Mrs. Theresa Jackson and Mrs. Esther Jones ..."

"On what charge?" Esther Jones had materialized beside her daughter.

"Perjury."

Esther gave a short laugh. "Perjury?"

"Yes, ma'am."

"I can't think why they would send two big men like you to bring in a couple of defenceless women on a charge of perjury," Esther taunted them. "You must think we are dangerous criminals!"

"Please, Mama!" Theresa said, now almost in tears. "We will not gain anything by talking back to policemen."

At that moment there was a commotion in the hallway behind them, and the women turned to see Ernest Exall, who had got into the habit of catching the streetcar home for lunch since they moved to Davie Street. "What's going on?" he demanded.

"They are here to arrest us," Esther announced, her voice acid.

"What for?" He moved to stand between the women in order to confront the police on the porch. "What are you arresting them for?"

"This doesn't concern you, sir," the sergeant began.

"It most certainly does," Exall said. "Mrs. Jones is my land-lady and—"

"They are arresting us for perjury, Ernest," Theresa Jackson said tearfully and, placing a hand on his arm, drew him back into the hallway. "I want you to telephone—"

"I'm sorry, Mrs. Jackson, but you'll have to come with us now. If Mr. Exall comes around to the police station, you can talk to him there. Of course, a third party will have to be present when you're talking—"

"Ernest, call Mr. Joe Martin," Esther ordered and stepped out onto the porch. Theresa hesitated for a moment longer then followed. They started down the stairs, the two officers coming after them, awkwardly trying to pretend that they were in charge. At the street where a small crowd had gathered, the women allowed themselves to be handed up into the paddy wagon and sat facing one another, Esther fixing her daughter with a stare that willed her to contain her emotions. There would be no crying or fainting on this trip. The police crowded into the wagon after them and the driver started the motor.

At the police station they were formally read the charges then taken to a side room where the jail matron, Mrs. Emma Raymond, searched them. Mrs. Jones had left her purse behind at the house, but the matron searched Theresa Jackson's bag and

MOTHER AND DAUGHTER
WHO WERE ARRESTED TO-DAY

Artist sketch of Esther Jones and Theresa Jackson printed in the *Province* newspaper on December 22, 1905. COURTESY OF REFERENCE DEPARTMENT, LEGISLATIVE LIBRARY OF BRITISH COLUMBIA.

found a little money, a watch and chain and a diamond ring, and this inventory was duly reported to the press. The two women were then taken downstairs and locked into one of the cells designated for women prisoners, the ones furthest from jailer John Grady's desk. Here lawyer Joseph Martin, K.C., found them an hour later, shivering in the cold, damp cell. Theresa Jackson was in tears, her mother barely holding back her own.

The man who became known as "Fighting Joe Martin" is an anomaly in British Columbia's early history because he came to this province with his reputation already well established. Born in Milton, Ontario, in 1852, the product of Irish and Scottish parents, he was educated in the grammar schools of Ontario and Michigan State before studying for two years at the University of Toronto and taking his law articles with an Ottawa firm. He then moved to Manitoba where he was elected to the provincial legislature and served as Attorney General, gaining notoriety in the debates over the Separate Schools Act. He followed this with a stint in Ottawa as the Member of Parliament for Winnipeg, all the while earning a nationwide reputation as a quarrelsome, feisty but exceptionally skilful lawyer with considerable debating ability and a biting wit.

When word reached Vancouver in March 1897 that he had eschewed politics in order to take an appointment as the CPR's solicitor in British Columbia, there was no welcome mat put out for him. In fact, John Houston, the editor of the city of Nelson's *Tribune* newspaper, urged Manitobans to keep Martin and "send on your blizzard." But Martin came anyway and soon cut a wide swath through the young province's political and legal life, within a year of his arrival gaining a seat in the provincial legislature as an Opposition Liberal candidate. Then, party allegiances being very loose at this time, he accepted the offer of the attorney general's job in the government of the Conservative premier Charles Semlin. In February 1900 Martin rejoined the Liberals to defeat Semlin's government and a few days later was asked by the lieutenant-governor to form a government. Martin was, however, now so unpopular among the political elite that he had great difficulty assembling a cabinet and his reign as premier lasted only until an election in early June of that year. He remained leader of the Opposition in Victoria until June 1903 when he announced that he was "disgusted with politics" and was quitting "for all time."

Joseph Martin, recognized as the cleverest criminal lawyer in Canada in his day, defended the two women when they were charged with perjury. When he tired of being misquoted by journalists, he started his own newspaper where he could choose what would and would not be printed. CITY OF VANCOUVER ARCHIVES PORT P1746

Thus it was that in December 1905 Joe Martin was concentrating on building up his legal practice as a partner in Martin, Weart and McQuarrie, with offices in the Fairfield Block on Granville Street between Hastings and Pender. In April of that year he had been appointed counsel to the City of Vancouver at $2,500 a year then had resigned six months later to earn a much heftier fee as general counsel in BC for the Great Northern Railway. He also represented the city's board of trade in a dispute with the CPR over freight rates and was suitably compensated when he won. But much as he liked money,

Martin was generous to a fault when it came to freely dispensing assistance to those whom he deemed to be in straitened circumstances or unjustly accused. Like everyone who read Vancouver's newspapers, he was thoroughly familiar with the Jackson/Jones case, so when Ernest Exall phoned him on December 22 to enlist his aid for Esther Jones and Theresa Jackson, he agreed to help. Within an hour he arrived by hack to interview the women in their basement jail cell.

When Martin emerged from that two-hour conference, he met with the waiting reporters from the *World,* the *News-Advertiser* and the *Province.* For Dennis Hopkins of the *Province,* the man who stood before them was not at all what he expected. In spite of his huge impact on BC's legislature and courtrooms, he was a surprisingly small man and seemed very vulnerable because he limped from a childhood accident. A ring of greying hair surrounded his bald pate, but he made up for the sparseness on top with a luxurious moustache and goatee below an extremely prominent nose. He fixed the newsmen with his large brown eyes and waited for silence before he spoke.

> I have no statement to make regarding this case, but one thing I will say is that these women are certainly suffering greatly in that cell from the cold. Mrs. Jones is shivering and is really extremely uncomfortable. There was no heat in the radiator. It appears to me that this is unnecessarily brutal. I don't think the law contemplates freezing prisoners to death even if they are accused of perjury. I spoke to the jailer and he laughed and said that he guessed someone had turned off the heat. I could not get any further satisfaction from him.

Fortunately for the press, it was just three o'clock when Martin delivered this statement and it could be included in that evening's papers. Both ran banner headlines that announced the arrest of the two women and a smaller headline that celebrated Fisher's capture at Blaine. But the *World*'s story also congratulated itself for the paper's part in the affair:

> While the police have until now been apparently idle since the inquest, they have really been working hard and persistently to throw some light on the poisoning mystery. However, these latest developments in the Jackson poisoning mystery are the natural outcomes of the investigations made by *The World,* which have already been published in part and by which the police have profited in their own inquiries. Their activity was concealed from the press by the police, but it was known to *The World* through its own investigations, which in part preceded those of the authorities and were the means of directing them.

For Nichol at the *Province,* this self-congratulatory piece was like waving a red flag. Although just two days earlier he had been able to publish young Hopkins's exclusive interview with the two women, thereby stealing his own march on the competition, the *World*'s claim to being the source of most of the police's information was a fresh challenge that could not be ignored. What the *Province* needed was an interview with Fisher himself.

"Hopkins?" he bellowed as soon as the young reporter entered the office the next morning. "Take the Great Northern down to Blaine and get an interview with Fisher!"

"Now, sir?" Dennis Hopkins stopped in the act of unwinding his scarf.

"Of course *now*! That hack outside is waiting to take you to the station."

"But it's Saturday, sir ..."

Nichol ignored his protest. "If you get a move on, you can make the nine o'clock train. I want that interview for tonight's paper."

Hopkins rewound his scarf and raced out the door. If he worked fast and caught the two-thirty train back to Vancouver, he might still be in time see the boxing match put on by the English Bay Bathing and Athletic Club at seven that night. It would feature the local boy Oscar "Battling" Nelson and Tacoma's Kid Merrifield at City Hall.

The constable behind the front desk in the Blaine police station shook his head when Dennis Hopkins asked to see Harry Fisher. "Not here," he said.

"Where is he?"

"Don't know," the constable said. "The commissioner let him go this morning."

"But I thought he was being held for extradition!"

"Can't extradite on a perjury charge. Couple of your cops came down here this morning to lay some more charges but Fisher was already long gone. Could be in California by now."

Hopkins's further inquiries elicited the information that Extradition Commissioner Montfort's hearing on the perjury charge had occurred very, very early that morning—at Marshal Kingsley's request—and Montfort had indeed dismissed the case since perjury was not, as the constable said, an extraditable offence. But a little more ferreting provided Hopkins with the additional information that shortly after releasing the accused, the commissioner had been advised that Vancouver's prosecutor would be arriving to lay more charges, and so he had given orders to Kingsley to round Fisher up again. Hopkins telephoned all of this news to his boss who told him to stay in Blaine until he got a statement from Fisher.

Nichol went to press with a headline reading "Fisher Gives Police Slip" followed by a couple of paragraphs describing his escape. He then made up for the scanty news on that front with a thorough report on the ongoing developments in Vancouver.

In the police court this morning Mrs. Jones and her daughter, Mrs. Jackson, charged with perjury, were remanded to Wednesday next. The two women, both attired in mourning, occupied a seat alongside the other offenders, mostly drunks who were sent down for periods covering the Christmas holidays. Both women were so deeply veiled that their features could not be distinguished. A large and curious audience listened to the proceedings.

Neither of the prisoners was asked to plead as this is a preliminary hearing, but Mrs. Jackson by mistake rose up to plead, momentarily removing her veil. She whispered something inaudibly and then resumed her seat. She showed traces of worry.

Mr. Killam, acting for Prosecutor J. W. deBeque Farris, asked for a remand to Wednesday. Then Mr. Weart, in the absence of Mr. Joseph Martin, counsel for the accused, said he would not object, provided that bail was allowed in a reasonable amount. Magistrate Williams, after a moment's hesitation, fixed bail in each case at $4,000 in personal bonds of $2,000 and two sureties of $1,000 each. The two women were then escorted to the women's quarters in the prison. Mrs. Jackson led the way, her aged mother with bowed head bringing up the rear.

Mrs. Jones and her daughter are now satisfied with their accommodation at the police station. Their ward was inspected today by Dr. McTavish, the jail surgeon, who pronounced it sufficiently well heated.

While the women were in court, their home was being searched by detectives Preston and Waddell who were ostensibly looking for proof that Fisher was Esther Jones's son and Theresa Jackson's brother, but they were even more anxious to find evidence that would convict one—or preferably all three—of killing Jackson. They were disappointed. When they were finished, they told reporters waiting outside that they had found neither beer nor Epsom salts on the premises and nothing else to point to the killer. There was also nothing to prove that Fisher's relationship to the women was anything other than they claimed. They then invited the reporters into the house to view some of the personal items— including piles of letters—they had found. This wasn't much to build a story on, but Nichol enhanced the notes his reporter had taken with a few suggestive phrases:

> A peculiar circumstance developed in a search of the Jackson residence by the police. They found many letters from Fisher to Mrs. Jones and Mrs. Jackson. Some of these were written three years ago. In none of these did Fisher refer in the slightest way to Mrs. Jones as if she were his mother. He referred to her in every case by her first name. The police devoted several hours to classifying and arranging the scores of letters found in the trunks of the two women. Mrs. Jackson especially seems to have had a mania for writing letters, judging from the number of replies discovered among her papers. Her correspondents were women friends in Victoria, Alberni, Cowichan, Brighton, England, and Toronto. The letters contained many favourable references to poor Jackson, who seems to have been a very popular person.
>
> One package of letters addressed by Fisher to Mrs. Jackson were written at Alberni when Fisher was engaged with Jackson at a mining camp. Frequent references to the good treatment he was receiving from

Jackson are contained therein. These letters bear the date of three years ago. In none of them did Fisher give any clue to his true relationship to the woman. He addressed them jointly as "Bess" and "Tess," signing himself, "Yours lovingly, Harry."

An insurance policy for $1,000 with Imperial Life on the life of Jackson in favour of his wife was found in one of the trunks. It showed that the premiums have been paid to date. Mrs. Jackson informed the police that she had yesterday made application to the insurance company for payment of the amount of the policy. Evidence indicating that the dead man also owns valuable mining claims on Vancouver Island and in the Skeena River district was also secured. Some of the correspondence respecting the mining property consisted of communications from mining recorders indicating that all the assessments to date had been recorded.

Fisher occupied a room upstairs in the back of the dwelling. He had evidently left in a hurry as various articles of clothing were piled on the unmade bed, and other garments littered the floor. His effects showed that he had been employed at Rae's store in New Westminster and in the streetcar service at Seattle. Fisher was apparently a smoker as he left behind three or four boxes of cigars and several pounds of tobacco. One of the drawers in the room contained several poems not designed to be read in public. The verses were apparently in Fisher's handwriting.

Some member of the household is apparently of a devout nature as the dwelling contains several Bibles and hymn books. A trunk in Mrs. Jones's room contained a number of prescriptions, strychnine not forming a constituent of any of the compounds.

Meanwhile, Harry Fisher had not set out for California. As ordered, Marshal Kingsley had rounded him up for a second hearing, and at two that afternoon the culprit again stood before Extradition Commissioner Montfort in the latter's office. The charges were presented this time by local lawyer W.B. Whitcomb who had been hired to conduct the case for Vancouver's twenty-six-year-old city prosecutor, John Wallace deBeque Farris, as Farris had no standing in the American court.

Born into a New Brunswick political family, Farris had received his BA from Acadia College, where he was captain of the football team, before taking a law degree at the University of Pennsylvania, where he became a noted debater. He arrived in Vancouver in 1903 and, almost before he had time to set up his law office with partner Cecil Killam, had been hired by the city for the job of prosecutor. By the time the Jackson/Jones case came along, he was already known as a fearless upholder of the law and a relentless foe of wrongdoers. For the extradition of Harry Fisher, he had brought along an impressive array of witnesses, and he was confident that he would step back across the border with the miscreant in handcuffs.

The first person brought into the office to testify was Colonel Whyte, warden of the penitentiary in New Westminster.

"Do you know this man?" Whitcomb asked, pointing to Fisher.

"I do," said Whyte. "He was under my charge from July 20, 1897, to January 12, 1900. He was received from Victoria under the name of Fred Jones. The next time I saw him he was working at Rae's Grocery Store in New Westminster and going by the name of Harry Fisher."

"You are confident that Fred Jones and Harry Fisher are the same man?"

"Yes, yes," the Colonel said. "I addressed him as Jones, but he told me he was called Fisher ... Harry Fisher."

"But you believe his real name is Fred Jones?"

"Yes. While in my charge he wrote letters to Miss T. Jones and Mrs. E. Jones—his sister and his mother."

"You read these letters?"

"It is my duty to read all letters written by prisoners before I post them."

The next person to stand before the commissioner was A.S. Burgess, who dealt in real estate from an office on Pender Street in Vancouver. He testified that he had attended school in Victoria nine or ten years earlier with Fred Jones.

"Do you see Fred Jones in this courtroom?" asked Whitcomb.

Burgess pointed to Fisher. "That's Fred Jones."

Sergeant Walker of the Victoria Police Department then identified the accused as the man he had arrested for theft in his city in 1897 and delivered to the penitentiary as Fred Jones.

At this point Montfort interrupted with considerable irritation edging his voice. "Mr. Whitcomb, I am quite willing to agree that these witnesses have demonstrated that Fisher and Jones are the same man, but as you well know there is no law on either side of the border to prevent a man from calling himself whatever he likes. What you have not produced is any shred of evidence to show that the man is guilty of perjury."

After a brief whispered consultation with Farris, Whitcomb argued, "But if we have proved that he is Fred Jones, we have de facto proved that he is the son of Esther Jones and—"

Montfort shook his head. "No sir, you have not proved that fact. What is more, you have not demonstrated that he ever swore that he was either the son *or* the nephew of Esther Jones, and I have no alternative but to let Mr. Fisher go."

John Wallace deBeque Farris, KC, was a hotshot young lawyer barely out of law school when he faced Joe Martin in the preliminary hearing for the Jones/Jackson perjury case in January 1906. IMAGE COURTESY OF THE ROYAL BC MUSEUM/BC ARCHIVES A02141

"But I have more evidence coming," protested Farris. "The holiday has delayed—"

"Oh, very well, Mr. Farris," Montfort said, checking his calendar. "The accused is remanded in custody for a full hearing at 2:30 on Wednesday, December 27. Take him away, Mr. Kingsley." And he waved them all out of his office.

Out on the street again, Dennis Hopkins caught sight of Burgess hurrying toward the Great Northern depot and he fell into step beside him. "Are you absolutely sure that's the same man?" he asked.

Burgess nodded. "Oh yes, quite sure. I didn't know him as Fred, of course. We called him Rufus or Brick—the nicknames he went by among the boys because of his red hair. But I'm certain that he recognized me as soon as I entered the room because he looked up and gave that involuntary sign of recognition that a man gives when he suddenly sees some old acquaintance unexpectedly. As soon as he saw me, he called his attorney over and whispered something to him. And then his attorney took a good look at me."

When Dennis Hopkins telephoned the details of the hearing back to his boss at the *Province*, Nichol demanded, "Where's the interview with Fisher?"

"He wasn't at the jail when I went there this morning ..."

"But he's there now, isn't he?"

"Well, yes, I guess so ..."

"Then go and get that interview!"

"Yes sir," Hopkins said. It was already past three o'clock and there was no hope of getting back to Vancouver in time for the Nelson/Merrifield boxing match. Sadly he wound his scarf around his neck again, pulled on his gloves and set off for the jail.

But Marshal Kingsley's idea of custody was not exactly as expected on the Canadian side of the line, so when Hopkins returned to the Blaine jail, he founded it empty. Kingsley had, in fact, taken Fisher to meet an old friend, George H. Westcott, a strange, Ichabod-Crane-like local lawyer with a messianic zeal for protecting the underdog. After hearing how this young American citizen—with a life of tragedy and abuse behind him—was being persecuted by Canadian authorities, Westcott readily agreed to represent him in court. He even offered to play host to him while he waited for his hearing.

It was not long before the two Vancouver police detectives who had accompanied Farris to Blaine also discovered that Fisher had not been jailed, and they began shadowing Kingsley. As a result, they soon discovered their quarry at Westcott's office. When Hopkins caught up to the detectives, they were standing in the rain outside the lawyer's office, staring through the glass at the young man and his new lawyer in deep conversation, both smoking big, fat cigars. Hopkins immediately went to the door to ask to interview Fisher but was turned away by the lawyer. A short time later Commissioner Montfort arrived and joined the two in the office, and for an hour the watchers outside could see Montfort and Westcott delving into the latter's law books, apparently trying to decide what the law really was in this case.

At six o'clock Hopkins telephoned the news back to his boss that he had failed to get the interview. Nichol was not pleased, but since the following day was Sunday and the next day was Christmas, he at last allowed the young man to return to Vancouver. Hopkins was elated. He had no family in the city but he knew that Mrs. Edna Smithers, his widowed landlady, would be providing a sumptuous Christmas dinner, and afterwards he and one of the other boarders would go to see the Roslan Comic Opera Company perform John Philip Sousa's operetta *El Capitan* at the opera house.

After Hopkins's phone call, Walter Nichol remained seated at his desk watching his employees leave one by one. When it was the turn of advertising manager Frank J. Burd to head for home, he stopped in Nichol's office doorway. "Good night, Walter," he said, smiling. Hewitt Bostock had recruited Burd and Nichol at the same time for his new *Province* newspaper back in 1898, and the two men had maintained a close relationship ever since. In fact, Burd was the only *Province* employee who ever addressed Nichol by his first name.

"I've got a problem, Frank," Nichol said. "The hearing for the women and the one for Fisher are both set for next Wednesday afternoon."

Burd understood. "And Kelly's not with us anymore."

"Maybe I was a bit hasty in firing him ..."

Burd was silent. He knew Nichol was not asking for his opinion on that one.

After a pause, Nichol said, "Young Hopkins is coming along and so far he's not taken to the bottle, but he still doesn't know how to take the initiative, figure out the angles. Besides, he can't cover a hearing in Vancouver and another in Blaine at the same time."

"Why not cover one of them yourself? You're no stranger to court reporting." Burd knew that before Nichol came to Vancouver, he had put in nearly ten years reporting for the Hamilton *Spectator,* most of it covering the courts.

"M-m-m."

"Farris will apply to get one of them adjourned, won't he?" Burd continued. "Go wherever he goes. Send Hopkins to cover the other one."

After Burd left, Nichol shrugged into his overcoat. He would decide what to do about Jones, Jackson and Fisher on Tuesday. Right now it was time to get home to enjoy the evening with his young family.

For the next three days, while Fisher was wined and dined as the honoured guest of lawyer Westcott and his family, Esther Jones and Theresa Jackson, not being able to raise bail, remained in their cell. It was reported that they ate a little of the Christmas dinner served by their jailer, Grady, although they later had a proper Christmas feast sent in from the Blackburn Hotel. And while Farris had taken the train back to Vancouver to enjoy his first Christmas with his new bride, Evlyn, the Vancouver city detectives he had left behind in Blaine to keep an eye on Fisher were given no such comfort. They spent the holiday in a rundown local hotel.

On Tuesday morning word came from Toronto that Thomas Jackson's next of kin had been located, and Nichol hired a Toronto "correspondent" to interview them. Jackson's brother, William, told this reporter that he had not seen his brother for eighteen years:

> Our home was in Palmerston, Ontario, and he left there when a boy, travelling through western Canada and the United States. He always appeared to be pretty

lucky, and I understood that he expected to make $60,000 out of his new mine.

All I know of my brother's death is contained in a letter I received from E.R. Exall that said he had died under distressing circumstances and that his wife had recovered under care. Next came a request from the insurance company asking for a declaration regarding his age. From no one have I heard any details regarding the circumstances of his death.

I am certain that he did not kill himself. My father, who is an aged man, said a few days ago after we heard of Tom's death that there had never been a suicide in the family.

Nichol's dilemma about which hearing to attend was resolved late on the afternoon of Tuesday, December 26, when word came that Farris had set off for Blaine with a freshly drawn-up complaint aimed at forcing the commissioner to issue yet another warrant for Fisher's arrest. Leaving orders for Hopkins to cover the Vancouver hearing the following morning, Nichol caught the next Great Northern train for Blaine, arriving in early evening to learn that Marshal Kingsley had refused to arrest Fisher. Instead, the marshal had told Farris smilingly, "Well, I guess Mr. Fisher will show up when he's needed tomorrow."

Farris was livid, but no amount of remonstrating could disrupt the marshal's complacency or persuade Montfort to force Kingsley to act. Farris, therefore, decided to go over Kingsley's head. At eight that evening he made telephone contact with the United States marshal in Seattle, and that worthy immediately wired Kingsley to hold Fisher in jail. However, when morning came, Fisher was neither in the Blaine jail nor in the commissioner's office.

"Where is Fisher?" Farris demanded.

"You think we're some kind of fools?" lawyer Westcott said. "The moment we let that young fellow out of our sight, you would have dragged him over the border!"

And Kingsley added, "If anybody had come for that boy last night, they'd have been dealing with my Winchester!"

Fuming, Farris contacted the Seattle marshal's office again, and at two that afternoon a deputy marshal arrived and went at once to Westcott's office. Walter Nichol and the Vancouver detectives stood watching while Fisher was escorted from the premises. They followed as the accused was taken to the town hall to appear before Commissioner Montfort. But Nichol, who was used to the pomp and ceremony of Canadian trials with robed and bewigged judges and lawyers, was taken aback by the lack of formality in the American courtroom. It also tickled his funny bone, reawakening his special talent for lampooning, and as soon as he got back to the *Province*'s offices in Vancouver, he began typing furiously. The ghost of a smile hovered around his lips.

> The locale was a bare, dirty little room with a gigantic round-bellied heater, a couple of lines of benches, a chair or two and a small table for the commissioner to take his notes upon. There was no carpet on the floor, not even oilcloth [the predecessor of linoleum]. An extra aesthetic effect was furnished by several large spittoons, which occupied prominent places for the convenience of court officials and loungers.

> The janitor having started a good fire, a few minutes before the hour half a dozen loungers sneaked in out of the rain and made themselves comfortable. The commissioner opened proceedings at three o'clock. The case being formally called, Deputy District Attorney Gardner of King County, who had arrived from Seattle to assist the Vancouver authorities to the

best of his powers, removed a fat black cigar from his lips long enough to announce that the prosecution was ready to proceed.

This was the cue for Mr. George H. Westcott, the attorney for Mr. Fisher, to get into the game. He commenced by entering objections to everything in sight. "We may owe a duty to our cousins across the boundary line," shouted Mr. Westcott as he theatrically waved his long arms in the direction of the half-dozen loungers, "but we also owe a duty to humanity in our country. Ours, thank god, is the home of the free and the brave, the home of liberty where every man is entitled to a fair trial, and thank god, there is no perversion of justice under the Stars and Stripes!"

By this time Mr. Westcott had assumed the strident tones a sea captain might use in an endeavour to make himself heard in a howling gale. The result was that he awoke several of the loungers and one of the witnesses from Vancouver. "Those people have come over from Vancouver for the purpose of depriving my client of his liberty. Two of my client's witnesses are held in jail in Vancouver in order that they may not appear before this court and give evidence in favour of my client. This is an indignity which I might suffer in silence, but when it affects the rights and interests of my client, never—never—NEVER!"

At this point Mr. Westcott stopped abruptly to reach out and welcome his second wind. While gathering in the frayed ends of his breath, he beamed approvingly at the commissioner and everyone else in the courtroom and then requested that the case be thrown out. The commissioner refused but granted him a twenty-minute recess to confer with his client. The Vancouver contingent took advantage of the respite to grope their way out through the engulfing wave of tobacco smoke to the fresh air. On the conclusion of the recess Mr. Westcott produced an affidavit to the effect that Fisher was an American citizen and claimed protection from United States authorities. He then argued for an adjournment because he planned to subpoena Mrs. Jackson and Mrs. Jones to testify on behalf of his client, and Commissioner Montfort obligingly remanded Fisher until Wednesday, January 3, at 2:30 and had him removed to the jail in Bellingham.

With anti-American sentiment running high on Canada's West Coast, Walter Nichol knew his story would add a nice bit of fuel to the flames. He concluded his story by adding that the Vancouver police had denied that Fisher was an American citizen as they had "certain information that just a few years ago Fisher had joined the militia at Victoria under the name of Jones," and had sworn allegiance to the queen. Nichol was smiling as he called for a copy boy. That evening his smile grew broader when he saw that the *World* had relied on a mere telephone interview with Farris to cover Fisher's hearing.

At nine o'clock on Wednesday, December 27, Esther Jones and Theresa Jackson had been ushered into a Vancouver courtroom. And exactly as Burd had predicted, before the court clerk had a chance to read the charge, Farris's law partner, Cecil Killam, had asked for a week's remand.

"Do you object to a remand, Mr. Martin?" Magistrate Adolphus Williams asked.

"I most certainly do," Martin replied.

"But counsel for the prosecution is absent, Mr. Martin," Killam explained.

"That is no excuse," Martin snapped.

The magistrate concurred.

"Could we have a remand until tomorrow then?" Killam asked.

Reluctantly Martin agreed and the two women were returned to their cell.

As a result, it was Thursday, December 28, when Farris stood before Magistrate Adolphus Williams in Vancouver City Police Court to battle with Joe Martin. But while Farris was a very fine, hotshot young lawyer, his opponent had been practising law for nearly twenty-five years, had argued—and won—cases before the Supreme Court of Canada and even the Judicial Committee of the Privy Council in London. He was at the peak of a brilliant legal career and renowned for his skilful questioning and provocative and incisive wit.

Long before the case against Esther Jones was called, close to five hundred people had arrived at the courthouse, pushing up the stairs, taking every seat in the courtroom and standing along the walls and in the corridor outside. Finally Chief North sent a constable to guard the entrance to the building and prevent any more from getting inside. They were all, according to the *World,* hoping for "sensational revelations, although they did not waste their time completely, for they received quite a liberal education on the nature of evidence, Mr. Joseph Martin, KC, who appeared for the defendants, contesting every point with all his ability and energy."

The *World's* reporter then launched into purple prose to describe the accused sitting side by side at the "top end" of the dock, next to them a "coloured woman" and beyond her "a girl painfully young to appear in such a place."

> Three men, one an ordinary victim of strong drink,
> the other two charged with vagrancy but looking
> anything rather than vagrant, completed the motley

assembly. Mrs. Jones and Mrs. Jackson endured the silent scrutiny of a hundred eyes. The former was pale but quite self-possessed, taking her seat later beside her counsel and following the proceedings with close attention. The younger woman, on the other hand, with cheeks blanched and distrait air, was entirely passive, as one who had wept until she could weep no longer, and whose mind had been numbed into indifference under successive shocks. The contrast between the apathetic widow of today and the vivacious girl who held her own in the witness box against the lawyers of the Crown only two months ago was as remarkable as it was painful.

For Dennis Hopkins of the *Province* the only person in the courtroom was Joe Martin, and from the spot where the young reporter stood close to the north wall he could watch every nuance of expression on the great man's face. He had to remind himself to take notes.

The first to give evidence was Dr. McGuigan who identified the depositions from the inquest over which he had presided.

"I object," said Martin.

"I am only introducing these depositions to show that an oath was taken in a regular judicial proceeding," protested Farris.

"No, no," said Martin. "This is just a very handy way of getting evidence accepted. If those depositions are in, then they can be used as evidence. My learned friend cannot justify this procedure, your honour."

"Then I will remove all the depositions except that of Mrs. Jones," countered Farris.

"That is just exactly my point, your honour," Martin responded. "My learned friend is attempting to introduce Mrs. Jones's deposition as evidence."

"Very well, I will introduce only a portion of Mrs. Jones's deposition."

"No authority has been shown for this introduction."

"I simply wish to show, your honour," an exasperated Farris replied, "that this inquest was a regular judicial proceeding."

"Ah-ha!" said Martin. "Now we have the point. But the coroner can do that."

"I am not taking any chances!" Farris said.

"I will allow it," interrupted Magistrate Adolphus Williams.

If Joe Martin was disappointed with the magistrate's ruling, he did not show it. He merely asked to see the offending portion of the document and then read it while making copious notes. When he handed it back to Farris, everything Mrs. Jones had said at the inquest was placed into evidence.

Satisfied, Farris returned to his witness, McGuigan, who explained that Mrs. Jones had taken her oath on the bible, that she had read over the transcription of her testimony and that he had watched while she signed it. Farris then read aloud that part of the deposition in which Esther Jones explicitly stated that Fisher was her nephew.

Colonel Whyte, the warden of the penitentiary, took the stand to reprise the testimony he had given at Fisher's hearing in Blaine. He finished with "While in custody Fred Jones addressed letters to Miss T. Jones, and Mrs. E. Jones—his sister and his mother. The letters addressed to Mrs. E. Jones were—"

"Where are these letters, Mr. Farris?" the magistrate asked.

"We don't have them, your honour, but we are—"

"Have you made all possible efforts to obtain them?"

"We have searched the premises and cannot find any trace of them ..."

"But she might not have kept them at the house," said the

magistrate and then grinning added, "She might even have them in her pocket right now …"

The spectators enjoyed his little joke and even Martin seemed amused—although no lawyer ever fails to find a judge's jokes anything but amusing.

"We are still expecting to obtain them, your honour," said Farris. "I wish to serve a search warrant on Mrs. Jones …"

Neither of the women showed that they had heard any of this continuing exchange. Studying them, Dennis Hopkins realized that the emotion reflected on their faces was indifference. *They know he won't find those letters! I'll bet they burned them!* And he felt a little surge of admiration for the two beleaguered creatures in the dock.

"But the letters will not constitute evidence anyway," Martin said. "Before you can serve notice on Mrs. Jones, you must connect her with the letters, and you have not done this."

Farris argued that Esther Jones was the only Mrs. E. Jones at the address to which the letters were sent, and the changes of address on the letters corresponded with Esther Jones's changes of abode. For the next fifteen minutes the two lawyers wrangled over this point of law with Farris pressing for an adjournment so he could obtain the letters and Martin insisting that no foundation had been laid for the introduction of the letters as evidence.

"The course adopted by the Crown," huffed Martin at last, "seems to be to arrest people and then see if any evidence against them can be obtained, a most unheard of proceeding!"

Instead of commenting on Martin's statement, the magistrate suddenly said, "I suppose Mr. Fisher will be a material witness in this case."

Alarmed, Martin said, "It could take six weeks to two months to extradite the man, your honour! Surely these women cannot be held pending the conclusion of that business!"

"Yes, yes," the magistrate said, nodding. "I take your point. This case and the one in Blaine do seem to be waiting on each other."

Eventually the magistrate succumbed to Farris's repeated requests to adjourn the hearing until the following Tuesday, January 2, 1906, so that the prosecutor could locate the missing letters. But Martin also had a request. "In the matter of bail, your honour, due to the notoriety of this case caused by the sensational nature of the newspaper reports, the accused have been unable to secure funding. We request a reduction."

"Very well, Mr. Martin," Magistrate Williams said. "We will cut bail in half. Will that do?"

"Thank you, your honour."

But even with the reduced sum, no bondsman was willing to put money on the line for the two women and they remained in custody. The *World* reported that the heating system in the court house/jail building was still malfunctioning, and as a result, the prisoners housed at one end of the women's section suffered from stifling heat while in the cell at the other end shared by Esther Jones and her daughter there was no heat at all. There the older woman sat huddled in a blanket next to the register, desperately trying to stay warm. The *World's* story continued gleefully:

> [Mrs. Jones and Mrs. Jackson] have not taken kindly to the regime in existence at our Hotel North, and now that the Hotel Blackburn, with its bill unpaid, has refused further credit for meals, thus putting the women on the prison diet, their admiration of the civic institution is certainly no greater. For a few days meals were supplied from the Blackburn, but when the bill was presented and payment refused by Mrs. Jackson, the supply failed promptly. Mrs. Jackson had a few dollars in her purse but she said she had assigned this to another creditor.

Mrs. Jackson was apparently misinformed regarding the jail regulations. She got very indignant when
Police Chief North refused to settle the bill with the
Hotel Blackburn yesterday and told him that her lawyer had advised her that she and Mrs. Jones had to be
supplied with everything they wanted while they were
awaiting their adjourned hearing. The chief told Mrs.
Jackson that she could have anything she was willing
to pay for or that friends might send her, subject to
police inspection.

SEVEN

———————

On Tuesday, January 2, Dennis Hopkins was again waiting in police court with his pencil at the ready when Esther Jones and Theresa Jackson made their next appearance. This time they heard testimony from a man named Robert C. Douglas to whom Fred Jones had written many letters while he was in the penitentiary. Douglas was followed onto the stand by Alfred Hooper who had known the family in Alberni and by Sergeant Walker of the Victoria Police Department who had arrested Jones in 1897. All insisted that Fisher and Jones were the same man.

Well, they can't all be wrong, Hopkins told himself. *So why doesn't the old girl just admit he's her son and get it over with?* And then it came to him: *She's counting on Joe Martin's fancy talk to save her!*

At this point Farris called Colonel Whyte to the stand again, but before he could speak, Martin rose to tell the magistrate that Farris had confided outside the court a few days earlier that he could not prove that Jones's letters from the penitentiary had actually been sent to either Mrs. Jones or Mrs. Jackson.

Farris was immediately on his feet, red-faced and blustering.

"That is taking mean advantage of my frank statement, your honour!"

"Have I said anything to his honour that is not true?" Martin inquired, smiling loftily. "Where on earth is the mean advantage in what I said?" Then turning to Williams he added, "Your honour would not possibly have granted an adjournment at the last session if it had been known that Mr. Farris's grounds were mistaken."

"That is true," said the magistrate.

"I knew all the time that he couldn't prove that they had been sent," Martin said.

"Then why did you not show him up earlier, Mr. Martin?" the magistrate asked, thoroughly enjoying Martin's little sideshow.

"I had to wait for my learned friend to *admit* the facts, your honour." Martin, pleased with himself, sat down.

Farris had just learned another lesson in law: don't put your head into the crocodile's mouth even if he does seem friendly. For a moment he stood, flustered and perspiring, then pulled himself together to request a remand for one more day as his star witness had been delayed. The magistrate, still visibly amused, granted it.

That evening, instead of giving front page coverage to Dennis Hopkins's report on Joe Martin's latest courtroom manoeuvres, the *Province*'s headline announced: *Police to Charge Women with Murder of Jackson!* But only a brief paragraph followed:

> New charges, this time of murder, will be laid against Mrs. Jones and her daughter, Mrs. Jackson. This is according to an announcement made this morning by Chief of Police North, who said that it had been planned to lay the new charges today, but later it was decided to delay action for a day or two at least. The chief was asked if any new evidence had turned up to support a murder charge, but he declined to make any statement on that subject.

In 1905 glass merchant Frederick Buscombe was elected Vancouver's eleventh mayor after promising to introduce sound financial management to the city's affairs. He was spectacularly unsuccessful at this task but is remembered for his war on the prostitutes of Dupont Street and for getting rid of both Police Chief Samuel North and jailer John Grady. CITY OF VANCOUVER ARCHIVES 99-3105

What the *Province* did not remind its readers—but every one of them knew—was that at this time in Canada's history the mandatory penalty for murder was death by hanging. And this remained the law until July 14, 1976, although the last hanging in Canada actually occurred on December 11, 1962; faced with a growing public aversion to hanging, all capital punishment sentences in the intervening fourteen years were commuted to life imprisonment. Between confederation in 1867 and that last hanging in 1962, seven hundred and ten persons were sent to the gallows, thirteen of them women. However, as of 1906, none of those hanged women had met their end in British Columbia, so the prospect of two women being convicted for the crime of murder in Vancouver provided fodder for speculation in every bar in town as well as behind the doors of private homes.

But the *Province*'s startling news on this occasion had much more to do with civic politics than with any advances in the police investigation of Thomas Jackson's poisoning. Police Chief North was now locked in what would prove to be his final battle with Mayor Buscombe who was trying to persuade the new provincially appointed police commission that the chief was incompetent and should be given his walking papers. North, on the other hand, knowing that the whole city was eager to see progress on the Jackson murder case, was retaliating by suggesting an imminent arrest, hoping thereby to persuade the public that he was the single rock upholding the law, in which case Buscombe's vendetta would fail. And there was another factor at work here as well: when the hearing in police court resumed the next day, it was more than possible that Magistrate Williams would dismiss the perjury charges, and the women would be freed. Of course, Esther Jones still had to stand trial for theft from Captain Sprague, but Exall's bail bond would allow her to await her court date for that charge at the house on Davie Street. But she could just as easily head south as Fisher had done as soon as the coast was clear.

Immediately on the case being recalled on Wednesday morning, prosecutor Farris put William Peden on the stand.

"You were acquainted with the family of John H. and Esther Jones some years ago," Farris stated.

"Ten years ago," said Peden. "They was living on Glenford Avenue outside Victoria. I made it my habit to go shooting in that neighbourhood and a number of times I spent the night at the Jones house."

"Did John and Esther Jones have a family?"

"There was two children, Fred and Theresa, and I always understood them to belong to Mr. and Mrs. Jones."

"And why did you understand that to be the case, Mr. Peden?"

"Because they called them mother and father."

Farris produced a photograph and showed it to Peden. "Do you recognize the children in this photo?"

"Yes," said Peden. "That there is Fred and that one is Theresa."

Farris showed the photograph to the magistrate and then to

Martin. "And when did you last see Fred Jones, Mr. Peden?"

"When him and me was working together at Major Wilson's feed store."

"That was in Victoria?"

"Yes."

"Do you remember having a conversation with Mr. John Jones in which he said something to the effect that—"

Joe Martin jumped to his feet. "Surely my learned friend does not plan to offer this conversation as evidence?"

"I certainly do."

"But what can something Mr. John Jones said have to do with us here?"

"Surely," Farris responded, "my learned friend will not contend that a statement by a deceased person respecting pedigree is not evidence?"

"That may be all right in pedigree cases, but this is a criminal case. Why, if one could admit evidence of what a dead man said, it would give all kinds of opportunity for the manufacturing of evidence!"

"You always insinuate that what I have to say does not amount to anything," Farris complained petulantly.

"That is probably true," Martin replied drily.

"Well, I have authorities on this subject," Farris countered angrily.

"My learned friend's authorities have a way of proving to be not very good."

"I am not asking you to judge my authorities!"

"Your honour, I object to the tone of my learned friend's response! I have—"

"Yes, yes, Mr. Martin. I take your point. Mr. Farris will mind his manners ..."

Farris then produced a volume of legal cases and read from it to prove that Peden's account of what the deceased Mr. John Jones had said about his relationship to Fred Jones was admissible as evidence. When he concluded, Martin took the book, studied it for a moment and proceeded to demolish Farris's argument.

"The case from which my learned friend is quoting states that the declaration quoted must be from a person related by blood to, or be the husband or wife of, the person to whom the declaration relates. The prosecution has, therefore, to first prove that the declarant, Mr. John H. Jones, was related by blood to Fred Jones before this declaration can be used in this court. In short, the prosecution has reversed the proper method of procedure."

But Farris was not giving up. "John Jones's declaration relates as much to Mrs. Esther Jones as it does to Fred Jones, and since it is acknowledged that Mr. Jones stood in the relation of husband to Mrs. Jones, his declaration meets the requirements of this rule."

Before Martin could open his mouth to rebut again, the magistrate interrupted. "I may be wrong," he said, "but I rule against you, Mr. Farris. You will have to prove that Fred Jones was John Jones's son before you can enter this conversation as evidence." Williams was hazarding the guess that Martin would be much more knowledgeable on such subjects than Farris. It was, therefore, safer to side with Martin.

Joe Martin allowed himself a small smile.

"Your honour, you must forgive my pertinacity," Farris pleaded, "but this matter is of the most serious nature. The rule appears to me to make this evidence plainly admissible ..."

"No, Mr. Farris, I disagree."

Then Martin, his voice laced with sarcasm, asked, "Did I understand that this man"—he pointed to Peden—"was to be the star witness for the prosecution?"

Farris's face was flushed with anger. "The case for the prosecution is closed," he said and sat down.

Astonished, the magistrate asked, "Is that your entire case?"

"That's the case," Farris replied.

"Then do you have anything to present, Mr. Martin?"

"I have no evidence to offer, your honour, but with your permission I will plead both cases at once—those against Mrs. Jones and Mrs. Jackson—if the court will first close the case against Mrs. Jones."

"Has the accused anything to say for herself?"

"No, your honour."

"Then you may plead, Mr. Martin."

"I submit, your honour, that no prima facie case has been made out by the prosecution. The only evidence that has been given is that the young man known as Fred Jones called Mrs. Esther Jones his mother. This amounts to nothing at all. There have been many cases where adopted children have called their foster parents mother and father. There are scores of cases in this city alone where women are called mother by sons-in-law and daughters-in-law and stepchildren and adopted children. No witness has sworn that he ever heard Fred Jones say that Mrs. Jones was his mother, and even if he did, it would prove nothing.

"In addition, it is not sufficient to show that a false statement has been made. In order to constitute perjury it must also be shown that it is corrupt and made for the purpose of misleading justice. There has been some attempt to show that this statement was false but not a particle of evidence has been produced to show an attempt to mislead justice. In addition, if the question was one in which the court was not interested and one that could not bear in any way on the issue before the court, then it could not be perjury. There is a provision in the code for this very thing. It is common sense."

Martin continued, "Supposing it to be true that Fisher and Jones are one and that Jones was the son of Mrs. Jones and that he had gone to the penitentiary, and on coming out, had decided to change his name—there would be nothing wrong in that. And supposing that on his coming out of the penitentiary the family had decided to let it be known to the neighbours that he was a nephew and not a son in order that he might get a fresh start, there would be nothing criminal in that either. It would, therefore, be perfectly natural after doing this for years to call Fisher a nephew at the inquest." He went on to point out that the best of citizens unintentionally make false statements from time to time and said that the statements in contention before this court were not material to either the issue or the evidence.

When Martin finished, Farris stood up. "First I wish to point out that, this being a preliminary hearing, the prosecution is only required to make out a prima facie case against the accused. It is not necessary that the evidence should be conclusive. I submit that the inquest was held to determine how Thomas Jackson came to his death, which occurred under suspicious circumstances. The only people in the house at the time or who could possibly have administered the poison were Mrs. Jackson, Mrs. Jones, Fisher and Exall. That being so, the relationships existing between these people is very material to the case because it affected the value that the jury would place on their corroboration of each other's testimony. I submit that a deliberate false statement was made to the inquest jury by these two people with the object of misleading the said jury." He hesitated a moment, cleared his throat as if he was about to add more, then abruptly sat down.

Dennis Hopkins closed his notebook and began buttoning his jacket. There was no point in waiting for Williams' verdict—the women were obviously going to be freed. He half-rose from his seat then, realizing that the crush of bodies behind him prevented an easy exit, he sat down again and glanced across at the *News-Advertiser's* Bruce Bennett who was sitting close to the opposite wall. He could see that Bennett's pencil was still poised over his notebook. He looked a little farther back to where the *World's* Norman Norcross was seated. Norcross was watching the magistrate expectantly. *Have I missed something?* Hopkins asked himself. He looked up at the bench. Williams was finger-combing his moustache and staring out the window at the cold blustery day. Hopkins reopened his notebook and waited.

Finally Adolphus Williams shook his head and returned his gaze to the courtroom. He was used to dealing with petty swindlers and thieves, prostitutes and drunks, sentencing and fining them routinely. He was sadly out of his depth in the legalities of the arguments put forward in this hearing. He was also very aware that Joe Martin knew the law backwards and forwards, and if he passed these two women on to the higher court, Martin would undoubtedly get them off. On the other hand, they really had lied in a court of law, and the public—urged on by the newspapers—was expecting them to be found guilty of perjury and sentenced to serve prison time. What to do?

"In a preliminary hearing," Williams began at last, "it is not my duty to weigh the evidence or to decide whether or not the accused is guilty. All I must decide is whether there is sufficient of a prima facie case to put them on trial. It is evident to me that ..." He paused to gaze around the courtroom. "That a prima facie case *has* been made out and I hereby transfer this case to the County Criminal Court ..."

Behind him, Dennis Hopkins both heard and felt the general sigh of satisfaction. This, he realized, was what everyone had been waiting for. The women would now be safely behind bars while the murder investigation continued, and with luck there would yet be a double hanging in the city. He tried to imagine these two little women in their tasteful black walking suits and their veiled and feathered hats swinging from a gibbet and he felt revolted. There was something wrong in all this, something wrong in the way that Martin and Farris and the magistrate were enjoying themselves so much, something wrong in how the newspapers were vying for the next sensational tidbit, something wrong in the indecent interest of the people who crowded the courtroom.

Hopkins watched as Farris, taken by surprise by Williams's verdict, registered disbelief then quickly recovered and beamed triumphantly at his legal opponent. Joe Martin merely smiled sardonically. He was too wise in the ways of police magistrates to have expected the decision to go in his favour. If he noticed that his clients were crestfallen by the outcome, he did not show it. He merely patted Esther Jones on the arm, told her not to worry, and proceeded to stuff papers into his briefcase as the women were led away. They disappeared down the stairs to be returned to the steel cage that constituted the women's ward.

To avoid the crowd, Hopkins headed for the same stairway, but at the top he turned in time to see Martin, seemingly unperturbed by the loss, shake Farris's hand heartily before following the crowd from the courtroom. Hopkins then returned his attention to Farris, still busily gathering up his papers. *He looks like the kid who has unexpectedly won all the marbles in the game,* he thought, *and he isn't quite sure what to do with them.* "When are you going to lay murder charges, Mr. Farris?" Hopkins called out to him.

Farris looked up to see who had asked the question then assumed his customary prosecutorial expression and stance. "The position of the Crown," he said, "is that now that the women have been committed for trial, they cannot possibly be released for some time to come, so there is plenty of time to lay new charges." He paused then added, "In fact, it is possible that nothing more will be done until Detective Sergeant Mulhern returns from Montana where he is giving evidence at the Dean murder trial." The statement was merely designed to give him breathing time before reporters began nagging him again.

As Farris walked out of the courtroom, down the main staircase and out into the cold, windy January noontime, he was a happy man. With the Jones/Jackson perjury case headed to Vancouver County Court, it would be the provincial prosecutor's turn to be humiliated by Joe Martin. His own job now would be to find enough evidence to bring charges for the murder of Thomas Jackson. He signalled to one of the hacks waiting outside the courthouse and was about to climb aboard when he suddenly changed his mind, turned away abruptly and began walking in the direction of Dr. Alfred Poole's surgery. Poole had done the autopsy and obviously this would be the best place to start reviewing the evidence.

A few minutes later, as Dennis Hopkins was mounting his bicycle outside the jail entrance, two policemen ushered mother and daughter out the door and handed them into the hack that Farris had rejected. Hopkins watched as it turned west onto Cordova and he pedalled after it until it stopped in front of Savard's Photographic Gallery at Number 8 in the block between Carrall and Columbia streets, and the women were escorted inside. Obviously they were to be photographed for the official "rogues' gallery" and he slipped into the studio after them to watch the procedure. Theresa Jackson endured it as though in a waking dream, but Esther Jones had no intention of submitting willingly to this further indignity, and each time the photographer was ready to snap the shutter, she made a sudden movement and held her head down so that her hat brim covered most of her face. After several botched attempts, one of the police officers held her head toward the camera, but even then she managed to thwart the process by "making faces" as the shutter clicked. At this point they gave up and escorted the women back to the hack.

Hopkins started to follow then turned back to speak to the photographer. "How much do you want for copies of those photos?" he asked.

"Who's asking?"

"The *Province*."

"Five dollars."

Hopkins reached into his pocket. "You've got it. How soon can you have them ready?"

"Come back at five o'clock."

As Hopkins pedalled off, he knew this was one time his boss would not be handing him any brickbats.

Meanwhile, the hack had continued to the tram depot at the corner of Hastings and Carrall streets, where the women and their guards alighted again and climbed aboard the 2:30 tram car. All around them people stared and whispered. Felons and even murderers—sometimes in leg irons—were routinely transported to the penitentiary in New Westminster in this manner, but it was rare to see women—especially stylishly dressed ones—treated this way.

But if the women had suffered indignities while in Vancouver's jail cells or as the centre of attention on the tram, it was nothing to what they would experience in the next stage of their incarceration. In all the three long years that Fred Jones had spent in the penitentiary, neither of them had visited him so they had no inkling of what to expect. As no special accommodations had been provided for women prisoners, they were housed in a roughly partitioned area at the end of one of the men's cell blocks. All incoming inmates—male and female—were given compulsory disinfectant baths then issued cotton uniforms. Meals were distributed on trays and eaten in the cells. A bell mounted under the building's dome announced escapes and head counts, meal and bed times and called the male inmates to work in the prison blacksmith shop or the vegetable gardens or to cut firewood for the furnaces. Unfortunately, there were no jobs designed for women.

For two women accustomed to a well-appointed West End home, their own cooking and their own comfortable beds, this experience of cold stone floors and walls, iron bars, a lack of privacy and the indignity of a disinfectant bath and a prison uniform provided the lowest point in their lives. The only compensations were the improvement in the quality of the food over that in the Vancouver city jail—the penitentiary inmates raised almost all their own meat and produce—and the opportunity to step outside once a day to exercise their legs.

However, they couldn't pass their days in quiet contemplation because from dawn to dusk their ears were assaulted by construction noise. The original, three-storey, stone and concrete penitentiary building, overlooking the Fraser River at Sapperton, had been completed in 1877 and the first twelve inmates brought from the provincial jail in Victoria and installed there a year later. However, by 1906 the population growth rate in the west—and the accompanying increased criminal activity—had exceeded all of the federal government's expectations and forced them to begin building an addition. Every day, workmen toiled on the construction of a new concrete cell block adjacent to the old building and on a two-and-a-half-foot-thick, twenty-four-foot-high stone wall to surround the entire prison complex.

The same afternoon that Esther Jones and Theresa Jackson were committed to the penitentiary, Ernest Exall visited the law offices of Martin, Weart and McQuarrie.

The photographs of Esther Jones and Theresa Jackson taken on Wednesday, January 3, 1906, for the penitentiary records appeared in the *Province* newspaper on Friday, January 5, 1906. COURTESY OF THE REFERENCE DEPARTMENT, LEGISLATIVE LIBRARY OF BRITISH COLUMBIA

"I want to withdraw my bail bond," he said.

"Does Mrs. Jones know this?" Martin asked him.

Exall nodded. "Tessie … that is, Mrs. Jackson … told me to withdraw it if she and her mother were sent up for trial in County Court. She said that since they won't be able to make bail in that case, her mother will have to remain in jail anyway, so there's no good my money being tied up any longer."

Martin said nothing but after a few moments nodded agreement. Exall stood up to leave.

"I'll make the application," Martin said then added, "You've been a loyal friend."

Exall stared at the floor for a moment before turning to leave.

"Where can I contact you, Mr. Exall?" Martin asked. "Are you still with the CPR?"

"Yes, but I work in the freight office now," he said. "But you shouldn't contact me at work. You can send a letter to me at the house on Davie Street."

"You're still living there?"

"Oh yes," Exall said as if this was the most natural thing in the world.

"I take it you will be visiting the ladies in the penitentiary, Mr. Exall?"

"Yes ... if I am allowed."

"I can arrange to have your name on their list of approved visitors. You will be allowed one hour only on Saturdays, Sundays and holidays," Martin explained then added a cautionary, "There will be guards monitoring all your conversations."

"I understand." And Ernest Exall went out without another word, leaving Martin frowning.

The next day Esther Jones, although already incarcerated, was formally ordered into custody on the Sprague theft charge as well.

With Martin's urging, the two women elected not to wait for the Spring Assizes where they would be tried by judge and jury since it was unlikely that an impartial jury could be assembled after all the publicity their case had engendered. Besides, it would mean sitting in jail for another three months before the Assizes began. Instead they opted for a "speedy trial" by judge alone and made the trip back to Vancouver on January 5 to appear at the imposing County Courthouse on the south side of Hastings Street between Cambie and Hamilton streets (the site of present-day Victory Square). Completed in 1894 and constructed from stone quarried on Nelson Island, this building was one of the finest in the young city and often provided a backdrop for official events, including the welcome to the Duke and Duchess of Cornwall and York in September 1901. (This courthouse was demolished after the new one on Georgia Street—now the Vancouver Art Gallery—was officially opened in September 1912.)

The judge on this day was W. Norman Bole, who generally presided over New Westminster County Court but was substituting in Vancouver during the absence of the sitting judge, Alexander Henderson. Bole, a brilliant criminal lawyer, came from a family of jurists in County Mayo, Ireland, and had turned up in New Westminster on holiday in 1877. He fell in love with the West Coast and never returned to County Mayo; within two months of his arrival he was called to the BC bar, the first lawyer to take up residence in New Westminster. By 1884 he had become the city's first police magistrate, was appointed a Queen's Counsel three years later, and by 1892 had become the city's first county court judge.

William Ernest Burns, the man who was to prosecute the two women, was a thirty-three-year-old from Milton, Ontario, and one of the rare Canadian lawyers to have a university degree—a BA from Toronto University—and to have studied law at a university—Osgoode Hall. He had arrived in the west in 1900 as the resident attorney for the Vananda Mining Company but soon set up his own law office in Vancouver with Knox Walkem as his partner. By 1903 he was also serving as one of the Vancouver County Court's prosecutors. While he had more court experience than Farris, he was still leagues behind the eminent Joe Martin.

Judge W. Norman Bole, KC, presided over the first day of the women's perjury trial with his customary wit and short temper. He came from a long line of eminent jurists in County Mayo, Ireland, and after arriving in New Westminster in 1877, became that city's first lawyer, then first police magistrate and finally first county court judge. CITY OF VANCOUVER ARCHIVES PORT P. 974

Having entered a plea of "not guilty," the women took their places in the dock. The newspapers reported that, as in their previous court appearances, both were dressed in mourning, but Esther Jones, "resplendent in a handsome sealskin jacket," was alert to everything going on in the courtroom. Her daughter stared at the floor, as if "sunk in sombre melancholy beyond the possibility of interest in the proceedings."

"Are you ready for trial, Mr. Martin?" Bole asked.

"We are, your honour," Martin replied and took his seat again to wait for the prosecutor to begin.

Instead, Burns rose to ask for an adjournment. Consulting his calendar, he added, "We would prefer a date sometime in the week of January 22—preferably January 24 or 25."

Martin bounced to his feet. "I am astonished, your honour, that my learned friend would ask for such a long delay! These ladies were arrested a fortnight ago and there has been adjournment after adjournment for reasons that in every case were found to be incorrect. It is a plain case of dawdling along because the Crown simply wants to keep them under lock and key for some ulterior purpose. In any event, the week mentioned is unfortunate for me as I will be appearing on another case and then I must go to Ottawa."

"Quite so, Mr. Martin, quite so," Bole said ponderously. "The Crown is asking for an adjournment that would make the term 'speedy trial' a *lucus a non lucendo*." The corners of his mouth turned up slightly at his little joke then returned to a thin straight line as he realized that the prosecutor had no idea what he meant. "It would make the term 'speedy trial' an *absurdity*, Mr. Burns, an absurdity … and that will never do. You will have to do better than that …"

"Many complications have arisen in this case, your honour," complained Burns, "and it is necessary to have time to put the case properly before the court. If the Crown is pressed to begin before the date mentioned, we shall not be ready to proceed." Then as an afterthought he added, "Mrs. Jones is also in custody at the present time on a theft charge, and as far as she is concerned, the length of the adjournment would have no ill effect as she would be in custody anyway."

All eyes turned toward Esther Jones who registered no change in expression.

"Mr. Burns, the court would not be influenced," Judge Bole said drily, "even were it a fact that the accused were also charged with treason."

"My words were not uttered with the intention of influencing the opinion of the—"

"Oh, get on with it, Mr. Burns," the judge snapped. "Get on with it!"

After interminable wrangling, the lawyers finally agreed to an adjournment until January 17, and the women were taken to the nearby office of the provincial police to await transport back to the penitentiary. Dennis Hopkins, who as a matter of course now covered all court proceedings for the *Province*, followed them and slipped into the room in time to hear Theresa Jackson pleading to be taken to the house on Davie Street for "just a short while."

When the guards refused, she began to cry.

"I just want to tidy up," she moaned between sobs. "I just want to tidy the house up."

Hopkins, overwhelmed with pity for her, opened his mouth to argue with the guards, but just at this point the door opened to admit Ernest Exall.

"It's all right, Tessie. It's all right," Exall said and would have taken her hand but the police matron stepped between them. "I cleaned up the mess after the police were there," he reassured her awkwardly. "It's all cleaned up."

"Oh, Ernest!" Theresa Jackson wailed. "They took my money!"

"What money, Tessie? Who took it?"

"At the prison. They took the rent money from my purse!"

"I'll pay it, Tessie. Don't you worry ..."

"Thank you, Ernest," Esther Jones intervened stiffly.

Her daughter took out a black-bordered handkerchief to wipe at her eyes and blow her nose. Then still sniffling, she echoed, "Thank ... thank you, Ernest. You are very kind ..."

"That's all right," he mumbled then shifted his weight from foot to foot, unable to find anything more to say.

Suddenly Theresa Jackson spied the telephone on a nearby desk. "Oh, do let me phone Mr. Springer at Imperial Life," she pleaded, directing herself to the police matron. "I must learn whether they have all the documents now." And when it appeared this request, too, would be turned down, she began to weep again.

"All right," the matron relented at last. "But just a few minutes."

Eagerly Theresa Jackson picked up the receiver and put through a call to the insurance company office. Five minutes later, reassured that all the documents had arrived that would allow them to pay out her husband's policy, she rang off and sat down to nervously pleat and unpleat her handkerchief. Exall stood uncomfortably, staring out the window.

The next time the door opened it was to admit a policeman who announced that the hack was waiting outside. But instead of heading directly for the interurban station, the hack drove the women and their police escorts to a restaurant where they lunched before they began the journey back to the penitentiary.

Dennis Hopkins detoured to the Commercial Hotel bar on Cambie Street between Hastings and Cordova before returning to the newspaper offices. Then he dutifully typed up the morning's events, trying not to let his sympathy for the women show.

City Prosecutor John W. deBeque Farris had now turned most of his time and energy into extraditing Fisher in the belief that, once he had the fellow back in Canada, he could make some progress on the murder charges. He was certain that the key to the mystery of who killed Jackson lay with Fisher, even though the press had generally concluded that Mrs. Jackson was the guilty party since she was the only person who admitted handling the salts after Jackson bought them. But Theresa Jackson had also said that the glass entered into evidence had not been the one from which Jackson drank. So who switched the glasses? And was the beer bottle that Fisher gave Preston really the one Jackson drank from? If he could get his hands on Fisher, Farris was convinced he could get the truth out of him.

At this point everything really depended on proving to the extradition commissioner that Fisher was Jones and that Jones was a British, not an American, citizen. It was, therefore, time to follow up on the tip that, sometime before Fred Jones was arrested for theft in 1897, he had been a gunner in the Victoria militia, Number Three Company, Fifth Regiment. If this was true, Jones would have taken an oath of loyalty to the queen and signed papers to that effect. So the same day that the two women made their first appearance in Vancouver County Court, Farris caught the steamer to Victoria to confer with a former militia officer who had recently been located there by the police. But Farris was about to be disappointed.

"It was my confounded housekeeper who did it, Mr. Farris," Major Arthur Hibben said apologetically. "She got to tidying and I think she burned the lot of them!" Hibben, though now retired, had long been the senior officer of the militia.

"Do you mean that Jones's loyalty oath has actually been destroyed?"

"It would seem so, sir. I told her not to touch nothing on my desk, but you know how women are when they get to tidying, sir. Regular menace, she was!"

Farris turned away. He knew that without this vital piece of paper he had nothing tangible to prove that Fisher was Canadian. But he was not giving up; if the commissioner would just control that idiot Westcott, Farris still had a chance.

On January 9 Farris had an early dinner and took the last Great Northern train of the day south to Blaine. Walter Nichol was on the same train, eager for another instalment in the Harry Fisher extradition farce. The two men sat together in the smoking car, discussing Vancouver's fractious politics before their conversation finally touched on the Fisher case, although Farris was obviously reluctant to talk about it.

The next morning Farris met with exactly the disappointment he had feared, and Nichol happily provided his *Province* readers with his own version of the proceedings in the extradition commissioner's office:

> As on the occasion of the first hearing in the Fisher
> case, G.H. Westcott, attorney for the accused, was the

star performer before the extradition commission. Mr. Westcott, when he thought of the cruelties, indignities and wrongs which had been heaped upon the head of his unfortunate client, wept elephantine tears. In fact, his feelings were so worked up over the case that large, salty blobs of liquid ran in torrents from his eyes, to the admiration of Fisher and the fear and inconvenience of those who were not wearing hip rubber boots. Mr. Westcott would be a hit in any melodramatic production where in a frenzied outburst the wronged mother petitions the villain to give back her child. Mr. Westcott, as the hero, could at this point rush in and drown the villain with his tears, the flood of which would make the Johnstown torrents look like an Arizona streamed in the dry season.

Nichol then explained how Westcott's tears had won the day and how the commissioner had flatly rejected Farris's extradition request. His story continued:

After Mr. Westcott had thanked heaven that Fisher was now safe under the Stars and Stripes, he told the story of his own life. He said he himself had been a stray wolf at six years of age, had found a home at six years and three months in the bosom of a happy Christian family, had learned to call his protectors father and mother as Fisher had done in the case of Mrs. Jones and her deceased husband and had lived with his foster parents until they died. Then, unable to bear the parting grief, he had gone forth into the cruel world and sought distraction from his sorrows by becoming a great lawyer.

At this point Mr. Westcott was so overcome that he nearly fell on the commissioner's neck. That party, however, ducked and by a little clever footwork got out of reach. The famous attorney wound up his speech by telling Fisher to keep away from all trains running into Canada as he might be kidnapped by emissaries of the Vancouver police.

Nichol concluded his story:

As far as the police are concerned, it is improbable that anything will be done regarding Fisher unless unforeseen developments occur. Today he is a free man and no effort is being made to shadow his movements. By the present time he may be halfway to Portland.

To say that Mr. J.W. deB. Farris, police court prosecutor, is disgusted at this turn of events is putting the matter mildly. "The next time we stop a man on the other side of the line," said Mr. Farris today, "we will let him go on to Bellingham. Blaine is no place to conduct an extradition proceeding. Last night's speech by Mr. Westcott, counsel for Fisher, was about the richest thing I ever heard. I kept count and he said "Thank god" six times in expressing his gladness that Fisher was in the United States and not in that awful country Canada. So what are we preparing to do now in the case here? Nothing at present."

But while Farris may have hit a dead end, the Vancouver newspapers were not ready to give up. As far as the publishers of the *Province* and the *World* were concerned, Theresa Jackson had murdered her husband and it was time for charges to be laid. A guilty verdict would mean hanging and a woman on the gallows would really sell newspapers. The campaign to have her charged was, therefore, renewed in the *World* on Friday, January 12.

It is understood that a charge will most certainly be laid against Mrs. Jackson in connection with the mysterious death of her husband by poisoning in

November, the authorities desiring to take steps to clear up the mystery surrounding that event. The question that remains to be settled is when the charge will be laid, and it is certain that the authorities will be guided by circumstances in this connection, always remembering that they can lose nothing and might gain much by delay as long as the person chiefly concerned is in custody.

Fisher is free and was seen in Bellingham by Sergeant Walker of Victoria on Thursday, so up to that time he had not gone very far. Mrs. Jones, no matter what the issue of the perjury trial may be, must remain in custody, unless she now gets bail, until the Spring Assizes on the receipt stealing charge. There remains only Mrs. Jackson. It is practically an open secret that the prosecution in the perjury case that is now in the hands of Mr. W.E. Burns for the attorney-general's department is not prepared with all the evidence it would like to have, and an application for an adjournment is expected when the case comes up before Judge Bole on Wednesday next. If his honour refuses to grant this and the prosecution is obliged to go on, then in the event of a dismissal of the case, Mrs. Jackson would be a free woman once more, and the hands of the city officials would be at once forced. In any event, a dismissal of the perjury case, whether there is an adjournment or not, would force this issue sooner or later.

But Farris remained silent. In fact, he actually had no hard grounds for charging Theresa Jackson with murder. All he had was the circumstantial evidence submitted at the inquest. First, there was no dispute that she had been the only person with Jackson when he took the fatal dose. On the other hand, doctors Poole and Underhill had proved that neither the beer bottle nor the glass that Fisher handed to Sergeant Preston had held any poison. In any case, Theresa Jackson had said that the glass was not the one from which Jackson drank. If this was true, what happened to that glass? In addition, since no fingerprints had been taken from either the bottle or the glass that had been entered into evidence, there was nothing to say how many persons in that household had touched them. Then there was the fact that she had become ill before her husband showed any symptoms, and the doctors had described it as hysteria. This meant that she knew he'd been given poison before he even began to react to it. But where had she obtained the poison that killed him? A diligent search had not turned up any shop in the city that had sold it to her—or to her mother. So while it was still possible that Theresa Jackson could have committed the murder all by herself, Farris was becoming convinced that all of them—Theresa Jackson, Esther Jones, Fred Jones/Harry Fisher and perhaps even that Exall fellow—had been involved in some way. If he could just get his hands on Fisher ...

EIGHT

By eleven o'clock on Wednesday, January 17, some three hundred people had jammed into the County Courthouse to see Judge Bole pronounce the two women guilty. Instead, the man who took his seat before them precisely on the hour was Judge Alexander Henderson, just back from conducting the Spring Assizes in Kamloops. Henderson was forty-six, a graduate of Toronto University who had completed a law degree at Osgoode Hall. He was called to the bar in 1889 and practiced law in Oshawa before coming to BC in 1981. He represented New Westminster in the legislature from 1898 to 1900 and served as attorney general. He was appointed County Court judge for Vancouver in 1904. A much more sober and sedate man than Bole, Henderson fixed a stern eye on the crowd as he asked Martin whether he was ready to proceed. When the answer was in the affirmative, he turned to the prosecutor.

"Are you ready to proceed, Mr. Burns?"

"No, your honour. Chief Provincial Constable Colin Campbell just left yesterday for Ohio to bring witnesses back to

Vancouver, and we request a fortnight's adjournment to allow time for them to arrive."

The two women in the dock exchanged a look and Theresa Jackson placed a hand on her mother's arm. Martin bounced to his feet. "Your honour, I fail to understand why my learned friend has not sent for these witnesses long ago! He has had this case before him since January third."

"Mr. Burns?" the judge inquired.

"We had some difficulty locating these people, your honour, but now that we have, Constable Campbell will make all haste to bring them here."

"I see. In that case we shall adjourn until ..."—he consulted the court clerk—"Wednesday, January 31."

"Your honour," Martin protested, "I am scheduled to appear before the Railway Commission in Ottawa at month end."

The judge frowned. "You might see about changing that, Mr. Martin."

"Since we are to be delayed again," Martin continued, "I request a reduction in bail for my clients."

"Oh, very well, Mr. Martin. What is it set at now?" When supplied with this information, he responded, "We can make that $400 for each of your clients in two sureties of $200 value." He peered at Martin then at Burns and back to Martin. "Is that everything?"

When Henderson stood up, everyone in the crowd automatically did so as well and waited silently until he disappeared into his chambers. Amid the hubbub of conversation that followed, Martin turned to his clients. Neither had moved but there was a new tension in their faces.

The days of waiting went slowly for the two women, with Esther Jones spending long hours reading and rereading passages from her bible and her daughter sunk in despondency. The newspapers, meanwhile, having failed to entice Farris or the police chief into making any fresh statements concerning murder charges, were compelled to fill their pages with other, less absorbing events. Then suddenly on Tuesday, January 23, there was real news to report. The previous day in the midst of a raging storm, Pacific Coast Steamships' 252-foot, iron-hulled passenger vessel *Valencia*, out of San Francisco, had struck a reef near Pachena Point on the west coast of Vancouver Island. A few of the crew and passengers managed to launch life boats and reach shore, but as would-be rescuers watched from ships that were unable to come close enough to take off the remaining pas-

County Court Judge Alexander Henderson, another alumnus of Osgoode Hall law school, was appointed to the bench in 1904 and became Vancouver County Court judge, although he also heard cases in the province's interior. He resigned shortly after the Jones/Jackson trial to run for a seat in the BC Legislature. When he failed in that endeavour, he accepted a four-year posting as Commissioner of the Yukon.
CITY OF VANCOUVER ARCHIVES, PORT P721.

sengers and crew, the ship broke up and all aboard were swept into the icy sea. Of the 154 persons the ship carried on that fateful voyage only 23 officers and crew and 14 passengers were saved; no women or children were among the survivors. For the following week the Vancouver newspapers carried little except news of the tragedy—accounts by survivors and on-shore rescuers, reports from government investigators and lengthy condemnations of the federal government for its refusal to provide the West Coast with lighthouses, a lifesaving trail along that rugged shore and a fleet of self-propelled, self-bailing and self-righting rescue vessels.

Meanwhile, in the tiny town of Madison, Ohio, BC's chief provincial police officer, Colin Campbell, was experiencing no difficulty in finding persons who had known the Jones family, but none of them wanted to testify in far-off Vancouver. It was thousands of miles from their town and too foreign. They also expressed themselves as being deathly afraid of the Jones family, especially John Jones, and the men who were asked to come and testify first wanted to know if he was still alive. Madison resident Sarah Walding claimed that the residents of Madison "were afraid they might be shot." A story in the *World* explained:

> When assured that it was not the custom to shoot witnesses in this country, she said it was different in Ohio. "In my country if I say something you don't like, you are liable to shoot me for it. Of course, they get arrested for it, but they don't mind that." When she was assured that in Canada the matter usually went further than mere arrests in shooting cases, she admitted that she had always heard that British law was carried out here. Time and again Chief Campbell was promised by different people in Madison that they would accompany him to Vancouver to testify, and time and again they disappointed him.

But Campbell finally arrived back in the city with two witnesses, and on Monday, February 5, after yet another adjournment requested by prosecutor Burns, Esther Jones and Theresa Jackson were once again escorted from the penitentiary in New Westminster to the Vancouver County Courthouse. It was just after 2:30 when they were ushered into the smaller of the two courtrooms in the building, which was, according to Dennis Hopkins's report for the *Province,* "packed to suffocation." Their arrival was "the signal for a buzz like that which issues from a disturbed beehive, and it lasted until Judge Henderson entered and took his seat." Hopkins, scanning the crowd as he took notes, recognized a familiar face in the front row. It belonged to a tiny, wrinkled woman, always dressed in the same shabby grey coat and hat, who had attended every hearing for the two women, worming her way through the throng until she got a seat near the front where she followed the proceedings avidly. *Madame LaFarge,* Hopkins found himself thinking. But he also noted that someone who should have been in attendance was not; Norman Norcross who always covered court proceedings for the *World* had been replaced by reporter John MacKay who normally covered sports. *So where is Norcross?* Hopkins asked himself. *Fired? Not likely. The guy's too good.* Of course, he could have been lured away for more money by either

William E. Burns, though a somewhat more seasoned lawyer than Farris, was no match for Fighting Joe Martin when he was called on to prosecute the women in County Court in February 1906. He was one of the few lawyers in the city to have both a university degree (from Toronto University) and a degree in law from Osgoode Hall. CITY OF VANCOUVER ARCHIVES 371-1535.

the *News-Advertiser* or the *Province*—and in the latter case, it would mean that Hopkins's own job was on the line—but the *World* generally paid its reporters more than the other papers did ...

At that moment, prosecutor Burns stated that he would take the case against Mrs. Jones first, and Hopkins had no more time to think about Norcross. Burns proceeded to call the same cast of characters who had given testimony at the preliminary hearing. The only new faces belonged to Thomas Kaulbach, who had known the family in Victoria and persisted in referring to the Jones children as Bessie and Eddie, and to Jesse Betts, the elderly man from the Kamloops Old Men's Home who had first raised the alarm about Harry Fisher's identity in a letter written to the *World*. Betts now could not remember the children's names at all but, when pressed by the prosecutor, said he thought the boy might have been called Harry.

However, Burns's star witnesses were the two ladies Chief Constable Campbell had escorted from Ohio. The first, Mrs. Sarah P. Walding, was, according to Hopkins's story in the *Province,* a woman "whose age might be set down as anywhere from forty-five to fifty by even a close observer" but who was a "remarkably well-preserved" seventy-three-year-old.

> She talked of things that happened fifty years ago as calmly as if she was relating what occurred the day before yesterday. She is very alert and active in her movements, and her mind is as clear and sharp as that of any quick-witted woman of thirty years. She was decidedly composed in her manner and speech and even under cross-examination by Mr. Martin, whose pointed questions have been the fear of many witnesses, she did not display the slightest sign of nervousness.

Mrs. Walding, dressed fashionably in black "except for white trimmings on her waist [bodice] and sleeves," mounted the stand confidently but for a brief moment seemed to be at a loss when the registrar held out a bible and asked her to repeat the oath after him. Then turning to Judge Henderson, she announced she would affirm instead. That done, she turned to face prosecutor Burns who asked her to state her name and address.

"My name is Sarah P. Walding of Madison, Lake County, Ohio, USA," she stated and then, just in case her audience had not understood the abbreviated form, added, "the United States of America!"

The *Province*'s story continued:

> Counsel asked her to have a good look at the prisoner, Mrs. Jones, and see if she could identify her. In a moment every person in the room was on the *qui vive*—many of them were also on their tip toes—and every eye followed the witness as she very deliberately stepped down from the witness stand, calmly walked across the room to where the prisoner was sitting and commenced her survey. In order that Mrs. Walding should have a good look at Mrs. Jones, the blinds in the room were raised their full length and the electric lights were turned on. Much as if she were matching a piece of dress goods in an uncertain light, Mrs. Walding approached the prisoner, bent down and calmly looked her features over. Mrs. Jones, by direction of the court, had raised her heavy black veil so that the witness could have a very good look at her. For fully fifteen seconds Mrs. Walding looked the prisoner over. "Yes, it's Ella Jones, though she is very much changed," finally declared the witness as she turned and recrossed the room to her chair on the stand.

The witness then went on to relate that she thought she had last seen Mrs. Jones in Madison in the spring of 1892. She declared that she had known the prisoner from the time of her birth. She knew her as a child, as a growing girl, as a woman, and she knew her at the time of her marriage to John H. Jones. Mrs. Walding said she knew of a daughter and a son born to Mrs. Jones and her husband John Jones. She used to see these children passing her house as they went to and fro between their mother's house and the school. Their names were Fred and Theresa Jones. She added that Mrs. Jones never had any other children by her husband, John Jones, but she had been married before her union with him to a man named James Burke, and she had heard that Mrs. Jones had had one child by this marriage but she could not testify to the truth of that report. The witness did not know Burke and did not know the sex of this child. The witness stated that John Jones had named his only son Fred after her own nephew Freddy Walding because Jones had boarded with the family of Freddy Walding prior to his marriage to the prisoner.

"I think Fred Jones was born in May 1876—the United States of America's Centennial Year. Mrs. Jones was a Fisher before her marriage, and she had one sister who died as a child and one brother, Henry, who married Laura Eberts. Henry Fisher and his wife had one child—a daughter named Kitty who is now married. No other children were born to Henry Fisher and his wife, and they separated when Kitty was still a child. He died without any other issue."

Mrs. Walding was just concluding her statement when there was a commotion in the back of the courtroom—a woman had

stood up on her chair in order to have a clearer view of the proceedings. This being entirely inappropriate courtroom behaviour,
Sheriff Hall rose and started toward her, intending to make her sit
down, but at that precise moment Burns produced a handful of
photographs taken from the house on Davie Street after the women
were arrested. Hall's attention was now diverted to keeping the
excitement in the crowd under control, and as a result, the woman
was allowed to retain her new vantage point. A few other women
quietly followed her example.

The first photo shown to the witness was one of Fred Jones
taken in recent years.

"I do see a resemblance to the Fred Jones I knew," said Mrs.
Walding, "but there is a great deal of change in his appearance.
When I last saw him in 1892, he was a fresh-faced boy with bright
red hair ... although the more I look at this picture the more I see
a resemblance." But when she was shown a photo of Jones taken
earlier in life, she was more confident. "Now this looks more like
Fred the last time I saw him."

As Mrs. Walding continued to examine photographs and
comment on them, Dennis Hopkins's gaze swung to the prisoner's
box. Esther Jones's face was still a mask of ferocious hostility, but
the arrogance that had underlain it was gone, and he recognized a
new emotion: fear. Inside his head he replayed his interview with
the two women in the days before their arrest. "Surely a mother
ought to know the number of children she has given birth to, don't
you think? Mr. Fisher is not my son. His father was my brother
and he died suddenly of a haemorrhage many years ago." Hopkins
remembered himself asking inanely, "You are positive you never
had a son?" And she had snapped, "Never! I only wish I had one
to help and defend me now in my old age. Mr. Fisher is not my son
and he never served a term in prison."

I'm such a fool! Hopkins thought. No wonder she and her daughter had expressly asked for him—they had recognized just how gullible he was. And just as they planned, he had come away convinced that they could not possibly have committed murder. He shifted his gaze to watch Theresa Jackson mindlessly pleating and unpleating her handkerchief and tried to imagine those little nail-bitten fingers putting the strychnine into her husband's glass. Anger grew in him for allowing himself to be duped.

Before Joe Martin began his cross-examination, he stepped over to the prisoner's box to confer with his client, then after a few minutes' earnest conversation he turned his attention to the witness. "What is your occupation?" he asked.

"I am a widow and I keep house for myself. My husband died twenty-four years ago."

"Are you a spiritualistic medium?" asked Martin.

"No, I am sorry to say that I am not a spiritualistic medium," she replied.

"You have never set yourself up as a spiritualist medium?"

"No."

"Perhaps you do not understand what spiritualism is," he said, his voice heavy with sarcasm. "Is it not believed by spiritualists that communication can be established with the dead?"

"Oh, I understood your meaning," Mrs. Walding answered coolly.

Of this Joe Martin was already aware because Esther Jones had just told him that Mrs. Walding made her living by staging séances. Since the middle of the nineteenth century the spiritualist movement had swept up the middle and upper classes in New England and California but had been accepted with even more enthusiasm in the upper Midwestern states. Many ladies and gentlemen there had given up tea parties and evening soirees entirely in favour of séances where automatic writing, table rapping and voices from the dead were demonstrated and "talking" or Ouija boards were consulted. Even Mary Todd Lincoln, grieving the loss of her son, had organized séances in the White House and her husband had attended them. Trance lectures had also become extremely popular, and thousands of believers attended state spiritualist conventions and summer camps. Then gradually as competition for paying audiences increased, showmanship became the most important element of the séances and lectures, and by the end of the century there had already been a number of sensational court cases where fraud practised in the guise of spiritualism was prosecuted—although even this did little to discourage determined believers.

However, in attempting to force Mrs. Walding to admit in front of a Vancouver judge that she was a spiritualist, Martin knew what he was doing. When it came to spiritualism, Vancouver was not the Midwest nor even New England or California. Here, where in the early years of the twentieth century society was still emerging from the pioneer phase, most people regarded the practice of spiritualism with considerable scepticism, some even suggesting that it was sacrilegious. (This would change a decade later when the city's *literati* became enamoured.) Martin was trying to suggest that she was hardly a credible witness. Unfortunately, he was not aware of spiritualist terminology and had asked her the wrong question.

"But you say you are not a spiritualist?" he continued.

The judge intervened here to say that Martin had actually asked the witness if she was a spiritualist medium, not a spiritualist. "That is how I understood your question."

"Are you a spiritualist?" Martin then demanded. "Don't fence with me."

"I believe in a person being possessed of spiritualism, but I don't give it the same definition you do. And I am not a spiritualist medium."

"And spiritualists are people who believe they can communicate with the dead."

"I make no such profession," she returned.

"And you have had nothing to do with people of that kind?"

"Oh, I have spiritualist acquaintances all around me," Mrs. Walding said calmly.

"Do you sympathize with them in any way?"

"You are asking me if I believe in the teachings of spiritualism, and I must say yes, in part I do."

"Well now, what part is that?"

"I believe in the hereafter."

"There are other bodies of Christians who believe in a hereafter. As a matter of fact, that belief is not peculiar to spiritualism, is it? Tell us something that does distinguish spiritualists from other people."

"They believe in communication with the dead."

"Ah, we are back to that. And what are your own views on that?"

"I cannot say."

The judge peered over his glasses at her. "You mean you have an open mind on the question?"

"Yes."

"Do you belong to a spiritualist church or similar body?" Martin asked.

"I told you I have a great many friends who are spiritualists."

"I have a great many friends who are spiritualists," Martin mimicked her, "but I do not believe one bit in it! Come now, tell me what special tenets of spiritualism you do believe in."

"I do not see what it has to do with this case, but if you had studied what science—properly understood—has developed on this question, you would believe in it, too."

"My views do not bear on the question. All I want from you

is a straight answer. What other tenets of spiritualistic creed do you believe in?"

"I don't think you could understand if I were to tell you."

"I see. Do your spiritualist friends have meetings in Madison, Ohio?"

"They did—years and years ago."

"But not now? Are there not enough spiritualists left in Madison to hold meetings anymore?"

"There are a good many there."

"But they do not all openly acknowledge it now?"

"I suppose that is it," she answered defensively.

"Were you ever at a meeting where they had intercourse with departed spirits?"

"I have been at what you call a séance."

"Only one?"

"Only one."

"When?"

"Twenty years ago. It was in Cleveland, not Madison."

"So what is your own attitude to this distinctive feature in spiritualism?"

She paused then said, "I think I am trying to know what it means."

"And how long have you been in this attitude?'

"Ever since the Fox sisters started out as mediums over fifty years ago."

"That's a long time to be hanging in suspense," Martin commented.

"There are certain phenomena that you cannot explain on any other ground except that there is communication with departed spirits."

"I see," Martin said and sat down. He had made his point: Mrs. Walding had finally confirmed that she was one of those goofy spiritualists. But was she goofy enough to convince Judge Henderson that she was not a credible witness?

As it was now five o'clock, Mr. Burns suggested an adjournment, claiming that his examination of the other Ohio witness would take twice as long as that for Mrs. Walding.

"But the two ladies will have all night to discuss the case," Martin protested.

"We shall keep them apart," said Burns with a laugh.

"Well, I am ready to continue right now," said Judge Henderson, "but I have received notice that the large courtroom will be available tomorrow morning and we could all be more comfortable there." He directed himself to the counsel for the defence. "Mr. Martin?"

"Very well, your honour."

"Ten o'clock?"

The first witness the next morning was Miss Lydia Brisco of Madison, Ohio, a middle-aged lady who was both desperately short-sighted and extremely hard of hearing. As a result, she had some difficulty finding her way to the stand and then could only respond to Burns's questions when he put his lips almost against her right ear. When he finally made it plain to her that she was to identify the prisoner, she had to be led to the dock where she poked her face to within inches of Esther Jones's nose.

"Yes, that's Ella Jones," she reported and was led back to the stand. "Her husband was John Jones. I understand he is dead now."

"How well did you know Mrs. Jones?" Burns asked.

"Oh, she was one of my firmest friends. I didn't know her before she was married, but I sewed for her when little Fred was born. That was in 1876—centennial year—in the month of May."

"When did you first see Fred Jones?"

"The day after he was born and every day for the next two or

three weeks. I was sewing for her before Fred was born and afterwards, too."

"Did Mrs. Jones nurse the baby?"

"Oh yes. And about two-and-a-half years after he was born,
Ella Jones had a daughter Theresa. I don't remember what year that
was ..."

"Did you know Mrs. Jones's family—her brothers and sisters?"

"She had a brother named Henry—whom I knew. He got
married and had a daughter named Kitty. He never had any sons."

"Did you keep in touch with Mrs. Jones after she left Madison?"

"I wrote to her once when I was living in New York, telling
her I was in a strange place and feeling very lonely, but she never
answered me."

"Where did you send the letter?"

"I addressed it to her in Victoria, BC ..." And she finished
sadly, "But she never answered."

Once again Burns brought out the photographs, and after Miss
Brisco had studied them myopically one by one, she pronounced
the young man in them to be Fred Jones. When it was Joe Martin's
turn to question the witness, she had even greater difficulty hearing
him, and the examination was finally accomplished by Martin
asking the questions and Burns repeating them into her right ear.
This process, however, elicited no new information.

After she was helped from the stand, Burns produced a transcript of a record of birth from the probate court of Ohio. It was
signed by a judge of that state under seal and certified to by the state
governor. The transcript was to the effect that Fred Jones was born
on May 1, 1876, at Madison, Ohio. His father was John H. Jones
and the maiden name of his mother was Ella Fisher.

"I object to this document being entered into court, your
honour," announced Martin. "I was not served with the required

ten days' notice that it was to be produced."

"You most certainly were!" Burns protested.

"It was not served on *me*," Martin contended. "It was served on a clerk in my office, Mr. William Harper, on January 26, but no clerk in my office has any authority to act for Mrs. Jones in any way, shape or manner. In any event, the notice was not served in time. January 26 is not ten clear days. This question has been before the Supreme Court of British Columbia in the case of Canadian Canning Company v. Fagan, in which the defendant distrained on the goods of the plaintiff, and it was held that ten days' *clear* notice must be given."

Burns responded vigorously. "If service was made on the offices of my learned friend, it was the same thing as being made on him. And that notice was served just as soon as I received the information. The statute declares that the reasonableness of the service rests in the discretion of the judge. From the time that notice was served on the office of my learned friend until the subject was brought up in this courtroom ten full days have elapsed!"

Martin's response was that "service on a clerk is not proper notice," and he begged for the judge's indulgence while he left the courtroom and proceeded to the law library down the hall. He returned with a half-dozen tomes to back up his argument. He then read from each of them, ending his presentation with the pronouncement that the ten full days must conclude before the start of the trial, not the date on which the document was introduced into evidence. "And besides," he concluded, "the certificate of the governor of Ohio is of no service whatsoever in this court."

Burns was furious. "We don't need the certificate of the governor! The mere production of the record of an American court under seal is good." He then took one of the tomes from Martin, read aloud the findings from another case and attempted to show how this ruling paralleled the present circumstances. Martin retaliated by pointing out the flaws in his reasoning and citing yet another case. And then to further frustrate Burns, Martin suddenly announced that the certificate the prosecutor wished to have entered as evidence first had to be proved. "My learned friend must show the court that this certificate is a record that is required to be kept by law, and he has not done so." Burns remonstrated. Martin cited more cases. An hour passed. Burns appealed to the judge.

"No, Mr. Burns," Judge Henderson said at last. "I am inclined to think that under the circumstances the section of the Canada Evidence Act applying must be strictly construed. I think the authorities cited by Mr. Martin have convinced me that 'not less than ten days' means ten *clear* days, and that the ten days expire on the opening of the trial. I cannot allow this new document to be placed in evidence."

Burns's protestations fell on deaf ears and he was forced to give up on the certificate and call his last witness, Norman Norcross of the *World*. At this point Dennis Hopkins finally understood why John MacKay had been covering the trial in Norcross's place.

"Mr. Norcross, will you please tell the court about events in which you took part on December 16, 1905?"

"I received instructions from my editor to go to the house at 615 Davie Street." Norcross did not bother to explain that his editor was his brother, James E. Norcross, who held the post of city editor for the *World* until 1916.

"The house occupied by the defendants?"

"Yes."

"Were you alone?"

"No. I was accompanied by Mr. Wintemute, a lawyer, who brought certain affidavits he had prepared."

"And what happened to those affidavits, Mr. Norcross?"

"Mr. Wintemute handed them to Mrs. Jones and Mrs. Jackson. I talked with Mrs. Jones and she said she could not understand why people were so interested in her affairs and why they should think they knew more about the number of children she had than she knew herself."

"And did you see the man known as Harry Fisher during your visit?"

"Mrs. Jones telephoned for him to come home, and after he did, all three of them signed the affidavits."

"Mrs. Jones, Mrs. Jackson and the man known as Harry Fisher?"

"Yes."

"Do you have those affidavits, Mr. Norcross?"

Martin was instantly on his feet. "What! Newspaper affidavits? Does my learned friend suggest that such documents could be evidence in this case?"

"I do so contend, your honour," Burns replied, his jaw set stubbornly.

Another long argument followed, but finally Martin's objection was sustained—although the judge did not absolutely rule out introducing the affidavit signed by Mrs. Jones into evidence. He would, he said, give his decision on that later.

And with that ruling, he called a recess for lunch. The defendants were removed to an anteroom where lunch was provided for them, though Esther Jones ate nothing. In fact, she had eaten nothing since setting eyes on Sarah Walding the previous day. Burns and Martin, both of them fully satisfied with the morning's vigorous jousting, called for hacks and hurried off to dine at home. Dennis Hopkins drank his lunch at the Boulder Saloon.

As soon as the afternoon session began, Joe Martin rose to announce, "Your honour, I don't intend to submit any evidence. The reason for my client calling the young man her nephew was for his protection. Further, no one at the inquest cared whether Fisher was the son or the nephew of Mrs. Jones. The question, when asked, arose from the fact that Fisher had kissed Mrs. Jones goodnight, and she had in reply to a juror's question explained this by saying that he was her nephew. Had she said that he was her son, it would have seemed even more natural that he should kiss her, consequently there was no object in her deliberately misleading the court on this point. And it is easy to see why she might inadvertently have called the young man her nephew on this occasion. There had been a family compact for years by which the young man, to cover up his penitentiary experience, was to be called Fisher, the nephew and not the son. It was a natural and justifiable one for the family to have carried out. There is nothing illegal about a change of name of this kind, though it is usually made for improper motives, but in this case the motives were proper. There is absolutely no evidence," Martin concluded, "to show that the false statement was also corrupt, which is required in order to constitute perjury. There was no guilty attempt on my client's part to mislead the court. I submit, therefore, that the prosecution has produced absolutely no evidence of my client's perjury."

Martin took his seat and the prosecutor rose to address the court. "Your honour, I submit that my learned friend's interpretation of the law regarding perjury is erroneous. He has implied that there is no other defence to a charge of perjury than that the perjurer had inadvertently made the statement. However, looking at this case in that light, it could not be possible for her, a mother, not to know that he was her son—her actual born son. As long as there was intention to mislead the court in that statement, it does not matter whether it was material or not. But I submit that this matter *was* material to the coroner's court because the actual cause of death was not the only matter of concern at the inquest. There is no question that the relationship of those who were inmates of the house where that death occurred was the concern of the jury. It seems to me that this was perjury of the strongest kind on a very material point."

Burns then turned to the matter of the *mens rea* or guilty mind of the accused. "This was shown by the fact that, when the accusation of perjury was made, she did not at once admit that she had made a false statement and that Fisher was her son and state her reasons for concealing this fact. It would have been the natural course for Mrs. Jones to have taken if she was innocent of intent to mislead the coroner's court. Instead of doing this, instead of disclaiming all intent to mislead, the accused hung back, and the Crown was put to the trouble and expense of bringing witnesses all the way from Ohio to prove the real relationship between herself and Fisher. She apparently hoped that the proofs would fail."

"Your honour," Martin said, returning to the fray as Burns took his seat, "I am surprised at the line my learned friend has taken. The Crown apparently wants a conviction on the ground that Mrs. Jones has caused great expense to this court—"

Burns half-rose. "Oh, no ..."

But Martin continued, "And according to his argument, had Mrs. Jones pleaded guilty, the Crown would not have prosecuted."

"Your honour," Burns said, "may I have leave to correct my learned friend?" And when he was given the nod, he continued, "I have not argued anything of the kind but only urged that the real relationship of Mrs. Jones and Fisher, had it been given by Mrs. Jones, would likely have materially affected the views of the coroner's jury."

"The relationship was of no consequence," Martin returned. "The transcript of the inquest offers no evidence to show that any of the inquest jury wanted to know anything about their relationship."

Judge Henderson joined in. "However, it does seem to me, Mr. Martin, that the question of the relationship was both material and important to the coroner's inquest."

"That may be, your honour," Martin replied, "but it was not asked for by any of the jury members. Mrs. Jones's response was elicited on the immaterial point of the kissing and not with a view to ascertaining the actual relationship. Her reply did not mislead the court regarding anything touching on Jackson's death. I ask that this case be dismissed."

Judge Henderson shook his head. "No, Mr. Martin, I am not prepared to dismiss this case ... which is, I think, tantamount to saying that I believe that the Crown has made its case."

"Assuming that the facts as alleged have been proved?" Martin asked.

"Yes." The judge paused before continuing, "Assuming that this is the entire data, I am not prepared to say that the offence of which Mrs. Jones is charged was done free from any intention to mislead the court. I can understand that under many circumstances—and even under the circumstances that exist in this case—this agreement made between Mrs. Jones and the members of her family that after being released from the penitentiary young Jones should be known as her nephew Harry Fisher was a praiseworthy one. I can understand that this arrangement was calculated to benefit the young man, to give him a fresh start in life and gain employment. But while that is true, Mrs. Jones should have been very careful what she said when making her statement before the coroner's jury. She should have carefully weighed what she said because Jackson died in a mysterious manner, poisoned by person or persons unknown, so that this investigation was not confined to merely the nature of the poison and cause of death. The relationship of the people in the house at the time was certainly of importance. Any relationship that might lead to a motive was especially noteworthy and of vital importance as a foundation on which to build a future case in this matter. Therefore, despite Mr. Martin's able and acute argument, I cannot look upon Mrs. Jones's statement as an innocuous one. The arrangement made years ago was an honest one, but when she appeared before that solemn tribunal that was endeavouring to ascertain how a human being had been snatched into eternity by the use of poison, she should have known that it was a time that demanded of her the truth and the whole truth, however bitter the acknowledgement might be. I can fully understand the feelings that prompted the shielding of the boy in the first place, but the terrible circumstances surrounding Jackson's death call for the whole facts. I cannot, therefore, grant a dismissal. Do you have any further evidence to present, Mr. Martin?"

"No, your honour. I leave the case in your honour's hands," Martin said.

"Then I find the accused, Esther Jones, guilty as charged. I reserve sentencing to tomorrow morning."

As there was no point in presenting and disputing all the same evidence against Theresa Jackson, Martin accepted it on her behalf and her trial was over in less than fifteen minutes. In pronouncing her guilty, the judge concluded, "To all intents and purposes it has been admitted that this prisoner made a false statement at a coroner's inquest under oath, and the evidence of Mr. Norcross has to my mind disposed to a great extent of Mr. Martin's argument that her statements regarding Mr. Fisher were accidental or inadvertent. What Mr. Martin has said on this issue holds great weight with me, but it is rather in the way of mitigation of punishment. However, if I may say so, this case has been well argued and presented on both sides. The Crown has presented a remarkably well constructed case, and I think that the public is indebted to Chief Provincial Constable Campbell for the fine work he has done and to Mr. Burns for the able manner in which he has handled the material before him. Mr. Martin's ability is so well known to the public that it is unnecessary for me to say more than that he conducted the case with his usual skill and foresight."

As the judge's speech ended, Hopkins half-expected the audience to applaud. It was just like attending the performance of *El Capitan* at the opera house at Christmastime. Just another entertainment. His attention shifted to the two convicted women being led from the courtroom, and he suddenly realized that their roles had been reversed. Theresa Jackson was now the stronger one, supporting her mother who seemed on the verge of collapse. Then remembering how the pretty little widow had controlled the interview the day he was asked to call on her and her mother, he thought bitterly, *That sweet little thing's helplessness was just an act all along. She killed her husband all right.*

Hopkins walked down the courthouse steps and onto Hastings Street, and as the cold February rain slanted into his face, he thought, *I don't think I want to be a court reporter. Maybe I don't want to be any kind of reporter. There's just too much evil out there.*

NINE

By 10:30 on Wednesday, February 7, several hundred people had crowded into the County Courthouse to hear Judge Henderson sentence the two women. When they were brought into the room and shown to seats below the prisoner's box, Dennis Hopkins could see that the shell of indifference and arrogance the mother had cultivated was completely shattered and she was suffering horribly from the suspense of not knowing her fate. The daughter, who kept a hand on her mother's arm, seemed to have better control of her emotions, but she kept her head down, refusing to look at the crowd. Neither looked up when the judge entered but were urged to their feet by the police matron, at which point Esther Jones sagged as if fainting and the matron allowed her to sit again.

As soon as Judge Henderson was seated, a police constable directed Mrs. Jones to enter the dock, but when she became so agitated that she had difficulty mounting the steps, he took her arm and assisted her. She stood then, hands clasped tightly in front of her, facing the judge, but her eyes were downcast. He cleared his throat, and the murmur in the crowd died to an intense silence.

"Mrs. Jones, the crime with which you have been charged and of which you have been found guilty is that of perjury, which is considered to be a very serious one. The punishment as laid down in the criminal code—the extreme limit of the code—is as follows: anyone who commits perjury or the subornation of perjury is liable to fourteen years' imprisonment. That is, I have the power to send you to prison for fourteen years."

Esther Jones swayed and would have fallen but for the steadying hand of the constable beside the dock. She reached out then and grasped the railing in front of her.

The judge continued, "But there are several reasons why I should not exercise that power and sentence you to that length of time ... or indeed anything like it. In the first place, I should consider your age. I do not know what your years are, but I can see that you are nearing the evening of your life, and for you the dark shadows are lengthening. Notwithstanding that this fact elicits some sympathy, public policy demands that your crime shall not be overlooked because it is certainly my experience that the crime of perjury is becoming more prevalent—although there are few convictions on that account. I must not, of course, hold you responsible for that fact." He paused, frowned and went on, "I have given the case of yourself and your daughter most serious consideration, and I do not think I should impose a sentence of less than twelve months in the common jail—in the provincial jail—that imprisonment to date from the time of your arrest."

Before he finished speaking, Esther Jones had broken into loud sobs, her hankie pressed to her eyes to stem the tears as she leaned against the half-wall beside her. A moment later the constable swung the door to the dock open and helped her down the steps and seated her again in the chair beside it. He then took Theresa

Jackson's arm and handed her up the steps. Until this point she had retained some composure, but when she turned to face the judge and saw the eager faces of the crowd who had come to witness her downfall, she began to weep silently into her handkerchief.

"To some extent," said the judge, "what I have said to your mother applies to you also, not because you have reached your declining years but because you are on the threshold of your life. Your career lies before you as your mother's lies behind her. Your counsel has impressed on me very strongly that your offence was not committed with the purpose of misleading the court but that it was to some extent due to inadvertence or error. I cannot give full effect to that, but I have taken it into consideration. I have decided to vary the punishment in your case slightly, and I shall give you a somewhat lighter sentence. I shall impose on you nine months' imprisonment, the sentence to date from the time of your arrest."

After one shuddering indrawn breath, Theresa Jackson recovered herself, stepped quickly down the steps from the box and walked rapidly towards the courtroom door by which she had entered, with a constable trailing behind her. Trembling, her mother stood up to follow, but when she staggered slightly, Chief Constable Campbell gave her his arm and supported her as she tottered after her daughter, with the police matron walking behind them.

The onlookers all stood as the judge left the bench and disappeared into his chambers, but as they began to disperse, all talking animatedly and happily about the verdict, Dennis Hopkins settled slowly into his seat again. He watched the reporters for the morning *News-Advertiser* and the evening *World* weaving their way through the crowds, eager to get back to their offices to type up their stories before deadline. He saw the Ohio witnesses, Mrs. Walding and Miss Brisco, gathering up their coats and gloves, preparing to leave the courthouse. Then suddenly out of the corner of his eye he caught sight of the tiny old lady in grey who had attended all of the Jackson/Jones court appearances. Instead of following the crowd out of the courtroom, she was making her way up to the rail behind which the two American witnesses were standing.

"Bless you, my dears!" she cried as she got close to them. "Bless you for coming all this way to make sure that justice was done!"

The women turned toward her, a little puzzled, somewhat wary.

The old lady then reached out and grasped Mrs. Walding's hand. "Bless you, bless you! You are a good woman!" And she continued to pour out her blessings as Mrs. Walding tried to extricate her hand. "Justice has been done this day because of your good works!"

Hopkins's gaze went from the scene playing out beside the rail to the people who were departing the courtroom. Some of them, pausing to see what was happening, were smiling and nodding. Yes, their smiles said, it had been a fine thing that the Ohio women had done.

Well, that old lady's right, isn't she? Hopkins asked himself. Esther Jones and Theresa Jackson lied and they're being punished for it. And while they are in jail, Farris will get the rest of the evidence he needs to convict them for murder. *And that's what we want, isn't it? They are evil women and they should be hanged for their crime.* He turned his attention to Martin and Burns, watched them chat together good-naturedly then shake hands. Martin then sauntered out of the courtroom while Burns stayed behind to speak to his Ohio witnesses.

Slowly Hopkins got to his feet and made his way toward the door where Esther Jones and Theresa Jackson had exited, planning to use it as a shortcut to the street, but as soon as he opened it, he could see that the BC Provincial Police constable who had assisted in the courtroom was now standing guard in front of a closed door at the far end of the hall. Obviously the prisoners had not left the courthouse yet. Hopkins knew he should ask permission to speak to them, attempt to get an interview, get the scoop on the rival papers that Walter Nichol would be overjoyed to receive. Reluctantly he made his way toward the constable, taking out his notebook and pencil as he went, but as he came closer, he realized that there was a veritable torrent of hysterical weeping and screaming coming from behind the closed door. In the forefront was Esther Jones's voice, shrieking oaths and maledictions. "I hope that god," she howled, "and I believe there is a god—will come down and paralyze everyone who has done this to me!" And one by one she named the judge, the prosecutor, the head of the provincial police and all the detectives of the Vancouver police department, adding suitable unprintable adjectives to each name. After that Esther Jones started on the witnesses, the newspaper reporters and her jailers. In the background of this entire tirade were the voices of the Provincial Police chief constable and the police matron attempting to calm her and above them was that of Theresa Jackson desperately trying to restore her mother to reason.

"Mother, you must stop this! You must!" the younger woman pleaded, her own voice thick with weeping. "I am as sad as you, but I don't carry on like this. If you don't stop, everyone will hear you ..."

"I don't give a ------- who hears me! I want them to hear!" And then Esther Jones howled, "I'll never live to come out of that jail! This will finish me ..."

The constable in the hallway, suddenly becoming aware of Hopkins standing beside him, said, "Oh, you don't want to go in there, Mr. 'Opkins. She's liable to add you to her list."

"I think I'm already on it," he said.

They waited in silence. From time to time someone would

pass down the hallway, look askance at the closed door and hurry
on. Then little by little the screaming ceased and Esther Jones was
reduced to merely sobbing with only an occasional outburst of blas-
phemy. At last Hopkins put a reluctant hand on the doorknob, but
at that precise moment he caught sight of a bearded man coming
down the hallway. The man's face was somehow familiar but for a
moment Hopkins couldn't place him.

"Good morning, Mr. Exall," the constable greeted him. "You
can go in. They're waiting for you."

It was Ernest Exall, the boarder, of course. Hopkins had not
seen him with a beard before. He stepped out of the way as Exall
brushed past him, and as the boarder opened the door, Hopkins
caught a brief glimpse of Esther Jones prostrate in an overstuffed
chair with her daughter hovering over her. The door closed again.

"What's Exall here for?" he asked the constable.

"Has to get instructions on what he's to do with the house.
Sell the furniture, maybe store it. Things like that."

While they listened to the voices beyond the door, quieter
now but still filled with tension, Norman Norcross from the *World*
suddenly appeared in the passageway.

"I heard the old girl's having a fit—is that right?" he demanded.

The constable nodded. "That Mrs. Jones, she's the hardest
female we've ever had in custody." He paused then added, "She's a
thoroughly wicked woman."

Dennis Hopkins left quietly as the *World*'s reporter pushed
past the constable and into the room.

Back at the *Province* offices, Dennis Hopkins sat at his desk
staring into space while all around him the room was filled with
the clatter of typewriters, voices shouting into telephones, and the
clacking of the printing presses from the adjoining room. At last he
took out his notes and began typing.

For genuinely artistic and scientific cursing of the variety usually associated in fiction with the poor woman who has been cruelly wronged by the arrogant villain, Mrs. Esther Jones captured the record this morning after His Honour Judge Henderson had sentenced her to twelve months' imprisonment. Her imprecations were delivered in a frenzied passion in the Provincial Police office in the County Courthouse, whither she had been led from the court after sentence had been passed upon her. The daughter of the old woman, Mrs. Theresa Jackson, who had just received a sentence of nine months' imprisonment for perjured utterances similar to those delivered by her mother, was calmer. Mrs. Jackson did her best to choke off the flow of maledictions issuing from her mother's lips but her efforts were unavailing.

Mrs. Jones, who is between fifty and sixty years of age, plainly showed that she is a past master in the art of cursing. Her outburst today was evidently not the work of a tyro. She distributed her curses promiscuously and finally wound up by handing them out to the individuals who were the particular objects of her wrath. The old woman even extended her prayers for evil so that they should include the families of all those she imagined had wronged her. Mrs. Jones, in the opinion of the police, is the hardest female character who has been in their charge for years. Her deportment today demonstrated that she is a thoroughly wicked woman.

Hopkins went on to describe the sentencing process and told the story of the old woman in grey who had congratulated the Ohio witnesses. He then reminded the newspaper's readers that the two women had been arrested at noon on December 22 and that their sentences would date back to that day.

The younger woman will regain her liberty three months before her mother is released. If they conduct themselves in an orderly manner while in jail, their sentences will be materially reduced by good conduct allowance, which amounts to five days in every thirty. Mrs. Jones declared today that she would never leave the jail alive—that the sentence would finish her. It is a fact that she is not in very good health, but this is attributed to the suspense she has been labouring under for some time. On Monday night she collapsed at the jail in New Westminster and her condition was sufficiently serious to necessitate medical attention.

Ever since Mrs. Jones was brought face to face with Mrs. Walding and Miss Brisco, the witnesses from Ohio whose testimony was of such a damning nature, she has refused to partake of food. It is the opinion of the police that now Mrs. Jones knows the worst insofar as the perjury case is concerned, she will brighten up. If she does and her appetite returns, she will undoubtedly live through her sentence.

Still hanging over the old woman is the charge of theft in connection with the trouble she had with Captain Sprague over a rent receipt. This charge has not been disposed of, but so far as indications are at present, it will be proceeded within the usual course at the Spring Assizes.

When he finished typing up his story, Dennis Hopkins headed for the Boulder Saloon again to drink his lunch. The fact that Walter Nichol was extremely pleased with his story had done nothing for his sense of failure. Nor did it help when later that afternoon Nichol read the *World*'s lacklustre coverage and was even happier with Hopkins's story. The rival newspaper had been reduced to self-congratulation again, though their lead story first waxed eloquent on the manner in which Judge Henderson had carried out the sentencing:

> One after the other the two women were placed in the dock this morning to hear their fate from the lips of Judge Henderson, and the solemnity of manner with which his honour gave sentence and impressed on the public in the courtroom the seriousness of what they had come to see was worthy of the best traditions and the highest ideals of a British court of justice. Before he was half through with Mrs. Jones, the condemned woman was sobbing and trembling in the dock, though the tones of his voice were those of sympathy and sorrow, with no trace of anything except the determination to properly fulfil a most painful duty. Mrs. Jackson, her face deadly pale and her eyes looming large in the realization of her position, took her mother's place in the dock after the older woman was sentenced and she too broke down and was ultimately removed, sobbing and trembling.

The *World*'s story then recapped the Jones/Jackson visit to that newspaper's editorial offices back in December when they came to demand a retraction of the statement that Fisher was actually Mrs. Jones's son.

> After this, events moved swiftly. The *World*'s special correspondents began pouring in the results of their investigations and, after consulting with the police and holding back the startling information they had gathered for a few days to enable the detectives to make some investigations of their own without

embarrassment, the story of the Jones family was published in the *World* ... On the morning of December
21 the *World* warned the police that Fisher had got
uneasy and was going to leave town that day if not
prevented. In the afternoon Fisher did slip away and
passed through New Westminster where he took the
train, arriving safely at Blaine before he was stopped.
The unsuccessful efforts to extradite him are still fresh
in the public mind.

Alarmed lest the women, too, should escape, and still
keen on the investigation of Jackson's death, the police
arrested the two women on the following day and
placed them in the city jail ... As the result of a preliminary hearing, which was successfully prosecuted
by Mr. J.W. deB. Farris, they were sent up for trial at
the higher court ... Mr. W.E. Burns was appointed
Crown prosecutor and he, working with Chief Constable Campbell, completed the chain of evidence
that during the past two days has traced Fred Jones
from the bed of his birth in Madison, Lake County,
Ohio, to Victoria and thence to the penitentiary, and
showed him to be one and the same as Harry Fisher.
Great credit is given to Mr. Burns for his energetic
and capable handling of the prosecution, pitted as he
was against possibly the best criminal pleader in the
west, and great credit is also given to Chief Campbell
in the way in which he secured in Ohio and brought
here absolutely the most valuable witnesses the prosecution could possibly have secured regarding Jones's
birth and early career.

Later that same afternoon Esther Jones was deemed sufficiently
recovered to make the journey with her daughter back to the

penitentiary in New Westminster to begin serving the sentence Judge Henderson had handed down. But as the days of her incarceration in the penitentiary slowly passed and spring came, Esther Jones's health did not improve, and the doctor who served as the provincial jail surgeon, R. Eden Walker, was called on many occasions to prescribe for a respiratory and heart condition.

Then one day in late April, with the opening date for the Spring Assizes drawing ever closer, Walker received a visit from his friend Dr. Wilfred Sprague who had heard rumours that the woman's health might preclude her appearance in court on the theft charge laid by his father.

"And how is your father?" asked Walker.

"Not too good," Sprague said. "Not too good. He's worried that this case will never come to trial. The woman is malingering, isn't she?"

The original cell block of the BC Penitentiary from inside the exercise yard, 1938.
NEW WESTMINSTER PUBLIC LIBRARY. ACCESSION NUMBER 1609.

"Well ..." Walker began, "she does have a heart condition ..."

"But it's not serious enough to keep her out of court ..."

"Well ..."

On May 1, Walker wrote a letter to the court on the stationery of the provincial jail and had it hand-delivered:

This is to certify that I have examined Mrs. Jones, prisoner in the gaol at New Westminster, and I consider that she is in a fit condition to be taken to Vancouver and to appear there for trial.

At two o'clock that same afternoon Dennis Hopkins, settling into his seat in the courtroom, suddenly became aware that the babble of voices around him had dwindled and then ceased entirely. As a shocked murmur began again, he looked up to see that everyone in the room was focussed on the prisoners' entrance. Chief Constable Campbell was poised awkwardly in the doorway, trying to enter with a large bundle of black cloth over his shoulder. From the bottom of the bundle dangled a pair of women's shoes. *Oh my god,* thought Hopkins, *it's Esther Jones!*

The headline over Hopkins's story in that evening's edition of the *Province* read: *Chief Constable Carries Mrs. Jones on his Shoulder.*

Weak and limp, carried over the shoulder of Chief Constable Campbell, Mrs. Esther Jones, who attained considerable notoriety last fall because of her conviction for perjury at the inquest for her son-in-law, Thomas Jackson, was brought into court this afternoon to face the charge of theft preferred against her by Captain Sprague. The aged woman, who has already served four or five months of her twelve-month sentence, was deposited in a corner of the prisoner's box. Her face was hidden from the crowded courtroom all the time as she buried it in her arm and never once raised it during the twenty minutes she was in the room. Huddled up in the box, the woman bore a greater resemblance to the effigy of a human being than animate flesh and blood.

As Constable Campbell pushed through the door of the court with his burden on his shoulder, a murmur of comment at the strange appearance she presented ran through the room. Once seated on the bench in the prisoner's box, Mrs. Jones seemed to collapse. Figuratively speaking, she stood before the Court of Criminal Assize without appearing to realize her position or care what happened.

After the Grand Jury had been sworn, His Lordship Chief Justice Hunter, who is taking the Assizes, charged them concerning their duties and then dismissed them. Mr. Registrar Beck called the case of Rex. v. Esther Jones. Immediately Mr. Stuart Livingston, counsel for Mrs. Jones, applied for an adjournment of her trial to the next Assizes on account of her weak condition. He said that at noon he had had his client examined by Dr. W.D. Brydone-Jack, and he wished to put him in the box to testify to her condition.

Mr. H.A. MacLean, deputy attorney-general, said that he had no objection to the trial being held over, but he had the word of the surgeon at the New Westminster jail that she was able to come to Vancouver and go to trial. Dr. Brydone-Jack then took the witness stand. He said he had examined Mrs. Jones and found her in an extremely weak condition. She was very much emaciated. Her mental condition was not such as to enable her to understand what would occur in the court. In reply to a question from Mr. MacLean the witness said that her temperature was normal but her pulse was a hundred, whereas a normal pulse is seventy-two. The witness denied that the excitement due to the expected trial would have had any effect on the rapidity of the pulse although it might on its volume. He added that the prisoner was in an apathetic state.

"Is it possible to feign this weakness?" Mr. MacLean asked.

"It would not be possible to feign the pulse. From what I understand from the jail matron, the prisoner has refused nourishment and as a result is very weak."

Mrs. Beattie, matron of the jail, then took the stand. In reply to his Lordship, she stated that the prisoner had refused to leave her bed for the past eight or ten days, saying that she was too weak. The jail surgeon had examined her and declared that, as far as he could see, there was nothing the matter with her. The surgeon had told her to get up, but she had refused on the plea of weakness.

His Lordship asked, "Do you say that she is shamming?"

"I would not like to say that," Mrs. Beattie replied.

"I see," said his Lordship. "I notice from the depositions that this is a case of oath against oath, and as there are no witnesses, I think I will stand the case over till next Assizes for trial."

Esther Jones was then removed from the courtroom the same way that she arrived—over Campbell's shoulder—and taken by tram back to the penitentiary. Since the earliest date she could be released on the perjury charge was October 23, the judge was satisfied that she would not get her liberty before the theft case came up again.

Meanwhile, J.W. deBeque Farris had resigned as Vancouver city prosecutor in order to concentrate on his law practice and his aspirations to become the Liberal Party's nominee for the upcoming provincial election. But before handing the prosecutor's job over to his successor, he had come to a dead end in his quest for the evidence that would allow him to lay charges in the murder of Thomas Jackson. He blamed this outcome on Detective James Preston who had allowed Fisher to collect the beer bottle and glasses used by the murdered man and his wife. If Preston had gone to fetch them himself, the prosecutor argued, he would have collected the right ones and they would have nabbed the killer. Preston, in turn, blamed Police Chief Samuel North for not instituting fingerprinting, which would have demonstrated immediately that Fisher had switched the bottle and glasses. And Farris condemned North for allowing Fisher—whom he was now convinced was as guilty as his sister—to escape from Canadian jurisdiction.

North, however, was too busy to worry about accusations by Farris or Preston because he was in the midst of the final phase of the city's continuing prostitution scandal—this time it was the small matter of who was paying whom in order to continue conducting business on Dupont Street—and by the end of June 1906 he was no longer chief of the Vancouver Police Department. His replacement was a man named Colin Chisholm, who had retired to Vancouver in 1899 after thirty-one years with Scotland Yard, having spent the last ten years of that time as superintendent of London's Metropolitan Police. By September, of the one hundred and fifty-three ladies of easy virtue who had been living on Dupont Street in forty-one separate establishments, he had moved "practically all" on their way to find new lodgings, and while the citizens of the West End and Fairview were up in arms over the ladies settling in their posh neighbourhoods, Chisholm found nothing wrong with this situation—after all, that was how it was done in London. He lasted as police chief for only nine months; he was accused by the Moral Reform Association of "favouring the ideas on the social evil question [prostitution] prevailing on the European continent." But before he left the job, he did introduce fingerprinting to the police department, although it was too late to help solve the mystery of who murdered Thomas Jackson.

The same month that North lost his job Walter Nichol fired Dennis Hopkins for missing deadlines and drinking on the job. The young man soon found employment selling shoes at Woodward's Department Store at the corner of Hastings and Abbott streets. He never went near another newsroom and he never drank again.

On August 8 a front-page story in the *Province* newspaper announced that Theresa Jackson, "whose husband was mysteriously poisoned in their Melville Street residence last November," was again a free woman, having fulfilled her sentence less good conduct days, and that she had returned via interurban tram to Vancouver. The story reminded readers that "her release recalls one of the most sensational fatalities that ever occurred in this city," then proceeded to outline the circumstances of Jackson's death, ending with:

> Mr. Jackson was fed enough strychnine to kill half a dozen men. How it came into his stomach is a mystery that has baffled police to this day. It was a point suggested at the inquest that Mrs. Jackson was not really sick but that she only simulated the symptoms of poisoning.
>
> Mrs. Jackson was dressed all in black. Her hat, her veil, her dress, her shoes, all were of sombre hue, but she was neatly attired. And no one who saw her, unless personally acquainted, would ever suspect that she

was the Mrs. Theresa Jackson of the famous poisoning case. Her features, however, stamp her as one who
has experienced sorrow, and the troubles which have
dogged her path have left their mark on her face.

Arriving in Vancouver, she hurried from the car and was
met on the platform by a woman friend. A carriage was
waiting, but as it was open, it was ordered closed, and
when this was accomplished, the two ladies were driven
rapidly away. She was driven to 914 Homer Street where
it is understood she has rented the small cottage and will
keep house there. Her mother, Mrs. Esther Jones, has
another couple of months to serve in jail.

In spite of Dr. Walker's assurances that Esther Jones had been
"in a fit condition … to appear for trial" at the beginning of May,
her health steadily worsened, and by the time her daughter was
released from the penitentiary, Esther Jones seemed near death.
This fact presented the judicial system with a problem: if she died
in the penitentiary, the province would be liable for her burial.
Her death there would also be seen as the direct result of sentencing an elderly and sickly woman to an excessive term in deplorable
jail conditions for merely lying about her relationship to her son.
And while the courtroom had been packed by crowds eager to see
the two women humiliated and punished, a large part of the city's
population—especially the female part—had apparently considered
the sentence handed down by Henderson excessive and a travesty
of British justice. It was expedient therefore to grant Esther Jones a
pardon on compassionate grounds, but first there was the matter of
Sprague v. Jones to consider. If she was released, there would be no
guarantee that she would turn up for her Assize date on that score.
Bail had been set at the previous Assizes at the sum of $400 and two
sureties of $300 each for a total of $1,000, and on Friday, August

24, two bondsmen—J.M. Peake and Samuel Wilkinson—put up the necessary funds, presumably having decided that a sick old lady was not likely to disappear before her court date. When Esther Jones was released on Saturday, August 25, she was met by her daughter, and the two returned to the little house on Homer Street where Theresa undertook to nurse her mother back to health. As he had during their penitentiary confinement, Ernest Exall continued to call on them regularly.

However, on September 26, with the Fall Assizes only days away, the lawyers Livingston, Garrett and King, who still represented Esther Jones in her unresolved battle with Captain Sprague, received a letter from Dr. Simon G. Tunstall of 709 Dunsmuir:

> I have examined Mrs. Esther Jones and found her in such a wretched condition physically that I ordered her removed to the hospital. She will not be able to come out for two or three weeks, if she ever does.

A letter from Dr. B.D. Gillis of 536 Hastings Street arrived the next day. Gillis concurred with Tunstall's decision:

> This is to certify that on the 24th inst. I saw Mrs. Jones and made a medical examination. I considered her seriously ill and recommended her removal to the hospital. She is suffering from a serious condition of her heart and vascular system. I consider that she is so seriously ill that the possibility of her appearing in court at the next Assizes is out of the question.

On October 2 a page-one story in the *Province* announced that Esther Jones was still too sick to attend the Assizes. Dr. Tunstall had appeared before Judge Henderson the previous day to explain that she would not be released from the Vancouver General Hospital in anything less than three weeks. Her "heart action is low and she is not yet able to take any solid food," he stated. And the *World*

reported—also on page one—that Tunstall had found her to be suffering from gastritis so that her "stomach was unable to retain any
nourishment," that her "extremities were cold" and her strength
"practically nil."

Two days later lawyer A.C. Garrett appeared before Judge
Henderson to ask that Esther Jones be freed on her own recogni-
zance because Peake and Wilkinson, the bondsmen who had put up
bail for her, were threatening to withdraw their funds. Henderson's
answer was no, but he did agree to reduce the bail to four sureties of
$100 each and one of $400. The two bondsmen were subsequently
persuaded to put up one surety of $100 each, while Theresa Jackson
and Ernest Exall paid the remainder. Thus, Esther Jones remained
free on bail though confined to hospital by her illness.

In spite of the two doctors' prognoses of her early demise, Esther
Jones gradually gained strength that fall, and just before Christmas
she was released from hospital into the care of her daughter again.
When spring came, her health was improved enough that the case
of Sprague v. Jones was once again scheduled for the Assizes.

Then very early on the morning of Tuesday, April 23, Ernest
Exall arrived in a hack at 914 Homer Street and was admitted by
Theresa Jackson. They spoke quietly for a moment before joining
Esther Jones in the parlour where she waited, already dressed for
the outdoors. She took Exall's arm and together they left the house,
negotiated the short path to the street and entered the hack. Theresa
Jackson watched them drive off then returned to the parlour. Hours
passed. She rose, made tea and toast and returned to the parlour.
At one in the afternoon there was a knock on the back door, and
Theresa opened it to a drayman and his assistant who stood on the
step, caps in hand. Behind them in the alleyway was their horse
and cart. Theresa beckoned them inside; they left again ten minutes

later, each balancing a trunk on his back.

A half hour later Theresa Jackson emerged from the rear door dressed soberly in her dark brown walking suit and a nondescript brown felt hat with a small veil. On her feet were sturdy Balmoral boots. She began walking north toward Hastings Street and, when she reached it, south to the interurban station at Carrall.

And so it was that, on May 2, 1907, Esther Jones made the *World's* front page news one last time:

> The first case on the list in Assize Court this morning was that of Mrs. Esther Jones, charged with the theft of a receipt from Captain William Sprague in September 1905. Prosecutor Lambert Bond said that he presumed that notice had been served on Mrs. Jones, and the court then instructed the sheriff to call for the prisoner.
>
> "Esther Jones!" called the sheriff loudly.
>
> "Esther Jones!" he repeated.
>
> A third time, "Esther Jones!" boomed through the courtroom, and it was repeated by criers in the corridor. But though the Hertz waves might have borne the sound to Mrs. Jones' retreat in Seattle, she failed to appear, and as the sound of the familiar name faded away in the courthouse corridors, the last echo of the famous Jones-Jackson-Fisher cases vanished—probably forever.

Esther Jones's bondsmen, J.M. Peake and Samuel Wilkinson, were notified that bail was estreated. Newspaper reporters soon ascertained that Esther Jones, Theresa Jackson and Ernest Exall had all disappeared from the city a week earlier.

EPILOGUE

Although Theresa Jackson was the obvious choice as the murderer of Thomas Jackson, and reporters for both the *Province* and the *World* delighted in informing their readers of her humiliations in court and her teary-eyed pleadings, she was to a large extent spared the vicious ridicule they usually ladled out for those charged with crimes. This was, perhaps, because she was young and pretty and she cried a lot—exactly as a womanly woman was supposed to react to misfortune. Instead, it was her mother, Esther Jones, who quickly became the target of the papers' most scathing and unpitying invective. She was not, alas, either young or pretty, and she never cried (at least not in public) until her final sentencing. But perhaps her greatest crime throughout her tribulations was her attempt to outwit the police, the courts—and the reporters. As a result, in the space of four months she went from being the "stylish American woman" charged with the theft of Captain Sprague's receipt to being the "thoroughly wicked woman" who was guilty of perjury—and possibly more.

Was she, in fact, the real mastermind behind Thomas Jackson's murder? After all, she had gained a reputation for a certain wiliness in many of her previous dealings. In addition, according to Sarah Walding, the people of Madison, Ohio, had been afraid of Esther and her husband, and she was reported to have fomented trouble among the partners who owned the Arlington Hotel in Alberni. But if Esther Jones did orchestrate the poisoning of her son-in-law, she made a very poor job of it.

Before the inquest opened, it had been proved fairly conclusively that the strychnine had not been in the beer or the salts when they left the premises of the local pharmacist and the beer bottler. Esther Jones also made it clear—perhaps unwittingly—that it was an inside job. She told the inquest that the house was locked up tight at night and whenever the family was out. On being questioned, she admitted that the pantry window had been unlocked, but since it opened from the top, no one could have entered that way, and that no one could have crept into the Jacksons' bedroom unheralded because the door stuck and had to be opened with force. The only possible entry point was through an unlocked door on an upper balcony, and the dog would have barked at an intruder coming into the house via that route. Her testimony therefore precluded any outsider adding the poison to the beer or salts once they had been brought into the house.

But why did Thomas Jackson have to die? Esther Jones seems to have had no direct motive for poisoning him and would have only gained indirectly if his widow inherited his wealth. However, she did know that Jackson had brought beer and Epsom salts into the house, knew they were in the pantry and had both time and opportunity to doctor them. And the fact that poison is favoured by female murderers points in her direction.

The only member of the household who would benefit directly by Jackson's death was his wife, Theresa, as she would collect his insurance, which eventually the Imperial Life Insurance Company was forced to pay out when no murder charges were laid against her. However, in answer to questions from the inquest jury about her finances, she said that, other than the insurance, her husband left her "no money to speak of, except outstanding bills" and that he had experienced bad luck with his prospecting during the past year or so. Although he had told her that he had located a property for himself that summer and had even brought back a small nugget, she said she did not know where the property was. Jackson's brother in Toronto told a reporter that the new claim was worth $60,000, but this could have just been one brother bragging to another. In any event, at the inquest his wife said that Jackson was still waiting for "papers concerning his new claim" to arrive on the *Tees*, a CPR steamship that made regular stops all the way from Skagway to Vancouver. In all probability, these papers were his assay results, which may or may not have proved the property worth developing.

There is a very strong indication that she knew her husband had been poisoned because on the morning he died she had a hysterical reaction before he demonstrated any poisoning symptoms. She is the only person who acknowledged handling both the beer and the Epsom salts but, perhaps to direct suspicion from herself, told the inquest jury that the glass that was checked for poison was not the one from which her husband drank, thereby suggesting to the police that they should be looking further for the source of the poison.

Who supplied the poison? Harry Fisher had access to strychnine because he had used it to kill rats in the Webster Brothers' warehouse, and he had access to the beer and Epsom salts in the family's pantry. He had an unhealthy controlling relationship with his sister and could have hoped to profit by her inheritance from her husband. He had also served time in the penitentiary, and although he had only been sentenced to time there for theft and forgery, it is a fact that the cell-sharing in that overcrowded institution allowed inmates to learn many new skills—including murder. And finally there is the fact that he headed for the border when the police began to focus closely on the members of the household.

Ernest Exall is the dark horse in this case. He was very obviously in love with Theresa Jackson and could have chosen to kill her husband in order to have her. When everyone else deserted the family after the women were charged with perjury, he continued to stand by them, even visiting them in the penitentiary. It is possible that he could have had access to strychnine as it was probably used in the CPR's freight sheds to keep down the rat population there (the police do not appear to have investigated this possibility), and he had access to the beer and Epsom salts in the pantry.

However, the fact that stands out in this entire story is that the murder—whether by a single member of that household or all of them working together—was poorly planned, timed and executed. Esther Jones was still in the legal spotlight because of the Sprague case so this was a bad time to commit murder, and the family was already hiding the guilty secret of the Fisher/Jones relationship. In addition, it would have made much more sense to kill Jackson after his new mining claim had been proved up and either Crown-granted or sold. Esther could have provided the entire household with an alibi by simply telling the inquest jury that the doors had been left unlocked so that anyone could have entered the house and gained access to the beer and salts, but instead she was quite emphatic that they were locked. Thus, it was not possible that any outsider could have committed the crime.

Who in the end gained from Thomas Jackson's death? Theresa Jackson received her husband's insurance benefits but paid most of that money out in bail for her mother in the fall of 1906, and because her mother failed to appear for trial, she forfeited those funds. As for Jackson's new mining property, it is doubtful whether his widow could have negotiated its sale, although Fisher, who had worked with Jackson in his Jolly Jack Mine and knew something about the industry, could possibly have found a buyer. However, if he did, the newspapers never got wind of it because it would have made front-page news. And since Jackson was no longer available to perform the assessment work that would have allowed him to obtain a Crown grant for his new claim, other prospectors who knew where it was located had only to wait for his claim to lapse before staking it for themselves. As for Ernest Exall, he appears to have also put up some of Esther Jones's final bail money and lost it, too.

Although the lawyers who defended Esther Jones in the Sprague v. Jones case were probably paid for their initial services, they are unlikely to have collected anything after she was released from the penitentiary because she and her daughter were more or less penniless by then. Joe Martin's services for the perjury hearing and trial seem to have been provided pro bono. On the other hand, both law offices received wide publicity and they undoubtedly gained enough from subsequent clients that they were grateful for the golden opportunity that the Jones/Jackson family troubles had provided.

The newspapers, giving front-page prominence to the story week after week, were, of course, the real winners, signing up avid subscribers by the hundreds, all of them eager to read the latest on the two women criminals. While in the aftermath of the Jackson murder, the *News-Advertiser* quickly sank into irrelevancy, the *Province* and the *World* continued to grow, battling for supremacy for another ten years, with Walter Nichol's *Province* triumphant in the end.

AFTER NOTE

Although I have imagined what went on behind the scenes in the Jones/Jackson/Fisher affair, most of the players in this little drama actually lived and breathed in the city of Vancouver in the years before World War I, and they all played exactly the roles I have assigned to them. Some acted out of an honest conviction that the letter of the law must be scrupulously upheld no matter the cost. Others, motivated by a mixture of raw personal opportunism and board-of-trade enthusiasm, acted with far less concern for the rights of the accused women than for the reputation of their infant city. Many of their faces give clues to which category they fall into—altruist or opportunist—but others are in deep disguise. And after the protagonists—Esther Jones, Theresa Jackson, Fred Jones (aka Harry Fisher) and Ernest Exall—had made their stealthy exit from the stage, some of these other players went on to more illustrious roles in the life of this province.

FARRIS, JOHN WALLACE DEBEQUE
Although Farris ran for the Legislative Assembly in 1906 and again

in 1909, he did not win a seat, but he remained a staunch Liberal and in 1914 became president of the Vancouver Liberal Association. He was finally elected to the legislature in 1916 and served as Attorney General in the cabinet of Harlan Brewster (premier 1916-18) and then in the cabinet of his successor, John Oliver. However, in 1921 he resigned his portfolio after a disagreement with Oliver and sat as a backbencher until 1924. He was appointed to the Canadian Senate in 1937 although he continued his legal practice, becoming known for his successful appearances before the Supreme Court. He died in Vancouver in 1970 at the age of ninety-one.

JOSEPH (K.C.) MARTIN

Although his real estate investments and legal practice in Vancouver earned him a comfortable living, early in 1909 Joe Martin left for England "because there is nothing there a person cannot have." The next year he won a seat in the House of Commons for St. Pancras, East Division, but by 1914 he had returned to Vancouver where he began publishing his own newspaper, the *Evening Journal*. He insisted that his editors should run nothing "unless you have it in black and white and properly witnessed." He died at age seventy-one in Vancouver in March 1923.

WALTER CAMERON NICHOL

Walter Nichol remained the publisher of the *Province* newspaper until 1924. As the paper had been a strong supporter of the war effort during World War I, in 1920 Prime Minister Robert Borden rewarded Nichol with the lieutenant-governorship of British Columbia. He retired from that post in February 1926 and, having sold his newspaper to the Southam family, remained in Victoria until his death in December 1928. He was sixty-two.

LOUIS DENISON TAYLOR

Throughout the Jackson/Jones affair, L.D. Taylor was in the midst of a romantic scandal, and his wife left him in the spring of 1906. After their divorce ten years later, he married the *World*'s long-time managing director, Alice Berry. Taylor was elected mayor of Vancouver for the first time in 1910 and repeated that feat eight more times (1911, twice in 1915, 1925, 1926, 1927, 1931 and 1933) to become the city's longest-serving mayor. But Taylor's *World* newspaper eventually lost the circulation race with the *Province,* and in 1915, due to financial difficulties brought on by the construction of his World Tower at the corner of Pender and Beatty streets, he forfeited the paper to Robert Crombie, owner of the *Vancouver Sun.* As a result, his World Tower came to be known as the Sun Tower. Taylor died a penniless recluse in Vancouver in June 1946.

The World Tower under construction at 500 Beatty Street (Beatty and Pender streets) in 1912. CITY OF VANCOUVER ARCHIVES, CVA 1477-5.

Upcoming release by Betty Keller

Better the Devil You Know
2ND EDITION
Fall 2011

Set in Vancouver in 1907, a small-time con man passes himself
off as an evangelical preacher. Together with the five-year-old
hellion left in his care by a former lady friend and a scrawny
hooker whom he reluctantly befriends, these three misfits
become involved with a cast of unbelievable characters: a lar-
cenous lingerie salesman, a Klondike miner bent on recovering
his stolen poke, a madam intent on revenge for past wrongs, a
pugilistic lady barkeep, two doctors determined to acquire a
cadaver of their own, a piano teacher with reforming zeal and
a handful of incompetent and corrupt cops. The pace is riot-
ous, the action continuous, and nobody—good or bad—ever
gets a break.

Historical Fiction
$18.95, paper,
6x9, 160 pages
ISBN 10: 1-894759-53-2
ISBN 13: 978-1-894759-53-3